THAT PLACE IN MINNESOTA

THAT PLACE IN MINNESOTA

Changing Lives, Saving Lives

Ed Fitzgerald

VIKING

VIKING
Published by the Penguin Group
Viking Penguin, a division of Penguin Books USA Inc.,
375 Hudson Street, New York, New York 10014, U.S.A.
Penguin Books Ltd, 27 Wrights Lane,
London W8 5TZ, England
Penguin Books Australia Ltd, Ringwood,
Victoria, Australia
Penguin Books Canada Ltd, 2801 John Street,
Markham, Ontario, Canada L3R 1B4
Penguin Books (N.Z.) Ltd, 182–190 Wairau Road,
Auckland 10, New Zealand

Penguin Books Ltd, Registered Offices:
Harmondsworth, Middlesex, England

First published in 1990 by Viking Penguin,
a division of Penguin Books USA Inc.

1   3   5   7   9   10   8   6   4   2

Grateful acknowledgement is made for permission to reprint
excerpts from the following copyrighted works:
"Blowin' in the Wind" by Bob Dylan. © 1962 Warner Bros. Inc.
All rights reserved. Used by permission.
"The Love Song of J. Alfred Prufrock" in *Collected Poems 1909-1962* by T. S.
Eliot. Copyright 1936 by Harcourt Brace Jovanovich, Inc., copyright © 1964,
1963 by T. S. Eliot. Reprinted by permission of Harcourt Brace Jovanovich, Inc.
and Faber and Faber Ltd.
"There Used to be a Ballpark," words and music by Joe Raposo. © 1973
Jonico Music, Inc. and Sergeant Music Co.
"Lonesome Cities" by Rod McKuen. Copyright © 1967 by
Editions Chanson Music. Used by permission.

LIBRARY OF CONGRESS CATALOGING IN PUBLICATION DATA
Fitzgerald, Ed, 1919–
That place in Minnesota : changing lives, saving lives / Ed Fitzgerald.
p.   cm.
ISBN 0-670-83317-7
1. St. Mary's Rehabilitation Center (Minneapolis, Minn.)
2. Rehabilitation centers—Minnesota—Minneapolis—Case studies.
3. Alcoholics—Rehabilitation—Minnesota—Minneapolis—Case studies.
4. Narcotic addicts —Rehabilitation—Minnesota—Minneapolis—Case studies.
5. Alcoholism—Treatment—Minnesota—Minneapolis—Case studies. 6. Drug
abuse—Treatment—Minnesota—Minneapolis—Case studies. I. Title.
HV5281.M6F58 1990
362.29′185′09776579—dc20   89-40678

Printed in the United States of America
Set in Primer

Love begins with L.

Happy Thought

The world is so full of a number of things,
I'm sure we should all be as happy as kings.

—Robert Louis Stevenson

Author's Note

Except for Debbie Chapman and me, the members of Debbie's group are my creations. They owe their existence to wonderful people I met at St. Mary's and are, I hope, neither better nor worse than they were. The members of the St. Mary's Rehabilitation Center staff appear as themselves, and I am grateful to all of them.

THAT PLACE IN
MINNESOTA

1

Last Exit Before the Toll Gate

This is a story for people who drink too much or who escape their troubles with hard drugs that don't blur their agonies at all but only replace the old ones with new ones. It's about them and about a place where they can go to find relief from their pain and hope for the years they have left to live, which will certainly be more than they would have been if they hadn't gone there.

I've been a reporter, a writer, an editor, and a publisher all of my life, and it's my book, so I'm going to be the recording secretary responsible for keeping notes on what happens in the twenty-eight days of treatment our group is going to experience at St. Mary's Rehabilitation Center on the west bank of the Mississippi River about a mile from the Metrodome in downtown Minneapolis.

It isn't heaven, but it isn't hell, either, and if you have a suspicion that it's the kind of place you ought to go to in an effort to straighten yourself out, you probably had better read the book and see if you don't think it's possible that a lunar month at St. Mary's might not only change your life but save it. As they say, if you think you may have a drinking problem, you probably have one. St. Mary's isn't the only place that does what it does; Hazelden, about forty-five miles north of Minneapolis, is probably better known nationally for doing the same thing in a slightly different way, and everybody knows that the movie stars and politicians and other people who live their lives on the front pages like to go to the Betty Ford Center in Palm Springs, California. But St. Mary's is where I went, so that's where you're going.

The least thing you can say about the treatment at St. Mary's is that you're going to go twenty-eight days without a drink, and when was the last time you did that? In my case it was probably during the war, although I'm not even sure of that. My infantry company liberated a few cases of Japanese red wine on Guam a few days after our D-Day landing there in July 1944; we bought some foul but potent homemade whiskey from enterprising Filipinos on Leyte; the Seabees were always ready to trade us one case of cold beer for two cases of warm stuff on the beaches of Okinawa; and you could buy Kirin on draft in the whorehouses of Sapporo after the shooting stopped.

So I don't know for sure when I last went that long without a drink but I know it wasn't lately and it certainly wasn't often. When I was fifteen I covered high school sports for the Yonkers (New York) *Herald-Statesman* for a nickel an inch and usually spent half of what I made drinking boilermakers with the mostly Slavic and Irish basketball players after bruising wintertime games in the sweaty little K. of C., YMCA and church gyms of the factory city where the fathers taught the sons how to drink straight shots of whiskey washed down by six ounces of draft beer. In 1935, when they were still selling apples in front of Trinity Church at the corner of Wall Street and Broadway, that was twenty cents worth of warmth and good cheer.

It might have been bad for your liver but you don't think about that when you're fifteen, and the fathers who inhaled a couple of pounds of dust working eight-hour shifts at the Alexander Smith & Sons Carpet Shop didn't think about it either.

After the war I worked for magazine and book publishing companies and found that my newspaper training was valuable not only because it had taught me how many characters of twenty-four-point Bodoni type could be squeezed into a one-column headline but also because it had equipped me to write intelligent copy after a two-martini lunch. Once, when I was working for Doubleday, the book publishers, my friend the president of the company nudged me into going to a luncheon I didn't want to go to at the McGraw-Hill offices by telling me with good humor, "Come on, Fitz, it's a drinking business. Drink or get out."

I drank.

Which is how come, in July 1988, three years after I had retired from active duty running the Book-of-the-Month Club for its owners, the renowned party givers of Time Inc., I found myself leaving on a jet plane for Minneapolis, Minnesota, in search of my health. Some wonderful people at the Freedom Institute in Manhattan, a not-for-profit alcohol and drug counseling organization that helps people put back together lives that have been soaked into numbness by alcohol or stretched to the tearing point by drugs, had sent me there. I wasn't convinced it was going to do me any good but everybody else was convinced and I was too weak to argue. Denial, they told me, is not a river in Egypt.

I probably wanted more than anything else for them to just put me on Northwest Flight 565 and leave me alone so I could get the friendly flight attendant to give me a drink. I made sure they bought me a first-class ticket so I wouldn't have to worry about the service being slow. Maybe I was going to hell but I wouldn't be thirsty when I got there. This book is about what happened to me there.

Actually, I made two trips to St. Mary's in search of a way to climb my Mount Everest. The first time, in the summer of 1987, I was an outpatient; I lived in a room on the eleventh floor of the main hospital, away from the Rehab, and it wasn't a good experience. I wasn't ready to give myself up to the monastery and it didn't help that I was living away from the rest of the consecrated brothers and sisters and rooming with a twenty-two-year-old kid whose idea of meditation was to smoke pot and talk to his girlfriend on the telephone while he watched "The Equalizer" on television. I never got into the program at all.

This time, to borrow from Richard Farina, I was down so far the Rehab looked like up to me.

2

The Way In, Which Is Also the Way Out

Whether they have been sentenced to or coerced into volunteering for the magic Minnesota cure, very few of the new arrivals at the plain red-brick building at 2512 South Seventh Street across from Augsburg College in southwest Minneapolis manage to present themselves at the admissions office without having swallowed something strong enough to subdue the raging demons that drove them there.

If you had enough willpower left to say no to a last drink or one more line of cocaine, you wouldn't be standing there shakily with your L.L. Bean carryon waiting for somebody to take your name, address, and serial number and relieve you of the card that will tell the computer who will pay for the $5,600 or so in bills you are about to run up at this midwestern purgatory.

You will learn to watch it with those religious code words. This place isn't religious but it's very religious. That is, you're welcome if you don't believe in God, but that's mostly because they are convinced they will change your mind before you get out and begin worrying about whether or not you ought to have a drink on the airplane back to New York or Memphis or Fort Smith or wherever you learned how to do all the bad things that got you here.

The one thing you didn't arrive with was willpower. You were wholly typical of the average arrival if you had three or four drinks on the airplane or carried a bottle on the train. Most newcomers, women or men, had a few last drinks at the airport or railroad terminal, and a few of them asked the taxi driver to stop at the bar closest to the hospital for a final jolt before going cold turkey.

Actually, I didn't do anything worse than have two double Bloody Marys on the airplane but that wasn't because I had suddenly had an attack of holiness but only because I was afraid it would be harder for me later if I had the straight vodka I really wanted. When I went in the door of what looked to me like Attica or Dannemora, I tried to make myself laugh by remembering the W. C. Fields line about being stuck in Pocatello, Idaho, for a week with nothing but food and water.

You never thought anything like this would happen to you, and it wouldn't have if you still had the strength to control your own life. But you don't, and as much as you resist admitting it, you know it. You're in such bad shape that, like a prisoner of the state who has just unexpectedly heard his sentence commuted from death by hanging to life imprisonment without possibility of parole, you are willing to go where they tell you to go and do what they tell you to do so long as they don't change their minds again.

When the woman at the desk tells you that you're in room 317 and it's a single room, it sounds unbelievably lucky, like being told at the Plaza that they have just one room left with a view of Central Park. You thank her humbly when she tells you to take the elevator up to the nurses' station on the third floor where somebody will show you where your room is. You know there won't be a bottle of wine in the room but just the same it sounds like they made a mistake and let you into heaven right away. Maybe they will even let you sleep for a while.

The first bad thing that happened to me was that I was told not to actually go to bed because they might decide to put me in a different room. So I just took off my shoes and stretched out on the bed and thought some long thoughts about how I wished I could drink like the civilians do and be satisfied with two martinis instead of always having to have one more. Then I fell asleep and the next thing I knew somebody was shaking me and telling me to pick up my bag and follow them to the room they had decided would be better for me.

When a nurse woke me up in the morning to take a blood sample, she said I'd been moved because they thought I would be more comfortable on this wing of the floor where "all of the seniors" were. I didn't care. I still had a private room, which was all my elitist soul cared about. The only problem I had was that I couldn't find my shoes. I looked everywhere, on the floor, in the closet, and in the bathroom, but no shoes. I felt helpless, nervous, desperately vulnerable. Being without shoes and having to run or walk on painful pebbles or rocks has always been one of my basic nightmares. I didn't feel very good anyway this unpleasant morning in this strange place, and the feeling that I had no control at all over what was happening to me got stronger and stronger. I asked the nurse if they had taken my shoes so I wouldn't leave—I meant escape—but she said no, they never did that unless somebody was violent. "You can leave any time you want," she said reassuringly. "The front door isn't locked." Then she had a brainstorm. "I'll bet I know where your shoes are," she said. "Weren't you in another room when you came in?" Of course. In two minutes, I had my shoes, and I felt better. Not good, but better.

"Do you want any breakfast?" the nurse asked. She knew perfectly well I didn't want any breakfast. They never do. "Well," she said when I confirmed her empirical judgment, "let's get started. First we'll take your blood pressure and then we'll fill out this form."

We didn't fill out the form for three or four hours because my blood pressure was one fifty-four over one hundred and they waved me back into bed and told me to swallow these two Tylenol tablets and try to sleep. "It's called withdrawal," the nurse said matter-of-factly.

I didn't wake up until the middle of the afternoon and I only woke up then because Liby was aiming the airplane she was driving in my dream straight into the George Washington Bridge after having just narrowly missed the Empire State Building and somehow miraculously flown under the Washington Square Arch. In a

747, mind you. It was much too soon for me to confront the question of why I had dreamed that she was flying the airplane and was clearly trying to get us killed.

What I woke up to was a standard real-life hospital room dominated by a high bed that could be raised or lowered at the pillow end, a night table with three drawers, a table and chair that could be used as a desk, a tall leather reading chair with a floor lamp next to it, and a wastebasket. There was a bulletin board with a patient's schedule thumbtacked onto it. The bathroom had a toilet and a sink with a large mirror that made it easy for you to see how bad you looked. It was more interesting to look out of the window which faced St. Mary's Hospital across a dead end street that accommodated an endless stream of delivery trucks. The west wing of the Rehab building was on my left and another red-brick building which proclaimed itself to be the College of St. Catherine was on the right. There were, I soon found out, always people to watch going back and forth, and happily the students at the college were all young and all female. Nothing about this place seemed like Attica except the implacable fact that it wasn't my idea to be here.

I understood that I could leave any time I wanted to but they had also made it clear that the price of going off on my own was that I couldn't come back, and I didn't think I was ready for that responsibility. I thought I was all right but I wasn't sure how all right. I wished I could have a drink. I wasn't dying for one; I just thought I would probably feel better if I had one.

A nurse walked in and asked me how I felt. I said I was all right and she asked me to hold out my hands. She looked at them and seemed satisfied. "Hold your palms against mine," she said, putting hers up as though we were going to make two high fives. I matched mine against hers and I thought mine were steady. "That's good," she said. Then she added, as she did almost every time she took my blood pressure and pulse, "Your hands are cold." My hands have always been cold. I remembered when my mother said to Liby, "I don't see how you've been able to stand those cold hands for forty years," which was how long we had been married then. "Forty-one," my wife had said brazenly.

Before the nurse left, I noticed that the last line on the chart she was carrying said, "Patient has cold hands." For some reason, that gave the patient a vagrant chill.

My first appointment was with Judy Wohlhueter, a short, intense young woman who looked like a political science major at Radcliffe. She seemed to know everything, so I let her direct the meeting and tried consciously to confine my answers to her questions and not fluff them up with my own opinions or pet digressions. Judy thought I was holding back and said so. Well, sure I was. But I had made up my mind on the airplane that I was going to hold tenaciously to a resolution not to show off. There wasn't any particular reason for me to think that a random group of people at a detoxification hospital in Minneapolis, Minnesota would be overwhelmed by the knowledge that I had been the chairman and chief executive officer of the Book-of-the-Month Club but I sensed that it wouldn't help my recovery efforts any if I took the attitude that I knew any more or was any better than anybody else here for the cure. The behavior that had got me here wasn't any better than the behavior that had gotten them here.

My experience going to Alcoholics Anonymous meetings, beginning three years before I got to St. Mary's, and listening to men and women scattering their gifts of evangelism and piety with the fervor and righteousness of a cockney communist on a soapbox at Hyde Park Corner made me wary of joining any group that would have the likes of them for members. I hated AA with a fierce passion and had viewed the countless meetings I'd gone to since drinking became an open problem for me after my retirement at the end of 1984 as a combination of penance and punishment. That's probably redundant, maybe tautological, but what the hell. I expected the worst and I thought the only way to stay sane and out of trouble while I was here was to keep my mouth shut as much as possible. I wasn't hostile, just wary.

I had never given up much of myself to anybody except the woman I married. That exception, I said guardedly to Judy, had something to do with my being here because the pressures that developed between Liby and me struck me with Force Ten devastation. Intensely private since childhood, I had nobody I could talk to about my feelings, so I took them to my one reliable friend and sat in the few bars that had become homes to me and drank.

Judy wanted to know everything I thought had a bearing on my condition so I bought her off with a little. It was all true; it just wasn't all of it. I told her I had married the first woman I ever touched and that I hadn't expected to ever argue or fight with her about anything and I was shocked when it turned out that she thought it was perfectly all right to argue and fight with me. "She yelled," I summed it up for Judy, "and I drank."

I admitted that we had fought an endless war over the different approaches we took to raising our children. Liby thought I was dangerously permissive and I thought she was an unthinking heiress to her Czech mother's old-world passion for rigorous discipline. But at least she always spoke her mind. I kept it all inside and rarely gave her a chance to find out what I was really thinking. Whenever we reached a new impasse, I just opened up another little room in my locked house of many rooms and buried it in an unused closet. She let out everything she thought and I kept it inside. And drank.

I didn't tell Judy how everything that happened on the night of our first date almost fifty years ago had been engraved in my head like a Rembrandt etching. The way she had moved over next to me in the car when it was time to say good night and had put up her face to be kissed, her beautiful knees unable to avoid touching mine. I didn't let go the streak of Irish poet in me and try to paint in words what I knew had happened, that this young woman had willingly but in a sense unsuspectingly provided the striking surface on which the head of my match exploded into an everlasting flame that lit up the sky for as far as I could see. As knowing Nora Barnacle had for the great writer Himself, Liby opened for me the door to paradise and gave me a sudden, unexpected look at the glories inside. But where James Joyce had been passive clay in the hands of his aggressor love, I rose to the charge and never called retreat. For me, recklessly pursuing the advantage I thought she had granted me, every day from then on was D-Day. I didn't tell Judy that when I kissed her and touched her and held her as though we were going down together on the Titanic I swore that I would never let go of her and that she would be mine and I would be hers forever and I would take care of her as long as she lived. "Ever wilt thou love," as the poet said, "and she be fair."

I didn't tell Judy that because she was from a different world than I was, and used to better things, I worked from that night on to make myself into the kind of man I thought she deserved. Everything I did, I did for her. I chose to love her and nobody else. Not surprisingly the devotional candles I lit for her generated more heat and light than she was ready for. But I just went on being determined to become worthy of her; I would create a man good enough for Liby.

"I never asked to be put on a pedestal," she said once. "I didn't like it then and I don't like it now." That may have been the night she tried to hit me with one of her hand-thrown pottery plates.

"Was it a good one?" a fellow potter wanted to know, trying to kid her out of her anger.

"No," she admitted, "it was a second."

Wasn't I entitled to a drink? I thought so. For a long time I kept my puzzlements and my sadnesses in an imaginary frame hanging over my desk. Like a doctor's license to practice, it was my license to drink.

I told Judy that I had been born on West Fifty-eighth Street in New York City and had been raised in Yonkers, a factory town just north of the city on the Hudson River. I had fallen in love with the newspaper business when I was a delivery boy trying to sell enough new subscriptions to win a dazzlingly red wagon with removable slats on the sides and I had made the newspaper office my hangout. I began covering school sports for the paper when I was in junior high school and later in high school. They paid me for whatever they printed of mine and they let me use a typewriter in the city room, which I would have paid them for if I had any money, and I didn't need a guidance counselor to tell me what I wanted to be when I grew up. When I got out of high school, with a general diploma instead of a college entrance diploma because I couldn't

pass plane geometry, I went right to work for the paper as an
assistant in the sports department. It seemed to the editor as though
I'd been there forever and I came cheap, ten dollars a week, so
there was never any doubt about my getting the job. By the time
the war came and I was drafted into the 77th Infantry Division, I
was the sports editor of the Yonkers *Herald-Statesman* and was
making thirty dollars a week. I wrote a column five days a week
and was happily romancing the only girl I had ever wanted. The
war took four years of my life and took me to Guam, Leyte, Ie
Shima, Okinawa, and Japan before setting me free. Liby had married me at Fort Jackson, South Carolina, and when some of us sat
around on Cebu after they dropped the atomic bomb and talked
about what kind of a world we hoped to find when we got back
home, I said I hoped I might make one hundred dollars a week
some day as a newspaper reporter in New York City. I didn't want
to go back to the Westchester paper. How can you keep them down
on the farm after they've seen Tacloban and Ormoc and Shuri, not
to mention Sapporo and Yokohama?

Judy asked me what was my happiest memory ever, and I wondered if she expected me to say the day I got out of the army, but
I didn't have to think because I'd thought about it so often lying
in holes in the ground in the Pacific. "The morning I woke up at
the Wade Hampton Hotel in Columbia, South Carolina, and looked
at my wife lying next to me," I said. "God, I'd wanted her so much.
I couldn't believe we were really married. I wanted to wrap her up
and take care of her forever."

I had to go back to work at the Yonkers paper for a while but
then I got lucky and got a job on a new national sports magazine
called simply *SPORT*. It all came out of a jewelry robbery in Bronxville, a rich suburb next door to Yonkers. There were always jewelry
robberies in Bronxville because that's where the jewelry was. The
city editor sent me to cover it because I had driven Liby's car in to
work that day. "Find Chief Brennan," he said. "He'll give you the
story. Then call me up as quick as you can and you can talk it to
Van. I want to make today's paper." The chief was a good-natured
Irishman who looked after me like a son and let me use the phone

in his own office to tell the paper what we knew, who had lost what, and the fact that, as usual, there were no clues. The sociologist police chief explained to me succinctly that "the stuff is probably being fenced in Harlem right this minute." When I was finished on the phone, and he had made sure I had spelled his name right, he pulled a bottle of Golden Wedding out of his desk drawer and poured us each half a water glass full. I would have asked for some water but I didn't want to look like a candy ass. Didn't I have a combat infantryman's badge for Christ's sake? While we drank the booze he told me how he used to read my column before the war (I wasn't in the sports department anymore) and what a big baseball fan he was. When he found out I was trying to get a job in New York he sent me to a friend of his at the *Sporting News*, the baseball weekly, and the friend offered me a job except that it was in St. Louis, where I didn't want to go. Then he sent me on to the Mac-fadden Publications people who were starting *SPORT*, and they hired me.

Skipping fast, and reminding myself that I had promised I wouldn't show off, I told Judy I had become the editor-in-chief of *SPORT* in 1951 and had stayed there until 1960 when another break got me the job of editor-in-chief of the Literary Guild book club at Doubleday. After that, I said, I went to the McCall Publishing Company for a few years and then on to the Book-of-the-Month Club where I stayed until I had to retire at the end of 1984 when I was sixty-five. I didn't say I'd been a senior vice president of Doubleday in charge of the book clubs and general publishing, and I didn't say I was the president of the McCall Publishing Company and the president of the Book-of-the-Month Club.

Some times it's more embarrassing to hold back on information like that than it is to admit it straightaway. But I wanted desperately to be as inconspicuous as possible here and I had an uneasy feeling that the professionals might think it was even more shameful for me to have had all the advantages I'd had and still become an alcoholic. The less attention they paid to me, the better I would like it.

What I didn't know yet was that at St. Mary's they pay attention to everybody all of the time. I knew from the summer before, when I was on my own as an outpatient, that the only place you could buy a copy of *The New York Times* was in the lobby of the general hospital; the lobby of the Rehab, which treated only substance abusers, had two newspaper honor boxes, one for the *Minneapolis Star-Tribune* and the other for the Gannett paper, *USA Today*. For me, the worst kind of New York chauvinist, there was only one newspaper, and neither of those was it. I slipped out of the side door of the Rehab and walked across to the side door of the hospital, made my way upstairs to the lobby and spent two of my precious store of quarters for a *New York Times*. When I got back I was stopped by Jim Maki, a generously warmhearted unit assistant who was notably friendly and helpful to everybody. "You were observed," he said sternly, "walking over to the main hospital. That's off limits. I'll get you a map of the grounds with the boundaries marked in red."

"I'm sorry," I said, "I just wanted a copy of *The New York Times*." I tried for a little black humor. "I'm an addict," I said.

Jim didn't laugh. "They have papers in the lobby here," he said patiently.

When Judy was finished with me she sent me back to my room with instructions to go to the lounge at three-fifteen to watch the indoctrination video film on the disease concept of alcoholism. I wasn't enthusiastic about that because I wasn't any more enthusiastic about the disease concept than I was about AA. I thought they were both gimmicks the professionals used to narcoticize their patients. I also thought the main reason for the overwhelming support the professionals gave the disease concept was because it got their bills paid. If alcoholism wasn't a disease, the government and the insurance companies wouldn't cough up the money to treat it, so it has to be a disease. Hadn't the Supreme Court already ruled in one Veterans Administration case that it wasn't a disease? Sure, it had.

I went to the film anyway and nothing changed. They still said it was a disease and I still didn't believe it.

It probably did me some good to stir up a disagreement with the established authority. It was better than being totally down, and I was pretty far down. I felt, lying on my bed in room 349, that life had finally caught up with me after all those good years. I felt diminished and demeaned. Was it only a couple of years ago that all those wonderful publishing people had come to a dinner for me at the Hotel Pierre on Fifth Avenue and said all those nice things about me? "We're losing one of the good guys," Dick Munro, the president of Time Inc., had said. "Doing business with Fitz was always a pleasure," Pat Knopf, the founder of Atheneum, had said. "You didn't need a contract. All you had to do was shake hands with him at lunch."

Well, I'd always had two martinis and sometimes a glass of wine, too, at those lunches. I couldn't have been drunk all of the time. Some of those lunch deals for big books cost the Literary Guild or the Book-of-the-Month Club more than a million dollars, and the record said I had made those companies a ton of money. What was wrong in this equation?

No alcoholic thinks it is all his fault. In fact, mostly he thinks hardly any of it is his fault. He can always begin by blaming her. She (and with the women it's just as surely he) may not have driven him to drink but she sure made it logical and even inevitable that he would drink. I had suggested to Judy Wohlhueter that I had always thought the perfect description of the warring couple was the question their friends always debated about Zelda and Scott Fitzgerald: "Did he drive her crazy or did she drive him to drink?"

I met my first peers when the loudspeaker in my room told me in the sweet voice of one of the astonishingly pretty nurses to go to the fourth floor lounge for an indoctrination meeting. I could see that there was a lot of indoctrinating done around here. But I was glad enough to go. It reminded me of the first few days in the army. You were so nervous and uncertain about what was going to happen next that it was a relief when somebody gave you an order and told you to get on with it.

There were more than a dozen men and women in the big lounge when I got there, all of them facing a nurse holding a clipboard.

It was, I decided, exactly like the army. Any minute now I was going to find out that I had been assigned to E Company and I should fall in behind the sergeant carrying the blue and white flag with the big *E* on it.

But unlike the army, it wasn't the officer with the clipboard who was doing the talking. It was all being done by a short, wiry, iron-haired man wearing a pink Lacoste golf shirt, complete with alligator, and light gray linen slacks. He was taking out his rage on the nurse.

"I know my rights," he was shouting. "You can't keep me here a minute longer than I'm willing to stay. So don't start pushing me around or I'll just get up and walk out right now. I'm a medical doctor and I don't have to take this kind of shit from anybody. In fact, when I do walk out of here I think the first place I'm going is to my lawyer's office and sue the pants off all of you. Beginning with my family. Do you people really think you're going to do me any good, you're going to help me, by kidnapping me this way? Jesus, they didn't even let me pack a bag of clothes. I don't even have a toothbrush or shaving stuff. That's a hell of a way to treat a man. Any man, much less a doctor."

It was pretty clear that our friend didn't want anybody to forget that he was a doctor and was not only entitled to special treatment but was damn well going to get it.

One of the other newcomers tried to kid him out of it. "You're just sore," he said, "because you didn't get a chance to slip a bottle into that bag you wanted to pack."

I was surprised that the doctor laughed. "I probably would have," he said. "Anyway, I sure would have taken a few good slugs while I was packing."

"Exactly," the nurse said. "Now, let's take the roll. Everybody give your name and your hometown."

The doctor wasn't bashful. "Doctor Bob Sommerfield," he said aggressively. "That's with an '*o*,' not a '*u*.' I'm from Duluth, which is in the state of Minnesota, just like this place, only they wouldn't tolerate an institution like this in Duluth."

Sarah Taunton was next. I thought she was probably younger

than she looked. Mostly because she looked like hell. She was tall, probably between five six and five seven, but she slumped over so much that she seemed round-shouldered. Everything about her shrieked that she was a beaten woman. She just didn't care how she looked. She wasn't wearing any makeup, not even a minimum slash of lipstick, and her face was so colorless and her hair so dull that you thought homely when what you were looking at actually was fairly pretty. She said she was from Baltimore. "A long way from home," the nurse said brightly. Sarah's head dropped a little lower. She knew she was a long way from home.

None of the other newcomers made any special impression on me and even Doctor Bob kept quiet as the nurse told us that we would all be assigned to groups as soon as the staff had a chance to go over our evaluation interviews, and that once we were in a group we would be expected to eat all our meals and attend all the lectures and films with the group. "Hang out with the other group members as much as you can," she said. "The more time you spend together, the better you'll be able to relate to each other in feedback." I wondered what you were supposed to do if you hated the other people in the group but I didn't think it would help my situation any to ask. The nurse said we shouldn't worry about finding out whose group we had been assigned to; either the counselor would tell us or make sure somebody else did. Right now, she said, we were free to go back to our rooms and hang around, but please stay in the building so that somebody could find us if they were looking for us. Otherwise, we should go to dinner with everybody else at five-thirty and to the lecture hall at seven. The nurse was cheerful and comforting, and when I walked out, I saw that her nameplate said EILEEN. No wonder she was nice; that's my daughter's name.

I skipped the elevator and walked down the one flight of stairs to the third floor. Jim Maki stopped me as I walked past the nurses' station. "Know your way around yet?" he asked helpfully. When I confessed I didn't, he showed me the points of interest. "That's the lecture hall," he said, pointing to the double doors at the end of the hall. "I see you've already found the stairs. I expect you'll find it's usually a lot easier to use them than it is to wait for the elevator. At least, going down. Your lounge is down at the other end, that's where the television is, and there's a coffee closet right near it on the right side of the hall going that way. Speaking of coffee, there's coffee and juice and food and ice cream in the day room, first door on the right that way." He pointed again. "Right inside the door are the telephones and the soda machine. You need a dime for the telephone, either for a local call or to get the operator for a credit card call, in which case you get the dime back. There's a blackboard for messages and everybody tries to answer the phone if they're in there when it rings. Be nice and write the message on the board."

"How much are the Cokes?" I asked him.

"Fifty-five cents."

I blessed the women at Freedom Institute who had sent me here for telling me to take a lot of change with me; I had a soft canvas bag filled with quarters. I could see that I was going to need them. I knew from my previous visit that there was a bank in the medical center, but, like *The New York Times* machine and the lunchroom in the lobby of the main hospital, the bank and its quarters was off limits to me.

Some of the stories I'd read about the famous places that did this kind of work had made me wonder if I'd been booked into another La Costa or Maine Chance, but it was pretty clear that this place was a hospital, not an inn on the park or a golf club with rooms for sleeping over. Apparently they didn't think it was necessary or advisable to treat drunks and druggies as delicately as fatties and anorectics.

I remembered that I had seen some people walking down the hall carrying look-alike plastic pitchers filled with ice cubes, so I asked Jim how I could get a pitcher and where you got the ice cubes. "Easy," he said in his laid-back way. He motioned for me to follow him and pushed through a glass door labeled STAFF ONLY. He took a pitcher off the counter and gave it to me. "The ice," he said, pointing to a motel-style ice-making machine just inside the door, "is right there. Just push the pitcher against that lever and fill it up."

I went straight from there to the Coke machine and bought two Cokes. Unhappily they were cans, not screw-top bottles, not so good for somebody like me who drinks a little at a time and likes to make it last all day, but I learned that if you put something over the top you were all right. I also learned very soon that if you seized one of the opportunities that are offered several times a week to go on a chaperoned walk to the nearby stores, you could buy a six-pack of sixteen-ounce screw-top bottles and have enough for a week. Cheaper, too.

Next I decided to see if the gift shop had anything I might want. There was a paperback book rack heavy on Danielle Steel and Jackie Collins but I found a Travis McGee novel by John D. McDonald and I was happy. I also bought a couple of Milky Ways and a couple of Hershey bars. Then I bought a thick notebook in case I thought of anything to write in it. When I sat down for a minute in the lounge across from the gift shop, I was glad I had the notebook because there was no way I could resist making notes on the earnest exchange between a young couple sitting on a sofa next to my chair.

She was about twenty or twenty-one, round-faced, a little over-weight, but just short of a Melanie Griffith look-alike. "Don't forget," she told him, "when you get paid, you owe my father three hundred dollars."

He was a few years older, taller and thinner, and it was easy to see that he was the inmate and she was the visitor. And clearly his visitor wasn't bringing him a jigsaw blade in a ham sandwich. "I'll give him what I can when I get the check," he said.

"Give him the whole three hundred dollars," she said.

"We're going to have to have some money," he protested. He was asking her, not telling her.

She was telling him. "If you don't pay him," she said flatly, "you'll use it." The way she said *use* had nothing to do with buying ham-burgers or ice-cream cones.

He fought back halfheartedly. "Jesus," he said, "why do you always have to nag me like that?"

That did it. "Nag you?" she threw it back at him. "Why do I nag you? Because I'm fucking married to you, that's why."

They kissed good-bye when they stood up but it wasn't Melanie kissing Don or whatever his name is that she keeps marrying. He turned left to go upstairs to his next meeting and she turned right to go out the front door. If she had brought a jigsaw blade with her, she still had it. I was struck by the difference between them. He was slumped over but her shoulders were straight back. Her ass missed being Melanie's only by maybe six inches too wide. You had to root for her. There were pieces to pick up and she was trying to pick them up.

I took my notebook back upstairs. Maybe I would write for a while. Obviously, for a writer this place was a gold mine. It wouldn't have taken John Cheever, who knew all about places like this and the people who went to them, an hour to make a short story out of that scene. But, except for the one thing we had in common, I wasn't John Cheever. But thinking of Cheever reminded me of the day we gave a lunch for him in the Book-of-the-Month Club board room. Knopf had just published his *Collected Short Stories* and we had made it a main selection of the club. I was happy that the first reviews were ecstatic because I had made an unusual fuss about pushing the book on our reluctant outside, independent judges who weren't sure that it was up to our standards to choose a book that was simply a collection of stories that had already been printed in magazines. In this case, mostly in *The New Yorker*. "Why not?" I had argued. "They've never been printed this way before. And, besides, they're great stories."

Cheever wasn't drinking. He had already been to Smithers, the Rehab in the old Billy Rose mansion on East Ninety-third Street between Park and Madison in what once was a fancy, then a decidedly unfancy, and now once again is becoming a fancy section of Manhattan's Upper East Side. His daughter, who wrote a book about him called *Home Before Dark*, said that after his twenty-eight days at Smithers, which he hated at first and later embraced, he never drank again. He handed drinks to friends but he had learned that for him it was a death sentence and he respected his unarguable need to leave it alone. He didn't look at all nervous or disapproving, or jealous, as I drank my usual two martinis in the board room's conversation pit before we sat down to lunch. I was nervous about it but not so nervous that I was going to give up my two drinks, carefully made for me by the caterer's bartender and probably loaded with a stunning four ounces of Smirnoff apiece. I had hired the caterer—actually, I had found him in the yellow pages of the telephone book—and I signed his checks and he took good care of me. I never had to ask out loud for a second drink; it was there when I reached for it.

"I'll bet I'm the only man in this room who never went to college," Cheever said when he turned to me after having a long discussion about first printing and reorder numbers with Bob Bernstein, the chairman of Random House, which owned Knopf, Pantheon, Ballantine, and various other publishing imprints.

"No," I said cheerfully, glad to have something in common with the distinguished author, "you're not."

"You didn't?" Cheever asked.

"I didn't. Gorton High School, Yonkers, New York, that's it."

He thought that over. "Well," he said finally, "I'll bet I'm the only man here who was in the infantry in the war."

Now we had a game going and I was happy to play. I had serious common ground with our guest. "No," I said, "you're not."

"What division?" Cheever wanted to know.

"The Seventy-seventh. And I know you were in the Twenty-second Infantry Regiment before you finally got lucky and got transferred to the Signal Corps. I looked it up. So we both survived infantry basic training."

Cheever looked as though he liked me better than when my old friend Bernstein had introduced me to him as the president of the Book-of-the-Month Club. But he had an ace in the hole. "Well," he said with some satisfaction, "I guess all that leaves me is that I'm the only enlisted man here."

"No," I said, "you're not."

"I was a staff sergeant," he said, and I wasn't sure then and I'm not now whether he wanted his rank to be higher than mine or lower. I know that I felt I had finally lost. "I was the First Sergeant," I said. "Maybe I could type better than you could."

Remembering all this lying on my bed in room 349 of the St. Mary's Rehab Center in Minneapolis, Minnesota, a city I'd been in only once before in my life when I gave a *SPORT* magazine award to George Mikan of the then Minneapolis Lakers as the Most Valuable Player in the National Basketball Association for 1950, I felt I didn't have much to be proud of about my life. I had done so well and had achieved so much that I was being taken care of practically hand and foot in what was not quite a hospital or a jail by skilled custodians who were paid to look after helpless people. I felt like eating something sweet that wasn't candy so I decided to see what they had in the kitchen. When I walked past the nurses' station, a good-looking, leggy blonde woman who had been my counselor for a couple of weeks my first time here, was standing there waving at me. I walked over to say hello and Debbie Chapman said, "I want you in my group."

"Okay," I said. "Have you got enough clout to get me in it?"

"I've got enough clout," she said grimly. "The question is, are you willing to work hard enough to make it work?"

I said yes, I was. "You tell me what you want me to do," I said, "and I'll do it." I meant it. I was determined not to be a clubhouse lawyer or doctor or whatever they called them in this place.

"Good," Debbie said. "This time it's going to be different." Debbie thought I had just given up the last time and hadn't really tried, and that was why I was back. She thought enough of my chances to want to be the one who kept me from coming back again.

Debbie, at thirty-six, was one of the youngest counselors on the staff but in the unpredictable way things turn out in even the most structured of worlds, she had become the Rehab's seniors' specialist. She liked working with older men and women and they responded to her. I know I did. I liked her forthrightness and her surprising mixture of compassion and toughness. I was both glad and nervous that she had volunteered to take me on—glad because I knew she was good and nervous because I knew she would ask a lot of me and I wouldn't be able to ignore her. It wasn't going to be a rest cure and I had to admit to myself that that was pretty much what I'd had in mind when I came here. But if somebody was going to push me around I was glad it was going to be Debbie.

Debbie disarms you even before she goes to work. You feel comfortable with her; you're not scared anymore. She looks as though she might have been the captain of her high school cheerleading squad twenty years ago and you think admiringly that she was probably the kind who cheated a little and hemmed her skirt a few inches shorter than it was supposed to be. She has an innocent worldliness that makes you speculate that she could have been one of those high school foreign exchange students who spent the summer in some place like Denmark or Finland.

In the movie, she should be played by Kathleen Turner.

Debbie is as refreshing as Coca-Cola and as bubbly as Canada Dry ginger ale, but, like Turner in *Prizzi's Honor*, you can see her taking on a contract as a hit man. There isn't anybody who doesn't like Debbie Chapman but it isn't because she's Miss Goody Goody Two Shoes. She's a restless, energetic woman whose five feet eight inches usually make her the tallest woman around even when she's wearing flats and who stands eye to eye with most men when she's dressed up and wearing heels. Either way, she has the legs of a Hanes stocking model. Her tallness helps give her a commanding presence which is strengthened by an easy confidence born of experience in the business at hand and by inquisitive green eyes that search skeptically right through your defenses. She is, as I said in one of the many letters I've written to her, a woman of limitless compassion and an unwavering sense of purpose.

Debbie comes from Wisconsin and her speech advertises her midwestern roots. She says "drinkun" instead of "drinking" and her voice level drops an octave when she confides in the group some personal asides about her own history as an addict. "I drank scotch and I ate pills," she says. "Lots of both." She says she's proud of the fact that she never helped break up any marriages when she was drinking but she thinks that if the liquor and the drugs hadn't slowed the guys down, she might have. "I was ready a lot of times," she admits, "when they weren't. They wanted to, but they were too stoned." That's one way Debbie lets you feel that you aren't the only one with guilty memories, watercolor slides flickering in your head of chaotic scenes that you're ashamed of but are curiously reluctant to let go of. It doesn't take long before you see Debbie as the combat-wise platoon leader who will find a way to get you out of here.

She was Miss Sheboygan when she was eighteen, but she's not about to tell that to her group. Some wise guy from New York or Chicago would be sure to sing, "I can see the judges' eyes when they handed you the prize, I'll bet you made the cutest bow . . . you must have been a beautiful baby, 'cause baby, look at you now."

Marjorie Noonsong, a nurse I remembered because I liked her so much, stopped me as I was getting ready to walk away from the station and said, "As long as you're here you may as well let me take your pressure." I tried not to tense up while she wrapped the band around my arm but it didn't do any good. "A hundred and eighty-two over a hundred and twelve," she said. It sounded like a death sentence. I was sorry about that last quart of Absolut I'd bought the night before they made me come here. But, then, why wasn't I sorry about all the other ones I'd bought before that one? It didn't make any sense. None of it made any sense. But it wasn't surprising that I didn't feel so good.

All Marjorie said was, "Make sure you come here after dinner for your medication." At St. Mary's they never call them pills. Maybe because that's what the inmates call them. I was pretty sure there wasn't much danger of my forgetting. I had hardly ever heard of a blood pressure reading that high.

"See you later," Marjorie said reassuringly.

I hoped so.

3

If My Friends Sent Me Here, Who Needs Enemies?

I had intended to skip dinner because I didn't want to take a chance on throwing up before I could get from the dining room table to the men's room in the hall just off the lobby, but Leona Geilfuss, a motherly nurse with a way of getting you to do what is good for you without turning you off by putting it that way, talked me into giving it a try. "They always have something that's like baby food," she said. "Go on, give it a try. Nobody's going to yell at you if you don't eat it all."

When I got downstairs, and stopped to look at the menu Scotch-taped to the wall outside the cafeteria, I decided to settle for the "Old-Fashioned Bean Soup." I certainly didn't want to have anything to do with the roast beef or the hot dog on a bun. But when I got inside and looked at them, I also picked up the mixed vegetables and the mashed potatoes. I waved off the gravy that the chef held up in an oversized tablespoon and, when I sat down, I mixed some of the potatoes into the dish with the vegetables. I ate about half of the soup and a little of my potato-vegetables creation and drank some iced tea while I met the people in my group. Mary Verkennes, a nurse I'd known from last year, who was as quick with a helping hand as she was with a friendly smile, showed me where Deb's group was sitting. She said she was sorry I was back but she was glad to see me.

I made a quick count as I walked over and saw that I was the ninth member of the group and that I'd already seen two of them, Doctor Bob and Sarah Taunton, at the fourth floor free-for-all. When I sat down, I guessed that four of us, Doctor Bob, two portly legionnaire types wearing plaid flannel shirts with wide suspenders, and me were in our mid to late sixties. The American Legion types introduced themselves as Ralph Woolard and Carl Bruhl. Two, Sarah and a tall, wiry man who looked dressed to go out and said his name was Ken, looked to be in their fifties. The only young man, who told me he was John Terranova, couldn't have been more than nineteen or twenty. The one who introduced himself as Denny Cravath was harder to place. Except that, seen close up, he had a tired, almost haggard look that he kept hidden by his quick grin and knowing eyes, Denny seemed to be in his late thirties, maybe even forty. I decided he probably wasn't more than thirty-five and just hadn't been here long enough to get a grip on his health. The flashing glitter in his eyes suggested to me that the stuff that had put him here more likely came in a powder or a pill than in a bottle. I had a lot to learn about Denny's experimental nature. He was what the ballplayers call an Edison, a young pitcher who can't wait to try every new pitch somebody tells him about. Denny was like that about stimulants.

Most of us left the table together, which was good for me because I had a chance to observe the common etiquette of garbage disposal and the return of trays, silverware, dishes, cups, and glasses. I hadn't learned all that the other time because I'd eaten either in the hospital cafeteria, where you just put everything on an endless belt for somebody else to worry about, or the coffee shop where you could always get a waitress to bring you either a hamburger or a hot turkey sandwich with mashed potatoes and gravy. After we squeezed through the narrow passageway from the dishwashing counter, we all played follow-the-leader and trailed the two sets of suspenders out past the gift shop, which I noticed for the first time was called St. Mary's Cupboard and seemed to have a window full of sweatshirts across the front of which was printed, "I Survived #*+%#* Family Week," through two sets of doors to the sidewalk. Judging from the dozens of people standing there in small groups, this was the Rehab's designated smoking area.

Maybe I was especially sensitive to the point because of my advanced years, but I was interested to see that there was no noticeable grouping by age. I wondered if, in this place, people gravitated toward each other because of shared experiences, or drug of choice, rather than age. There were more women than I had thought, nowhere near half and half but maybe two-thirds, one-third. The average age of the women seemed to be a lot younger than the average age of the men. I stopped playing sociologist when I reminded myself that I had only been here one night.

Denny Cravath and Mac Mackenzie had just started off together, walking in the direction of the open field next to the Rehab, when Mac stopped and called back to me. "Want to go for a walk?" Denny waved as if to say, yeah, come on with us. It was exactly what I felt like doing and they both seemed like nice guys. "We can't go on the big walk," Denny said. "Not enough time before the lecture. But if we feel like it, we can do that after. I love to walk," he explained without apology. "Me, too," Mac said, just as I said, "Me, too." We all laughed and that organized our walking group for the rest of the month.

"What's your real first name?" I asked Mac as we walked across the field toward the riverbank. Denny looked as curious as I was; he said he'd been wanting to ask, too. "Everett," Mac said, "but nobody except my parents has called me that since the third grade. And they're dead now. It's just a name for my driver's license and social security card and, I guess I may as well tell both of you right away, for the bulletin board outside my church. I don't want to scare you guys, but I'm a Presbyterian minister. From the smallest town you'd ever want to see, West Castleton, Vermont."

"I'm retired," I said. "I used to be in the book business."

"I'm in the trucking business in Odessa, Texas," Denny said, with just a trace of the Texas "bidness" in the way he said the word. "Actually, it's my father's business, and it was his father's before him, but I'm runnin' it now with the old man lookin' over my shoulder whenever he hasn't got anything better to do." Denny had been here a week already and he knew how everything worked.

When we got over to the riverbank we looked through the bushes at the narrow stream that didn't look to me as though it could possibly have any connection with the mighty Mississippi of song and story, or even with the river I'd seen from the deck of the paddlewheeler we'd been on in New Orleans, the same day we'd ridden on a streetcar named Desire. "Not much of a river up here," I said. "I guess we're a long ways from Natchez or Memphis or wherever the hell the big boats are. Maybe even Hannibal, Mo. I got hooked on all that romance reading Richard Bissell's novel *A Stretch on the River*. This canal here doesn't look big enough to float a towboat with a string of barges behind it."

"There's a riverboat over there," Denny said, pointing through the trees to a paddlewheeler tied up on the St. Paul side. "I guess it's a dinner theater or something." We could make out MISSISSIPPI RIVER CENTENNIAL SHOWBOAT on the side.

Mac said, "Too bad it's on the other side. If it was on this side, we could slip down and get on line for a drink before the show."

When I think back now on that first walk in the summer Minnesota evening, as breathlessly hot and muggy as any I remembered from basic training in the lowlands of South Carolina, I marvel at the serendipity with which like-minded men find each other. I'm sure Mac and Denny and I would have made it through St. Mary's without each other but it would have been harder and we wouldn't have got anywhere near as much out of it.

We talked, on that first walk, about how we had got there.

I told them my wife and kids had got the Freedom Institute in Manhattan to arrange for St. Mary's to admit me and to expect me the night of July fifth. Then they set up an appointment for me that afternoon with our family doctor, Jerry Shevell, at his office in New Rochelle. They settled on a time toward the end of the day when Jerry, who had been a family friend for a long time, would have enough time to spend with me if it turned out to be hard to talk me into going. I didn't give them any trouble. If they wanted me to go, I would go. I was tired and I didn't have much hope any more that things would ever get any better. I had spent a few days at my friend Roger Kahn's house in Croton-on-Hudson drinking slowly but steadily, even keeping a glass of Absolut on the night table next to my bed in Roger's downstairs guest room. I could keep it cold because Roger had thoughtfully put a refrigerator in the guest room. I don't think I ever got drunk while I was in Croton, but I was never sober, either. The main thing I felt was sorry for myself, and when I feel sorry for myself, I drink. I know there's a theory that some people drink the way manic-depressives behave; they can stay sober for a long time, but when they fall, they fall hard. It's all or nothing, and I was in an all period. No wonder Liby had got scared and called for reinforcements.

My doctor wanted to know why I was so despondent. "I'd rather you were mad about it," Jerry said.

"I feel diminished," I said. "Diminished and, I guess, demeaned. I hadn't expected to end my life this way."

Mac had also had a friendly intervention. The people at his little church, where he made up the whole clerical staff, had been worried about him for a long time. They had seen him unsteady and stumbling over words at meeting after meeting, sometimes even at services. They had mourned his increasingly frequent flash "illnesses" that made him miss appointments they were privately sure he had simply forgotten or slept through. "The truth was," he said as we turned right at a kids' wading pool and headed out toward the street for the walk back to the hospital, "I missed some of them just because I wanted to show them I didn't care."

"Maybe," I said, "it was a *cri de coeur*."

"What the hell is that?" Denny wanted to know.

"Literally a cry from the heart," I said, "but really a cry for help. Drunks are very good at that."

"I guess in a way it was," Mac said. "I knew I couldn't go on like that. Anyway, they finally did something about it. There's this one woman in particular who has a lot to do with the church who found out about St. Mary's and made all the arrangements with one of my sons. They just called me in and presented me with a fait accompli. Before I knew what was up, I was on my way to the airport. I didn't even get a chance to ask how everything was going to be taken care of. They said all I had to worry about was coming here and getting well." We walked along quietly for a while. "I hope," Mac said, "it's as simple as that."

Denny had a different story to tell. He was out on bail on a drug bust and he was here because his lawyer had convinced his family it would not only straighten him out but would also help convince the judge, when he came up for trial, that he was really trying to clean up his act. And his family had convinced him.

"They have a lot to say," Denny explained, "because it's still really my father's business and he can throw me out any time he wants to. There wasn't a whole lot I could say when he told me to get my ass out here. They were all pretty upset, me bein' all over the television news all the time. Of course, it made a pretty good story, me coming from what you might call a prominent family and all that. Shit, I'm a member of all the businessmen's clubs and I'm the president of the university boosters' club and I got me a good-lookin' wife and she's got two pretty daughters from her first marriage and it just made one hell of a story. No wonder everybody wanted to get me out of town. I guess, as a matter of fact, I was glad to get the hell out of town myself."

Denny had been grabbed by a combination of federal agents and local cops when he picked up a package of cocaine at a Federal Express office. He had bought it from an old friend who had moved from Odessa to California and had made a heavy connection there and had bragged about it to Denny when he had seen him on a visit back to the old hometown. But the feds got onto the man in California, where apparently he'd been doing a little more selling than is considered excusable by the law enforcement people as just dealing to friends, and they had trailed Denny's package from the day it had been mailed. "I was really stupid," Denny said. "He kept putting off mailing it and I kept calling him up and yelling about it, telling him I needed it. I should have known something was wrong but the only thing I thought about was getting the goods. I got it all right, and so did the cops."

Denny's worst mistake was agreeing to go to the Federal Express office to make the pickup. "I didn't see why our company mailman couldn't pick it up like he always did but they said no, it was the insurance (Denny said *in*surance the Texas way) or something and I had to come and sign for it myself. I was pretty nervous and I stayed nervous until I had the package safe in the car and had started out of their parking lot. I drove a little ways down the road and then I pulled over and stopped because I just couldn't resist opening the package and taking a peek. Just when I had ripped the wrapper open, I was surrounded by half the police cars in the state of Texas and one cop was leaning in the door with a great big gun up against my face. I was scared shitless. So I got arrested and fingerprinted and all that crap and I was the star of the eleven o'clock news that night. I was the best thing that had happened to the Odessa television since they arrested an eighteen-year-old hooker in the lobby of the Marriott Hotel on the night of the debutante cotillion. I was on my way out here forty-eight hours later."

Mac summed it up when we got to the front door of the Rehab. "Well," he said, "we're really some kind of a consortium, aren't we? The preacher, the writer, and the prodigal son from the Ponderosa."

Odd trio or not, we became best friends and we logged a lot of miles that month taking the rectangular walk around the park. We often made the short loop after breakfast and lunch and the long, leisurely, close to a mile walk after the seven o'clock lecture when we sometimes saw the line forming for dinner at the riverboat across the way. It was hot those July nights and the burnt grass underfoot was as dry as we were after a day with nothing except coffee, Coca-Cola, and iced tea to drink. I felt a little faint after the exercise and I was glad to get back inside the air-conditioned building. I made it through the lecture, which was a movie on AIDS starring Mike Tyson's on-again, off-again sweetheart, Robin Givens.

"We're going to talk about sex," Robin said from the screen, fixing her melting brown eyes right on you. "You may get embarrassed, but that's okay. I'm going to tell you the stuff you need to know, beginning with the fact that AIDS is hard to get. It's especially hard to get if the guy wears a condom, which he should always do whether it's for vaginal sex or anal sex. Either way, guys have to wear them and girls have to make sure they do."

Most of us alcoholics slept through Robin. Out on the sidewalk, Ralph and Carl, the suspenders twins, talked about their Family Week experiences like a couple of old infantrymen talking about D-Day. Denny said it was his turn next week. We listened nervously to everything they said; God knows it would be our turn soon enough for the dreaded confrontation with our Loved Ones. At St. Mary's, Loved Ones always sounds capitalized and it gives you an uneasy feeling as though you should genuflect or at least number your rosary beads. Doctor Bob shattered that spell. "Loved Ones, shit," he said bitterly. "They're the ones who put us here. I'd like to see every one of mine hang by their thumbs for a week."

"In your living room?" Denny teased him.

"Hell, no," Doctor Bob said. "I wouldn't let them inside the house. Out on the front lawn would be the right place. I'd build stocks for them like they had for the Salem witches."

For a medical man, Doctor Bob was impressively creative.

"Doc," Mac said admiringly, "you are really tough. You're pretty sore at them, aren't you?" Sarah and I looked at each other and she rolled her eyes. Like Mac, we were remembering what we'd heard on the fourth floor.

Leona Geilfuss stopped me at the nurses' station when I was on my way to my room and reminded me that I was supposed to take my medication and have my blood pressure taken. Curious, I asked her what the medication was. "Ativan," she said, and spelled it out for me. "It's for hypertension." Then she took my pressure and said, "One seventy over one sixteen." She looked at me with her steady eyes and said, "Better go lie down and give the medicine a chance to work." I didn't mind. I felt awfully sick to my stomach. Withdrawal is no fun.

When I stretched out with the book I had brought with me, Brenda Maddox's biography of James Joyce's wife Nora, resting on my stomach, I thought about my situation. I'd always been proud of being a self-made man who had made his way pretty far in the world without any formal education. But here I was in a world I had never expected to live in and I wasn't here as a reporter; they said I belonged here. I wished I had the half-full bottle of Absolut I had stuffed in a box of old books in the basement before I left the house for the airport. Mostly I wished I didn't feel I needed it.

When the idea of going to a treatment center is first proposed to a serious drinker he resists it automatically, even though he knows in his heart it is time to stop making jokes about how necessary booze is to him and do something about it. That place in Minnesota, or the one in California, or even the one that John Cheever went to and the Mets sent Dwight Gooden to, Smithers, is for the movie stars who use vodka to wash down those pills they take or to soak up the dryness after they've inhaled a line of white powder off a hundred-dollar bill. Those places aren't for a happy martini drinker who just likes his Absolut on the rocks before meals. And maybe a little wine with his food. And, okay, a little brandy after dinner; sure, a couple of stingers maybe. What's so terrible about that? Well, yes, lately there have been a couple in the morning to get started, but that's only been just lately and only because you haven't been feeling so good. Mostly you just drink when it's time to have a drink. Sure, you probably drink more than is good for you but so does half of the rest of the world, and, anyway, you've had your reasons. What man wouldn't drink with a wife who complains if he declares a Bloody Mary day at a quarter of twelve on Saturday because it's snowing outside? Or raining. Or so hot, or so cold. Or because it's such a perfectly beautiful day.

My family began talking about it two years before I was willing to consider it seriously. Even as a threat. I thought they were exaggerating the problem. I was still the family optimist. I was always ready to get up and get on with the new day; I was always sure that something good was going to happen, that there were still better things to do than I had ever done before. I was sorry that I had had to retire from the job I loved, running the Book-of-the-Month Club, when I got to be sixty-five, but I would make up for it by writing a good book. The book I'd already written about my life in publishing, *A Nickel an Inch*, was only a warm-up. I was a long way from finished. How many people alive today could say they had created a brand-new book club, the way I had with QPB, the paperback club? If I could do it once, I could do it again.

The talk about a hospital, which is what it was no matter what they called it, and God knows it didn't look like anything but a hospital, made me mad. Why should I accept the identity of an alcoholic? (The inmates refer to themselves as drunks. It doesn't make much difference if you're one of them.) I didn't like it and I hadn't thought I would ever have to deal with it. I had thought that if they made my life so miserable by insisting on a hospital I would just go away by myself, rent a little place, preferably by the water, somewhere like Amagansett or Truro or one of those rockbound towns on the coast of Maine, and live the way I wanted to live. I could get by fine with some frozen food, a case of Progresso soup, and some fresh bread and cheese. Add a case of Absolut and some good French wine and I wouldn't have to go out for anything except *The New York Times*. I'd want to go to a bookstore once a week or so but if I got snowed in I could always use my credit card for my favorite British bookstore, Waterstone's, 193 Kensington High Street, London W8. My mind ran in practical channels.

At one of our author luncheons somebody had asked John Kenneth Galbraith why he thought so many of the great American writers had been alcoholics. "I don't know," he said, "but they sure were. Fitzgerald, Faulkner, Hemingway, Sinclair Lewis, Eugene O'Neill . . . it's a hell of a list. You can go back as far as Edgar Allan Poe and up to John Cheever, with Ring Lardner and Dashiell Hammett in the middle, and it does make you wonder. I remember somebody asked James Thurber the same question once and Jim said he thought he knew one answer. "They were all such good writers," he said, "that they made a lot of money very fast and they could afford to buy liquor by the case."

I remember Bennett Cerf telling me at lunch one day in the Bull & Bear at the Waldorf, probably while I was having my second martini, that he hadn't known anything about writers and drinking until he had given William Faulkner an office at Random House to work in while he was finishing *The Reivers* and every day he would see the great author sipping slowly from a water glass of

Jack Daniel's while he typed. Bennett thought that Faulkner's problem was that his thirst was infinitely greater than his capacity,
although it was never a good idea to tell him that, and if he started
a little too early and kept it up a little too long he would drift into
a full-scale bender and would be helplessly drunk and probably
missing for three or four days.

When it came to that, Faulkner wasn't the first and he wasn't
the last. He purely liked to drink; he always said he liked anything
with corn in it. Here, behind these austere but safe brick walls, I
wondered if anybody had ever tried to talk Faulkner into going to
a place like St. Mary's, and if they had, if it might have helped him
live longer than the sixty-five years he managed astonishingly to
survive before his body surrendered to the regular assaults he made
on it and he died at his home in Oxford, Mississippi, in 1962. The
folks at St. Mary's probably would have agreed with his contention
that "there's a lot of nourishment in an acre of corn" but they might
have persuaded him to take it in succotash.

I was in my pajamas and under the covers and I didn't even
know what time it was when Leona walked in and asked me to
hold out my hands. I did, and she seemed satisfied, because all she
said was good night and I went back to sleep. This time I turned
off the light.

4

You Can Run,
but You Can't Hide

The new day, I learned, got under way paradoxically in a more leisurely fashion if you got up early. Then you could take your shower before the last-minute rush.

The hardest thing about the shower routine for me was not getting up but managing the soap business. You had to bring your own little cake of soap with you, which I didn't mind, but then you had to take it back with you, and that was hard. Wet soap is slippery, and it's messy; even if you wrap it in your wet towel, it tends to end up on the floor. I solved the problem by shamelessly stockpiling every cake of soap I could lay my hands on, begging some from the chambermaid, swiping some from the linen closet when nobody was looking, and even, when things got tight, stealing some from empty rooms before the new tenants moved in. Then I simply left the used cake of soap in the shower. After all, I rationalized, somebody else would use it.

I was usually in the shower room by six and shaved and dressed twenty minutes later. Then I went downstairs to the lobby and bought the *Star-Tribune* so I could have something to read while I waited my turn in the vital signs lineup scheduled for seven o'clock. We took our own temperature and waited for third floor head nurse Mary Scanlan or one of her staff to do the blood pressure and pulse measurements. To me there was something chilling about the announcement that echoed down the hall: "Please report to the lounge for your vitals." It always made me wonder if I'd left them somewhere.

It was at least a week before I got a respectable report card from the morning readings. On my second full day Mary, so pretty a young woman that her picture appears five times in the magazine-style brochure St. Mary's publishes describing its work, looked at me with a frown and said, "Not so hot. One seventy-two over one thirty." Not so hot? It sounded like Good-bye, Ed, it's been nice to know you. I had always thought anything over ninety on the diastolic was bad and over one hundred was catastrophic. But I was still walking around, so I decided I wouldn't get any more excited about it than Mary was.

In fact, I did too much walking around. I didn't see how I could face the day without my precious *New York Times*, so I kept slipping out the side door before breakfast and walking swiftly across the road to the main hospital and upstairs to the lobby where one of the boxes coughed up a *Times* in exchange for two of my quarters. That made me feel I was back in the real world. But one morning, when I walked past the nurses' station on my way to my room, I got caught again. Connie Krantz told me sternly that I had "been observed walking over to the hospital" and didn't I know that was against the rules? I pleaded guilty with an explanation. "All I did was go over to buy a newspaper."

"They have newspapers downstairs here," one of the other nurses said.

"I already had the *Star-Tribune*," I said, trying to be patient with the provincials.

She wouldn't give in so easily. "They have the *USA*, too," she said.

"That," I said with the authority of a lifelong *Times* reader, "is not a newspaper."

I always thought it was a tribute to the intelligence level of the alcoholics and druggies that the *Star-Tribune* box was empty by the late afternoon of every day but the *USA* box was never empty.

The Gannett evangelists for graphs instead of words had made few converts among the hard drinkers of America.

Denny, Mac, and I said the hell with the cholesterol and had what the menu described as "soft cooked eggs" for breakfast, with bacon and toast. There is no such thing as soft-cooked eggs at St. Mary's, neither at the Rehab nor the main hospital. All eggs are cooked for ten minutes before they are taken out of the water. That's fine with me because I don't like them runny anyway but the purists grumbled ritually every morning. The truth was we all knew we shouldn't be eating eggs anyway, in any form. I seldom heard anybody in the group claim to have no cholesterol problem and I was interested that practically everybody, regardless of age, was aware of the crusade for an egg-free diet.

When I was running the McCall Publishing Company, in the early seventies, Bob Stein, a brilliant editor and a wily observer of the human comedy, used to say he allowed himself "one visible egg a week" because you got enough of them in hidden ways. Bob was years ahead of his time, and he was right. When I left St. Mary's, my cholesterol count was higher than the Empire State Building.

You can't win no matter how you look at it. Every recovering alcoholic knows that if you associate with a lot of other recovering alcoholics at AA meetings or group programs of any kind you are exchanging the threat of death by alcoholism for death by nicotine poisoning. Reformed drunks smoke until their fingers are yellow and scarred with burn marks. The Minnesota Clean Air Act wages militant war on smokers but there is a last stand being waged inside and outside the walls of 2512 South Seventh Street in Minneapolis that rivals the defense the Japanese put up for Shuri Castle on Okinawa.

I couldn't go for a walk before the lecture that morning because I had an appointment with Dr. Amer. Since I had met him a year ago, Dr. Gregory S. Amer had been appointed medical director of the Chemical Dependency Unit. He is a soft-spoken, confidence-inspiring gentleman whose natural courtesy masks a perceptive probing into exactly what is really going on inside the experienced liar and cheat presently impaled on his stethoscope. He likes to hear what you think about how you feel, but it's a waste of time to try to convince him that the information he gets from his instruments, his eyes, and his skilled fingers is less reliable than your opinions.

Dr. Amer was a baseball fan before he arrived in Minneapolis and the success of the Twins has raised the temperature of his enthusiasm, so we always had something to talk about besides the weather and my alcoholism. But today we didn't have much time to spend on the Twins' inconsistencies. Dr. Amer wasn't happy with my blood pressure readings. He wanted to know if I had told the truth about how much I'd been drinking before I came to the Rehab. I told him I didn't remember what I had told anybody since I had gotten here and that seemed to tell him what he wanted to know.

"We'll have to keep you on the Ativan for a while," he said, "and the Tenormin, too, for your blood pressure." He wanted to know if I'd been taking any medication at home and I said, no, not for a long time; I'd taken Dyazide for a while but my blood pressure had been good for a couple of years and I wasn't taking anything when I got here. "Except vodka," he said with a slow smile. "Except vodka," I agreed.

"I'll want to see you again if your pressure doesn't come down," he said, "but it probably will with a few more days of the Ativan. Try to eat as much as you can. If you have any problems, just tell one of the nurses you want to see me."

He made me feel so optimistic that my pressure was probably down ten points by the time I got to the lecture hall for a film on the evils of marijuana. The closest I've ever been to pot in my life was contact highs from other people's smoke, so I didn't stand to gain much from this one. Because it's hard to concentrate on a sin you haven't committed, I spent the hour daydreaming carelessly about some I had. There's a difference between careless daydreaming and serious daydreaming. That kind is an occupation common to all writers and a particular specialty of mine since the third grade. But you have to want something powerfully, or need desperately to avoid something, to do your best work in that area. I was ready for the kind of time wasting that massages the ache out of your back and lets you feel easy after a hard time. Only I had the uneasy feeling that most of the hard time was still in front of me.

A wayward rewind of the VCR in my head gave me a quick laugh. A man in the film had just said you can't rely on somebody else putting a stop to your pot habit; you've got to make that decision for yourself. I thought about Arch Murray, a baseball writer for the *New York Post* in the forties and fifties who was known as The Tiger because of his dedication to the teams of his alma mater, Princeton. Arch was one of the most famous drinkers in a Manhattan press corps that included some pretty good ones. Arch got to the ball park late one day and had to ask the man sitting next to him to bring him up to date on the game so far. "Reese walked," his buddy said, "Robinson laid down a sacrifice, Snider hit a ground ball to short and Schoendienst made a sensational play." Arch interrupted him. "I'll be the judge of that," he said.

I felt chilly. The air-conditioning in this room was turned up high enough for the polar bears in the Central Park Zoo. I was glad when the movie was over and we could go outside where it was hot. Our gang decided to settle for walking over to the statue of St. Mary between the Rehab and the hospital. Denny was going to have to talk in group today about the work he had to do over the weekend to get ready for his Family Week next week, and, although he was about as religious as Mikhail Gorbachev, he thought it might not hurt to stop by the lady and see if any of her forgiveness might rub off on him. "I'm not going to get forgiven much by Emma," he said philosophically. "She's got the idea fixed in her head that I was gettin' off on somethin' besides coke when I stayed out all them nights with the guys."

"Were you?" Mac asked forthrightly.

"I thought you were a Presbyterian minister," Denny said. "You fellows don't do confessions, do you?"

St. Mary didn't say anything. She just stood gravely behind the low iron fence and between two wooden benches, looking serene. You had the feeling that nothing she had heard since she had been put there, according to the plaque, on June 18, 1931, had surprised her. We all agreed on that and then we agreed that we had better start back before Denny became the first person ever to do it.

I felt I was lucky I'd already met the people in the group because I don't see how anybody could walk cold into a room like that, knowing the kind of painful honesty that's required of you in there, without feeling shaky. It helped when Debbie came in and sat down in the middle of the circle of chairs and said, "Who wants to read the Thought for the Day?" I was astonished when Denny, of all people, said he would. Well, why not? A lot of people in Texas can read. His voice was strong but soft and his reading so true that I wondered if he had already read it through:

"We had become hopelessly sick people, spiritually, emotionally, and physically. The power that controlled us was greater than ourselves—it was John Barleycorn. Many drinkers have said: 'I hadn't gone that far; I hadn't lost my job on account of drink; I still had my family; I managed to keep out of jail.' True, I took too much sometimes and I guess I managed to make quite an ass of myself when I did, but I still thought I could control my drinking. I didn't really believe that I was an alcoholic. If I was one of these, have I fully changed my mind?"

That lay there on the floor like a live rattlesnake that nobody was brave enough to touch. Just the word jail had slammed into me. I was right back in the Yonkers City Jail, where I had covered police news for the daily paper before the war, and where I had been taken last year in a police car charged with drunken driving. They didn't arrest me but they were going to keep me until they thought I had sobered up and they opened a cell door and motioned me in. The room was already crowded with four black whores who looked big enough to be linebackers in a Grand Guignol NFL, and I backed away. "No," I said. One of the cops laughed and opened the door to an empty cell next door. "Sleep it off in here," he said. "Nobody will bother you here."

Well, had I changed my mind about being an alcoholic?

Debbie reminded Denny that he hadn't introduced himself. The person who does the reading hardly ever remembers to do it. "My name is Denny," he said, "and I'm chemically dependent." They went all around the circle.

"My name is Ralph and I'm an alcoholic."

"My name is Carl and I'm an alcoholic."

"I'm Mac, and I'm an alcoholic."

Debbie spoke up clearly when it was her turn. "I'm Debbie," she said, "and I'm an alcoholic and chemically dependent."

"My name is Sarah, and I'm an alcoholic."

"My name is John and I'm an alcoholic and a drug addict."

"My name is Ken, and I'm an alcoholic."

Denny, who was sitting on my right, leaned over and whispered, "He's leaving tomorrow. So is Carl."

"My name is Bob, and I'm an alcoholic."

That left me. "My name is Ed. I'm an alcoholic."

I sat there wondering if I had actually said that, but Debbie didn't give me any time to think about it. She said, "Do you want to tell the group something about yourself and how you got here?"

"You don't want me to tell my life story, do you?"

"Just enough," Debbie suggested, "to give everybody a feeling for who you are and what's been happening to you."

"What happened to me," I said, "is that I knew I'd been drinking a lot but I guess I didn't know what a lot was until my wife and two children got me into the doctor's office without telling me what they were doing and talked me into getting on an airplane for Minneapolis a couple of hours later." I thought for a minute and plunged on. "As a matter of fact," I said, "when I was in the evaluation counselor's office I saw a piece of paper on her desk with my name on it and naturally I looked and I saw a line in big print that said 'Wife and children intervened on him.' It was, no pun intended, very sobering. I thought it was strange it didn't say intervened for him. Anyway, that's how I got here. I didn't see any point in fighting about it."

Debbie interrupted. "Do you wish you weren't here?"

"I'm sure we all wish we weren't here," I said. "But I'm willing to admit that I need it. I was in bad shape. I'm not in very good shape now."

"I should tell the group," Debbie said, looking around the room, "that I worked with Ed last year when he was here as an outpatient." She turned back to me. "And I should tell you that I remember you as a stallion, bucking and fighting, and now you look like you're beaten. You're flat. You don't seem to care anymore."

"I said in the doctor's office that I hadn't expected to end my life this way," I said. "I don't feel proud of myself, and I used to."

"You're not finished yet," Debbie said. "In fact, here, you haven't even gotten started yet. You just have to want to work for it."

"As I already told you, just tell me what you want me to do," I said, "and I'll do it."

"That's fine," Debbie said, "but don't sound so much like a prisoner of war. I want more from you than your name, rank, and serial number. I want you to care enough to work through all the pain you obviously feel and come out on the other side."

"Fair enough," I said. "Done." I had to admit to myself I sounded like a subordinate who didn't agree with his boss and was saying 'I'll do my best' just to shut him up.

Debbie knew an evasion when she heard one. "Okay," she said, "now tell the group as much about yourself as I know."

I almost said "That won't take long" but I didn't want to be a wiseass this early in the day. "I'm sixty-eight years old," I said, "and I've been in the publishing business all of my life. My last job was at the Book-of-the-Month Club where I stayed until I had to retire at sixty-five. The conventional wisdom is that I couldn't stand not working, so I made a career out of drinking. Which, I guess, I'd always excelled at anyway."

It seemed a good time to lighten things up so I told the story about the time I'd taken a three-week trip to Europe with the president of Doubleday, John Sargent, who had become a good friend. "We went to London, Frankfurt, and Paris," I said, "and we did a lot of eating and drinking in fancy restaurants and hotels. By the time we got home, we were pretty tired. Living well may be the best revenge but it can be exhausting, too. Anyway, the first Monday back in the office I told my secretary, Penny—this was so long ago they were still called secretaries, not assistants—that I was going to have lunch at my desk and try to catch up on all the mail. Unhappily, just before twelve, Sargent walked into my office and said, "Sorry to have to do this to you, but we're going to McGraw-Hill for lunch. Curtis Benjamin is going to London tonight and he wants to talk to us about the English book club before he goes."

"You go," I said. "I'm having a Coke and a tuna on rye right here. The last thing in the world I want to look at today is another drink."

But John was firm. "Come on," he said, "you've got to go. Curtis wants to talk to both of us, and he's an old friend."

I went to lunch, but it didn't work out well. Harold McGraw and Curtis laid on a lovely lunch for us in their private dining room but I never got to eat it. The martinis John and I ordered looked deceptively attractive as they sat, all shimmering silver, in their Baccarat glasses, but the first sip hit me the way the two-minute warning buzzer alerts the quarterback in a pro football game. I should have quit right there but that's not what dedicated martini drinkers do. I kept on bravely until I knew that the only place for me to go next was not to the table but to the men's room. Fortunately, it was only a few steps away.

When I came back, visibly pale, things got worse fast. I told our hosts that I thought it was best that I leave now, and naturally, they were solicitous. "We've got a wonderful medical department here," Harold said. "I'll call Doctor Burbank and tell him you're coming over and he'll give you something to fix up your stomach."

Jesus, I thought. Doctor Burbank was all I needed. He was the father of my son Kevin's steady girl, Jane, who probably spent more time around our house than I did. It would make Liby wonderfully happy to have Jane's father tell her all about how he had had to treat Kevin's father for an acute hangover. I settled for having Harold's secretary call me a radio cab to take me back to the security of my own office. Maybe I could reheat the soup that I had asked Penny to order for my lunch.

Everybody laughed but not out loud. One way or another, they had all had the same experience. Their reaction, I thought, was more a kind of wry understanding than delighted laughter. They weren't outside looking in, they were inside, looking out.

"I guess that's about it," I said, willing to let somebody else take center stage. "The first year after I stopped working, I wrote a book about the publishing business and then we went to Italy for four months." But the confessional mood of this chamber pushed me on. It suddenly seemed dishonest to pretend that the Italian trip had been as simple as getting on an airplane and flying happily to the little town in Tuscany where we were going to live in a borrowed house and go where we wanted to go when we wanted to go there. "I guess I ought to say that if I'd had any doubts about the kind of shape I was in before we took off for Italy, I didn't have any by the time we got there. We had a couple of Bloody Marys in the Clipper Club while we were waiting to board the airplane, and because I made the drinks myself they weren't very bloody. Especially mine. I remember drinking down half of mine while I was making Liby's, and then fixing mine all over again before I carried them to the sofa we had pre-empted after turning over our tickets to the club hostess. Then there was champagne on the ground before takeoff; we had mimosas, on the serious drinker's wistful theory that the orange juice eases the effects of the alcohol. And, in no time at all, we were airborne with dry martinis in our hands made scrupulously according to our directions—not too much ice, vodka up to the brim of the glass, and a mere *soupçon* of dry vermouth. 'Just bow,' a fellow conspirator across the aisle instructed the stewardess, 'in the direction of France.' There was wine with dinner, probably red for me while Liby had white, and brandy after. Liby always has coffee after a meal but I had a second brandy. I'm sure Liby looked disapproving, and may very well even have sounded it, but I don't remember for sure.

"I do remember that we had to change planes in London for a short flight to Pisa, where we were to pick up a rental car and drive to the little village of Camaiore, near the city of Viareggio on the coast, not far from Lucca. The first thing I did when we sat down in the London terminal was tell Liby I wanted to buy a couple of newspapers. I headed straight for the nearest bar and quickly put away a double vodka on the rocks. A little later I suggested to her that a Coke might be a good idea, and when she agreed, I went back to the bar and ordered the Cokes and another double vodka. The trouble was, my wary wife had followed me, and she caught me red-handed. She had caught me before, at the golf club, at New York theaters, once between races at Belmont Park when I was supposed to be buying a ticket for the next race, and God knows how many times in the kitchen at house parties, but she had never been this angry before."

I didn't think I ought to take time to fill them in on all of the reasons why Liby might have been expected to be distraught at this raw evidence of my inability to go a minute more than necessary without a glass of vodka in my hand—I assumed there would be plenty of time for that—so I settled for filling them in on what happened. "She made me give her her passport. 'Do anything like this again and I'm going home,' she said. 'I don't care whether you stay or not, but I'm not going to live in a foreign country with a drunk. In fact, I'm going home right now if you don't promise to give up booze while we're there.' Liby hadn't lived through my rapidly escalating alcoholism without learning her lessons. 'It's obviously easier for you to stop altogether than it is to regulate how much you drink. So either you stop or I go home. It's up to you.' None of this was said righteously, more in a flat tone of resignation mixed with firmer notes of resolve when she talked about what she would do. I said okay, I would do it. I was scared; I wasn't sure I could go four months without a drink. But I didn't want the trip to be blown out from under me before it even got started, so I said yes and I hoped dismally for the best.

"I had my first taste of the fires of hell on the British Airways flight to Pisa. When the stewardess offered us drinks, I had a Coke. I think the first time I felt a breath of relief was when we sat down to the housekeeper Lydia's dinner of *penne*, the broad strips of pasta that are so common to the Italian table, short strips of macaroni and a thick tomato sauce aromatic with oregano, bay leaves, basil, onion, and garlic. Well, don't take my word for the ingredients.

Besides the food, what I remember from that first night in the house we were going to live in for two months before moving on to San Gimignano was that Liby pushed the bottle of homemade

Chianti across the table to me after she filled her own glass. That was how we made the deal that we kept from April to July. Wine with dinner, and a glass of beer when we wanted it with lunch, but no booze. Liby didn't have any, either. She was willing to share the stresses of abstinence with me, and, besides, she didn't trust me."

When it was clear that I didn't want to say anything more, Debbie said, quietly, "How do you feel about being here?"

"I think it's where I should be," I said carefully. I could think of a lot of places I'd rather be.

"You look all used up," Debbie said. "As I said before, you look like you're beaten, physically and mentally. Is that how you feel?"

"I don't feel very good," I said. "I feel discouraged, and I've never been discouraged in my life, so I don't like it."

"Well," Debbie said, "if you're willing to work for it, we're going to help you feel good about yourself again. We don't do any magic tricks here but we can help you find a way to live successfully without alcohol. Live happily, I should say, because we don't think we'd be doing much for you if we sent you back home sober but miserable. Everybody else here has already heard me on that subject but I'll have a lot more to say about it as we go along. For now, I want you to think about positive things, like feeling better and being able to do the things that alcohol has kept you from doing, and not about negative things, like not going to parties and drinking all night. There is a world without liquor. I ought to know, and I'll tell you more about that, too."

The door opened then and a short, husky, middle-aged man stepped part-way in, looking not only hesitant but disapproving. "Sorry to interrupt," he said as though he wasn't sorry at all. "I'm Richard Ernst. They told me to come here. You're Debbie Chapman?"

"I'm Debbie Chapman," our counselor said. "Come on in and meet the group."

The new man seemed even more nervous about closing the door behind him than he had been to open it. "I'm not sure this is what I should be doing," he said. He wasn't apologetic; his attitude was more challenging, even hostile. Like a lot of shorter than average men, he seemed Napoleonic in his imperiousness. The rest of us might be here for help but not him; you felt that he had just dropped by to see if he could do anything for anybody. He was carrying a leather envelope fat with papers that, considering the butter-soft look of the case and the agitated way he clutched it, should have been at least on their way from the president to the general secretary.

Debbie had met his type before. She wasn't unfriendly but she wasn't trying to sell any Girl Scout cookies, either. "Sit down," she said. "We just finished meeting one new member. The way we do it is to have the new person tell us a little about himself and how he got here. That usually gets us off to a good start."

Ernst ran with the ball. "I really don't think I ought to be here," he said rapidly. "I've already been to some of the finest treatment facilities in the country, and I've consulted some of the most famous authorities about what I should do. I'm the head of an internation- ally respected company and my time is very valuable and I have access to all the best sources of help. I don't think I'm going to find what I want here."

That was too much for Denny. "Maybe us common folk know something your high-priced friends don't know," he said in his best aw, shucks Texas drawl.

"I don't mean any offense," Ernst said. "It's just that my problems are somewhat special. . . . I've got a beautiful young wife and that's a delicate situation for an older man . . . and I've got to look after my company while I'm trying to help myself, and I don't see how I can do that if I'm an inpatient here." Maybe, I thought, he figures that will get him off the hook and he won't have to say he doesn't think he belongs with the likes of us. "I think," he finished, getting up and heading for the door, "I'd better go back to the office and talk to them about becoming an outpatient." He liked that idea so much he walked right on out.

I didn't notice that Debbie's feelings were hurt. "Well," she said, "we're batting five hundred for the day. Ed stayed and Richard dismissed us." She looked at her watch. "We've got enough time

for some work on your first step, John, if you want to go over it
with us. Even if you're not entirely finished, I think you ought to
make a start. Your family's going to be here next week."

John Terranova, the kid, was nervously eager. "It's okay," he
said. "I guess I'll never be really ready. But I think I've got enough
of it together to be able to go over it pretty well." He had a looseleaf
notebook in his hands and he flipped through the pages to find the
place where he wanted to begin. He was a good-looking young man
with a slender, sharp-featured face dominated by piercing dark eyes
that were perpetually restless. He was like a wounded bird, quick
to shy away, to draw back from an encounter. Debbie spoke to him
as an equal but you could see that she was trying to draw him out,
to reassure him, to avoid scaring him off. She wanted him to know
that he could wait until he was ready to try to fly again.

"I guess I've been having the most trouble with my drinking
history," John said. "I don't remember everything as well as the
rest of you people seem to."

"If we don't remember it," Ralph encouraged him, "we just
fake it."

"I guess I can remember enough." He remembered enough, all
right. John had begun drinking beer with the other boys, and a few
of the girls for that matter, in sixth grade. He must have been about
twelve then. He and his older brother, Andy, spent as much time
as they could out of the house because they were scared to death
of their old man, who sounded like a regular Captain Bligh, complete with the rope's end remorselessly wielded for the slightest
infraction. "The other kids," John said, "began to call him The
Hawk because when they saw him out looking for me that's what
he looked like. And he'd pounce like a hawk, too." So as soon as
John thought he could take care of himself alone, he skipped out.
He didn't bother to stay for his high school graduation—"which,"
he said, "probably broke my mother's heart,"—and didn't take much
with him. As soon as he was eighteen, he just left home one morning and never went back. "I just had fun," he said. He had already
sharpened his thirst with uncountable cans of beer and whatever

stronger spirits came his way, and now he was free to drink as much as he wanted to. He liked the way it made him feel.

John worked when he had to and tried to stay out of public shelters because he was afraid they would send him back home. "I've never been lazy," he said, "but I hated to stay in one place too long and I was afraid to let anybody get too close to me for fear they'd somehow get in touch with my parents. I wasn't sure if eighteen was the legal age everywhere."

He had left in the springtime, and when the night air got chillier in October, he headed for the West Coast. He had decided to spend the winter in Southern California, not in Los Angeles but somewhere in that part of the state. He ended up in Santa Monica, hanging around Muscle Beach. "I thought there were so many young guys there," he said, "that the cops wouldn't pay any attention to me. And I stayed away from the gay guys cruising because I didn't know what kind of trouble that might get me into."

He stayed so far away from the gays that he got attached to a pretty young runaway from Ohio, "a dark blonde," he said, "with a real neat figure and everything, and she worked as a waitress whenever she could, which was most of the time because you could always get a job in a McDonald's or a Burger King or a Wendy's, so we made out pretty well." She was just as afraid of being picked up by the police as he was, so they never stayed long in one place. Mostly they lived in the parks and on the beach. "We liked the beach better," John said, "because you could have more fun and you could stay clean"—and it was easier to make love at night without being interrupted by the cops and their ugly searchlights.

"Most of our money went for beer and pot and pills, anyway," he said, "and then we began to get into coke, so that used up just about all the money we could make, that and the beer. We pretty much stayed on the beach."

Until one day another guy, older and bigger than John, made a move on the girl, Peggy, and she said no and John told him to fuck off. The guy didn't do anything right away, but that night, while John and Peggy were sleeping under the old army blanket she'd had when he met her, the guy came back with a knife. John pushed Peggy away and told her to run like hell, but he was helpless on his back when the intruder slashed at him with the knife. "He stabbed me five times," John said, "but the one that almost got me was a deep one right under my heart. One of them, and I suppose it was that one, knocked me out, and I didn't know anything until I woke up in the hospital. I only stayed awake long enough to see that there was a cop there, and no sign of Peggy. I was in there for six weeks and she never did come, but I could understand that. She didn't want to be involved. What she did finally was get one of the orderlies to bring a note to me. She said she'd know when they were letting me out and she would be outside to meet me.

"She was, too. She had stayed friends with the orderly and she checked with him every day until finally he said one of the nurses had told him they were going to discharge me tomorrow. It made me feel pretty good to see her standing outside the hospital like that, with her army blanket under her arm and her canvas tote over her shoulder, all ready to go. We didn't waste any time getting out of Santa Monica. The cops had gotten tired of asking me if I knew the guy who had stabbed me, so there wasn't anybody waiting for me. I told the woman in the office that I was going to Austin, Texas, to visit an older brother there because my parents had split up and I didn't know where either one of them was, and that was good enough for her. I guess they might have sent me someplace where I would have been given some stuff, maybe even a little money, but I was so glad to be on my own again that I didn't want to check in with anybody. Anyway, it turned out that Peggy had been working and had figured we'd want to go away and had saved up a couple of hundred bucks. So that night we scored some coke and splurged on a Motel Six and really celebrated. I wish we had stayed there for a few more days because then we would have missed all the shit that came down on us."

It was riveting listening to this slender, serious-faced young man, sounding like a modern Tom Jones, talking about his picaresque adventures as matter-of-factly as if he were telling us about his senior class outing. John's narrow face had hardly any cheeks and the gauntness was relieved only by a Cary Grant dimple in the middle of his chin. He hadn't been at St. Mary's long enough for even the baby food diet there to have had a chance to soften either his face or his body. But he was a good-looking boy and his eyes defied you to take yours off him. It was easy to see why Peggy had carried trays and saved her money and waited for him.

"I drank an awful lot that night," he said. "We brought two six-packs into our room when we checked in and it couldn't have been much later than eight o'clock when we killed the last one and I had to go out for more. There was a convenience store in the gas station next to the motel, and while I was in there, this guy who looked to be about forty . . ."

"Real old," Denny said.

"Yeah," John said. He didn't laugh. To him he was real old. He was busy remembering the trouble that old man had brought to him. "He said he had seen me and my girl come in before and he asked where we were going. I was a little suspicious at first but then I couldn't see any harm in him, he didn't look like a con at all, and I told him Texas, in fact San Antone. We hadn't actually made up our minds to go there yet, but it was the most likely. So it was what I said. And he said, 'That's where I'm going, too. Hey, I wonder if I could talk to you about it.' I didn't know what there was to talk about but I said sure and I took my two fresh six-packs of Coors Light and waited for him outside. What he wanted to know was if I, well, that is, we wanted to ride along with him. 'I figured you didn't have a car,' he said, 'because I saw you get off the bus when you came.' I agreed that we didn't have a car, and he pointed to a 1986 battleship gray Cadillac parked halfway down the row of front doors of the motel. 'That's mine,' he said, 'at least it's mine now. I got to tell you right up front I stole it up in Bakersfield. I switched the plates on it, knew a guy who sold me a set that were on a car that got sold for junk, and I figure it ought to be safe. But I wouldn't feel right not telling you. The thing is, I want to go to Laredo, right on the border, and I could drop you guys off in San Antone on the way, and it would be great for me because we could drive all night. We could stop only when we wanted to eat. You

and the lady would get where you're going real fast and be in out
of the rain. Sound good?' Then he suddenly thought and he asked
me if I had a license. I said sure, and I showed it to him, and by
then I had made up my mind to do it. I told him to wait for me,
I'd go talk to Peggy, and I'd come right back and let him know. So
I did and she said why not, and we agreed we'd be ready to go at
six o'clock in the morning. Peggy and I had a good night's sleep
in one of the two queen-size beds in that Motel Six room, and we
figured life was finally treating us good.

"That was all we knew. We ate coffee and doughnuts with our
new friend, who told us only that his name was Marvin, we didn't
find out his last name until we got arrested, and then we hit the
highway not much after six. Pretty good for me and Peggy, but we
thought we ought to show him we were reliable.

"Everything went all right the first twenty-four hours or so. He
drove through Palm Springs and into Arizona and I took over then
and got us past Phoenix and all the way to Las Cruces, New Mexico.
We stopped once for gas at an all-night, but even though the lights
were on, the place was closed, so I just siphoned some gas for us
out of the tank of a pickup sitting in the lot. It didn't seem like that
was doing much harm. Marvin never asked if Peggy could drive.
I knew she could but I didn't want to volunteer her until I caught
him once playing with her tits while she was sleeping. Then I said
I thought she ought to sit up front with me and make sure I stayed
awake, and when I slept she could sleep. I didn't care if he took
offense or not. I wasn't going to have him messing with her while
I couldn't see. But we never had any trouble after that and we got
through the night with him and me taking turns about four hours
each. We were hungry in the morning, so we stopped at a Dairy
Queen kind of a place for coffee and something to eat. That's when
the shit hit the fan. We'd only been there about five minutes when
a Highway Patrol car pulled into the parking lot. Marvin got nervous
right away but at first I thought they were only having coffee, too.
But one of them stayed outside looking over the Caddy, and we
knew we were in trouble. The one outside waved to the one inside
and he came right over to us and asked whose car that was. Marvin

said it was his and the trooper asked for the registration and his license. Marvin showed him his license and said the registration was in the car and the cop said to go get it. 'Actually,' Marvin said, 'it's not my car. A friend of mine loaned me it for this trip because I'm going to do him a favor.'

" 'What's his name?' the cop asked him.

" 'Everett Sampson,' Marvin told him. I was surprised that he knew it but when he came back with the registration the cop just nodded. 'Everett Sampson,' he said, looking at it. 'That's it, all right. That's the name of the man who reported this car stolen. Let's go, all of you.'

"Well, I argued right away that Peggy and I didn't steal any car, that we'd just hitched a ride from him in exchange for me driving some, but the cop wasn't interested. 'Just come along with me, son,' he said, 'you and the young lady. My partner will go with your friend in the Caddy.' "

"I don't have to tell you all the details but what it was was that somebody in the filling station had called the cops and described me as the kid who had siphoned gas out of their truck, and had described the Caddy, and they put Marvin away for two and a half to five years, because he had a record, and me for six months to a year because I didn't have one. Or hadn't had one until then. They let Peggy go home after they called her parents and told them they were putting her on a bus and they should meet it. I had a trial without a jury and I was in the county penitentiary before I knew what was going on. I guess they had a Public Defender represent me but it was the judge who ran the whole thing. They let me say good-bye to Peggy and I gave her my home address and she gave me hers so we'd have a way of trying to find each other later. Then I went to jail.

"I have to admit it wasn't so bad. We lived a lot better than I'd been living in California. Except for the beach. The food was all right and there was plenty of it. The worst thing was the coffee, which I knew was always mixed with chicory. That's when I started going to AA meetings because the people who ran them always had real coffee, so it was worth listening to all the bullshit twice a week to get the coffee and the homemade doughnuts and sometimes even pies."

Debbie wanted to know what was so bad about the AA meetings. "What kind of bullshit exactly are you talking about?"

"All that religion," John said. "It was like going to a Salvation Army meeting, or even worse, sometimes you thought you were at one of those revival meetings with an evangelist and everything." He was thinking hard; you could see that he wanted to be fair. "But the coffee," he said, "was always good."

Sarah had a mother's question. "Did you let your folks know where you were?"

"No. I didn't want to risk having The Hawk come down there. I had a few California postcards in my stuff and whenever somebody left the jail and said anything about going to California I'd write one of the cards and get him to mail it for me from there. They never found out until I finally went home last month and they put it all together to send me here."

"It never occurred to you to call them before your trial?" Debbie asked.

"Oh, it occurred to me, all right. I knew they would get me a lawyer and all that stuff. I just figured I'd rather do some time than face my father."

Debbie had heard too much of this kind of pain to look horrified but she looked as sad as I'd seen her look so far. "You'd rather spend six months in a Texas prison than face your father who you know loves you?"

John wasn't uncomfortable, just remote somewhere inside himself. His voice didn't have any emotion in it. "I'd run away from home to escape him," he said. "I wasn't going to go back to being a kid getting punished again."

"Were you afraid he would hit you?" Debbie wanted to know. "Or do something worse to hurt you?"

John was quick to answer. "No, no way. I guess he smacked us some when we were little. Probably my mother did, too, and she's the sweetest lady you'd ever want to meet, but neither of them ever hit us when we got bigger. It was just that I didn't want him being

God anymore, he was always laying down judgments from on high. He just terrorized me, that's all. I wanted to stay as far away from him as I could. Anyway, like I said, the jail wasn't that bad. If I was in jail in Turkey or even Mexico or some place like that, I might have thought about asking for help. But as it was, I thought I'd just live through it."

"Does the group have any feedback for John?" Debbie asked. I'd read in the "Guidelines for Group Therapy" that feedback is your own personal reaction to what has been said or what's happening in a group session. I also remembered that the guidelines had said you could give feedback, or ask questions, or remain silent. I made up my mind I would keep my mouth shut. Who was I to tell this kid what I thought about his hair-raising story? But, when nobody else said anything for a minute, I asked him how he had gotten here.

"I wrote Peggy's parents and they gave me her address, she was living in South Bend, and she wrote me back and we began to stay in touch with each other. Then I got sick and I went to see her but I couldn't work much and I needed something all the time, Valium, speed, ludes, heroin, crack mostly, but I didn't have any money and I didn't want to steal. I had stomach cramps all the time and my mouth felt like cotton and I was dizzy not just when I woke up in the morning but off and on all day. Peggy figured I'd gone as far as I could go, so she sat down and wrote my father and he came and got me inside of twenty-four hours."

We all sat there thinking about the power of a parent's love for a child, and feeling glad that Peggy had let his father know where he was.

Debbie thought he had talked enough. "That's very good work, John," she said. "We've still got tomorrow and Monday to do some more to get ready for when your parents will be here next week. I'd like you to think about how you're going to tell your father all the things you told us this morning."

"No way," John said, looking worried.

"Oh, yes," Debbie said. "That's the only way we're going to help you work your way out of this and get you on your own feet. You two have got to face the way things were so you can make them better together."

John didn't look convinced but he didn't have to say anything because suddenly Richard Ernst was back with us again. This time, I noticed right away, he was carrying two briefcases. The second one was just as genuine-leather-looking as the first one but approximately twice as thick. Mac, surely one of our least caustic members, said, "Looks like you brought the whole office with you."

Ernst didn't see anything to laugh at. "Just about," he said. "It's incredible how things pile up when I'm not there." He put the cases down on the floor and confronted Debbie. "No offense," he said, "but I've decided there's no way you people can help me."

5

God Grant Me the Serenity

Ernst looked straight at Debbie and said, with what he probably thought was endearing candor, "I guess I mean *you* can't help me. I just don't think a regular counselor is good enough, I mean knows enough, I need somebody who's specially trained to deal with my particular problem."

Debbie didn't say anything, so Ernst rushed on. "I've been to some of the most famous people and places there are, and nobody's been able to help me. From what I've been able to see here, and reading the literature they gave me, this certainly isn't going to do it." He stood up and retrieved his briefcases. "Maybe what I'll do while I'm looking for the right place is sign up here as an outpatient. Then I can take care of my business while I try to get myself in better shape before I go somewhere else." When nobody said anything, he turned and walked out the door.

"Well," Denny said with the right touch of awe, "that's sort of like being told the man can't hire you to shovel the shit out of his barn because the barn is bigger than a little guy like you can handle."

"I come from Wisconsin," Debbie, who was only a regular counselor, said, standing up and reaching out her hands for Ralph and Carl, who were on either side of her, "and they have a lot of cows there." That was all the critique she was going to offer of Mr. Ernst's bravura performance, but it was enough. Debbie looked around the circle. I was holding hands with Sarah on one side and Mac on the other. "God grant me the serenity," everybody recited, "to accept the things I cannot change, the courage to change the things I can, and the wisdom to know the difference." I knew the Serenity Prayer from AA meetings but somehow it seemed like more of a prayer here. We really were all in it together.

I hadn't been in my room more than a minute, I'd barely had time to go to the bathroom, when the loudspeaker came on and one of the nurses said, "Ed, report to the nurses' station, please, so we can take your blood pressure." I went right away, but I wished I hadn't. Marjorie Noonsong, the softest voice of them all, broke it to me gently but there wasn't much she could do to make it better. "A hundred and seventy," she said, "over a hundred and eighteen." It was a good thing, I decided as I met Denny and agreed to go downstairs for a breath of fresh air before lunch, that I wasn't thinking of asking for an overnight pass.

We talked about John as we walked around the block. Denny slowed down going past the junior college because three of the girls were setting up a barbecue grill between their building and the Rehab and he wondered if they needed any help. They didn't, but it certainly was thoughtful of him to ask. We agreed that Mr. Terranova must be a holy terror for the kid to prefer six months in jail to letting the old man maybe get him off.

"We don't even know his first name," I said, reminding myself to ask John.

"His first name," Denny said, "is The Hawk."

We both thought Debbie had done a good job with him, getting him to open up the way he had. "You don't know the half of it," Denny said. "It's taken her a week to do it. I got through with my first-step data last week, I guess I couldn't wait to talk about all the fun I'd had, but John kept saying he just couldn't put it all down in his notebook. Deb didn't rush him. She said all he had to do was tell us the things that he thought really mattered. He didn't have to write a book. And it worked. She knows what she's doing, all right."

We talked some more while we waited on the chow line. Denny said he was really looking forward to seeing his wife next week. "Emma's a real good girl," he said, "and this is the most I've been away from her since we got married. I'm not a man who does without very easily." He became even more homesick when we looked at the food that Clark and Isabelle, the manager and assistant manager, respectively, of the Rehab cafeteria, had on display. It didn't look like home. But, as we reminded ourselves many more times before the month was over, we hadn't come to St. Mary's for the food. Anyway, the boiled potatoes were fine and there is no vegetable I like better than canned peas.

My stomach was improving but I still didn't feel up to another walk before the lecture, so I hid out in room 349 and lost myself in the story of Nora Barnacle's first date with James Joyce on the evening of June 16, 1904, immortalized in *Ulysses* as Bloomsday. Ducking into a doorway in the docks area of Dublin, "she unbuttoned his trousers, slipped in her hand, pushed his shirt aside, and acting with some skill, made him a man." I felt so bad I couldn't get too excited about what I thought was an unsatisfactory way for a male of twenty-two years to become a man, even in straitlaced Ireland, but I am a Joyce addict and I felt glad, before I fell asleep with my very different kind of hypertension, that my hero had finally made it. Jesus, I remember thinking, when I was twenty-two, I was married. I must be a poor Irishman; I'd still had a living mother I could have stayed with.

The twelve-thirty lecture was a film, which earned a low-pitched wave of approval from the captive audience. The inmates always like films better than live speakers because it's easier to sleep through them; the tapes don't complain about your inattention. This one was my first exposure to Father Joseph Martin, a witty Catholic priest who apparently had made alcoholism his life's work. You didn't have to agree with everything Father Martin had to say to enjoy the way he said it. I didn't, for instance, agree at all with his insistence that Jews never become alcoholics because they have a reverence for wine that comes from its place in their religious history. "They wouldn't dream of abusing alcohol," the good father said with a touch of awe. "He's full of shit," I thought irreverently. "He's never known any Jewish writers." I was reminded right away of the world-famous author who agreed to do a television interview in the Book-of-the-Month Club offices one Saturday morning and was escorted into my office by the producer of the show who hoped I might be able to provide the star with a hair of the dog to get him through the ordeal. I set out a bottle of vodka, for which he had expressed a preference, and got him a glass full of ice cubes and watched him do away with two healthy glasses of straight Smirnoff before he straightened his tie and went in to face the world on cable television.

In a minute I decided Father Martin was just plain prejudiced because he got a cheap laugh with the line that "whenever you see four Irishmen talking together you can be sure you'll find a fifth." He was all right, though. He sent us off to our group meetings with a marvelous collection of drunk stories that ended with two that even Jackie Mason might not throw away.

There was the Irish cop who yelled at the motorist for ignoring a sign pushing him from the left-hand lane into the right. "Don't you see those great big arrows right there?" the cop demanded. "Arrows?" the sloshed driver said. "I didn't even see the Indians."

Then there was the drunk who was walking along the sidewalk doing his best to keep on a reasonably straight line when he saw two nuns coming toward him. He straightened himself up as well as he could, just in time for one nun to swing around him on one side and the other on the other side. Painfully, he turned and looked back over his shoulder. "How did she do that?" he asked nobody in particular.

Then we were back in room 355 for another hour and a half of soul-searching. Debbie gave the floor to Carl Bruhl. He had asked her for it. He would be leaving tomorrow and he wanted to have one more chance to get feedback from the group. He began by apologizing for having asked to have his meeting with his family in private. "I know all of you saw me walking around some with them last week," he said, "and I know I'm the only one who didn't have the tough meetings with the whole group sitting in, like Ken did. But I just didn't know what would happen. I told you I was afraid that I was going to lose my whole family after this and I didn't want anything to happen that might make it more likely." Carl was an earnest lumberjack of a man, deep-chested, broad shouldered, a middleweight fighter gone to seed. I was surprised when I found out that he was a cattle farmer with a huge ranch in Montana but you knew he was a strong man. Even when he had just shaved, he looked like he needed a shave. I wouldn't want to take a lot of money from him in a poker game.

"Well, my wife has left me. She said, Debbie knows this, that she's glad I'm going to stay sober now and she hopes it makes the years I have left better ones for me, but she says it's too late for her. She thinks she's paid her dues and she wants to be on her own. Matter of fact, she's already moved her stuff into an apartment she rented in town. So far she hasn't even told me where it is, though she says she will."

Carl waited a minute while he got himself together. I was sure that nothing could induce him to reach for one of the packages of Kleenex that are visible every place you look at St. Mary's, but he fooled me. He did, and he not only blew his nose vigorously but he even wiped his eyes. "I'm glad to tell you my kids are another story," he said. "They aren't going to abandon me." He didn't apologize for leaving the impression that he thought his wife had. "I'm going to live alone in the house. It's too late for me to start over someplace else, and I love the ranch. The kids have promised they're going to come and visit me. I can take them out to dinner once a week or so, maybe to a ball game or something like that once in a while. So I don't have to look at nothing but being alone, and I just can't tell you how much better I feel about that." He looked around the room. "I know you all didn't agree with me all the time about some of the things I've said, maybe the way I said them, but I want you to know you've been great for me. I couldn't have gotten through this month without you."

"Better not use up your good-bye speech today, Carl," Debbie warned him.

"Don't worry, Deb," he said. "I've got plenty more left. But you're right. I'd better save it. Anyway, I did want you to know that things look better for me than I had been afraid they would. I haven't lost my kids, that's the main thing. And if the way to keep them is to stay sober, then that's what I'm going to do." You couldn't doubt that he meant it.

Debbie turned next to Doctor Bob who had been looking as though he would rather be anyplace else in the whole world than where he was. His weatherbeaten face was tight and his lips were pressed together as if he had just tasted something unpleasant. "Have you made up your mind yet about staying, Bob?" she asked him.

"No," he said, "I haven't. You said I could take my time." He made it sound like an accusation.

"You can take all the time you want," Debbie said pleasantly. "The longer you take to make up your mind, the longer you're here."

"It's nothing against you," Bob said. "I just hate to give her the satisfaction of having me put away like this." Debbie started to say something and Bob interrupted her. "I know, I know," he said, "the front door is always open."

"I want you to stay," Debbie said, "because it's a good program and because you're lucky to be in what I think is a remarkable group. Maybe you can work your way through your problems here, everybody helping each other. And anyway, you won't have a drink for twenty-eight days and the least you'll get out of it is feeling like a new man when you leave."

"Well, I'll tell you," Bob said, spitting out the words as though he had carefully memorized them one by one. "If I do decide to stay, it'll be because I can put the month to good use figuring out how I can keep that bitch of a wife of mine from getting any of my money. I intend to see to it that she doesn't get a dime from me that she doesn't need the help of the law to extract."

"Just because she organized the intervention?" Debbie asked.

"Well, my God, it was the way she did it. There were eleven of them, a whole goddamn army, all stacked up in the living room of my house. My kids, the people I work with, my best friend, everybody. I felt like they were the posse and I was some kind of a mass murderer. And they packed me off here without even a toothbrush, like they were afraid I might escape or something."

"At least they didn't lie to you," Debbie said. "They did what they did right out in the open. I've known some interventions where they told outrageous lies to the alcoholic, and then they were surprised that all through treatment he focused on their lies instead of on all the lies he'd told about his drinking. I mean, he wasn't as bad as they were, right?"

I thought about the angry Doctor Bob at the fourth floor meeting that first day. If he was any less angry now, you would need a very fine instrument to measure it. Debbie didn't try to soothe him. She let him have his say. "Just let me know when you make up your mind," she said. There was no judgmental edge to her voice. "I hope you decide to stay." There was no pleading in it, either.

Next she looked at Mac and asked him if he had gotten in touch with the counselor who was in charge of the grief group in the Rehab. Mac said he hadn't met him yet but he had left a message that he would like to know about the next meeting. That was the first I knew that Mac had had a death in his family. He was sitting next to me so I leaned close and asked, "Your wife?" "Yes," he said. "Last year." Debbie said she had heard good things about the results people had obtained from sharing the pain of a death with others who had gone through the same thing and had, like Mac, used it as an excuse—maybe not the only excuse, but one of them—to drink. "Do you think you can tell us," she asked him, "what it is about it that has been hurting you the most? I've found that sometimes it helps to focus on a specific thing and try to work with that."

Mac never answered a question without thinking about it carefully. "There is one thing," he finally said. "I get a lot of pain from the fact that I never had a chance to ask her forgiveness before she died. I wanted to, very much, but I just never seemed to have a chance, and the later it got, the fewer chances I had." He was

quiet for a long minute. "I wish I had done that," he said. "I suppose
what I mean is that I just wish I had had a chance to say a proper
good-bye to her."

"Do you think she would have forgiven you?" Debbie asked.

Mac was sure of it. "Yes," he said, "she would, I'm sure of it."

"Just because she knew she was dying? Or do you think she
would have done it anyway? Do you want to talk about it?"

"I don't think I'm ready to talk about it yet," Mac said. "But I
think it's good that you're making me face up to it."

Then everybody began to talk at once, and that was the first time
that had happened. Debbie sat back and let it happen. Everybody
had something to say about grief and good-byes and forgiveness,
and the words scrambled over so much ground and kept coming
together so persistently that nobody could have missed the point
that we all shared the same worst and best feelings and experiences.

"I think this was good for all of us," Debbie said.

"I know it was good for me," Mac said.

The nurses told me that Dr. Amer wanted to see me at three-
thirty, so I couldn't go walking with Denny and Mac, but Denny
told me a long time later that Mac had made an important confession to him when they walked after that group session. "He said
he had never forgiven himself for having gone to a massage parlor
one afternoon when he'd had a few drinks and decided it was time
to find out what that kind of paid sex was like," Denny said. "And
it ate him up that he'd never had a chance to apologize to his wife
for that. I told him there was no reason to, that she couldn't have
been hurt by something she not only didn't know about but that
had nothing to do with her anyway, but he wasn't so sure. He
thought she had a right to know."

"He's crazy," I said. "That's only taking his guilt and giving it to
her. That's supposed to make her feel better?"

"That's what I said," Denny said. "At least, I think I made him
think about it."

Dr. Amer told me he thought the Twins would do better next
week not only because they were home for a ten-game stand but
also because Kirby Puckett's bad ankle was supposed to be better.

"I hate to think a hitter like him is trying to pivot with a bad ankle," he said. I didn't know how much better Puckett felt but I knew I felt better having somebody taking care of me out here in the snow and ice country who thought it was important that a strong right-handed hitter had good wheels. He took my blood pressure and it was one hundred forty-two over ninety-two. Baseball helped. So did Ativan.

I relaxed with Nora Joyce for a while before I decided a little air might help me eat better. When I stepped outside the front door and looked at the cigarette smokers and the romantic couples, I saw that the most intense pairing was Richard Ernst, the important businessman who couldn't be bothered with our "regular" counselor, and a beautiful young woman who wouldn't, I decided, be listening so intently to what he was saying unless she was the young wife he had said was his special problem. If he thought she was a problem for him, I wondered, what does she think he is for her? None of my business. I turned away to do the around-the-block walk and, as I passed them, all I heard was her saying, "No. How many times do you want me to say it, no?"

Dinner was a choice of baked ham or baked chicken with au gratin potatoes and carrots. I ate more than I had eaten so far and that was encouraging. But my good mood didn't last long.

The seven o'clock lecture was scary enough to make Ernest Hemingway never want to take another drink. It was on the physical consequences of alcoholism and the doctor who gave it used slides to illustrate his stories of what the bogeyman would do to you if you didn't watch out. He talked mostly about the liver and how dangerous it was to think complacently that it would always regenerate itself if you just stopped drinking for a while. "There comes a time," he says, "when you've used up all of its regenerative powers, and when that happens, you've had it. There is no treatment, no medicine, for a rotted liver. When it's gone, it's gone." He showed us slides of livers partly destroyed, almost completely destroyed, and just plain destroyed. They were frightening. What made it worse for us was that Cal Scheidegger's group had a man who was suffering from cirrhosis and whose skin actually glowed with a bright yellow color. I tried not to look at him as we walked out of the hall. According to the lecturer, he was a dead man. Just as surely as if he was walking to the gas chamber at San Quentin, he was on his way out of this world. Jesus.

I stopped at the nurses' station and took my pills from Connie Krantz, went into my room and fell asleep in less time than it takes me to read two pages.

I never took my clothes off. All I did was pull the blanket over me.

I remember wondering what it would feel like if they made you close the lid of your own coffin, and if you were as yellow as that man, would you act like an electric bulb and light up the inside.

6

All Alone and Feeling Blue

I've always had trouble with the first line of the "St. Louis Blues." Is it that she hates to see that evenin' sun go down or that she loves to see it go down? " 'Cause my baby, he done left this town." Then there's what comes next. "If I'm feelin' tomorrow like I feel today, I'm gonna pack my trunk and make my getaway." I wonder if she was thinking of making her getaway to Minneapolis, Minnesota. She would have to have a blood level count of over .10 to get in, but I guess Billie Holiday and Libby Holman and Bessie Smith would never have had to worry about that. If they came in July they wouldn't have to worry about it being cold, either. No wonder they treat alcoholics here; they know all about extremes. I'd hate to come here on a cold day in the winter time.

My daughter Eileen said it was a cold day in the Village when a uniformed cop walked into their storefront dharma temple. Their first thought was that they were going to be busted and they wondered how many of the kids were holding. Then they thought maybe he had just come in to get warm. But when he took off his helmet and laid his nightstick on the floor and knelt down with everybody else, they realized he was just another Buddhist. "A chanting cop," Eileen explained to me disbelievingly. So you never know. Anyway, Eileen's Buddhism gave me one of the best stories I ever broke up a Time Inc. meeting with. The first time Andrew Heiskell, the president of the company, and Pat Lenahan, the treasurer, toured our office after the merger, they were interested in a group of Buddhist artifacts I had on one wall. I explained what they were and Pat said, "You mean Eileen Fitzgerald is a Buddhist?" And when I said yes, Pat turned to Heiskell, the quintessential Wasp, and said, "Well, Andrew, it's better than being a Protestant."

But that doesn't explain how my life, which began on West Fifty-eighth Street in Manhattan sixty-eight years ago, had taken me here. Where am I going to place this on my list of important places? Paris is the most romantic city, London the most historic, Tokyo the most chaotic, Shanghai the most exotic, Hong Kong the steepest, New York the most exalting. Right now, Minneapolis is the scariest.

When I was a kid, working in the newspaper city room, we used to roll up our sheets of copy paper in a tube and clap the tube into a pneumatic pipe that shot it up to the composing room where they set it in type. Are they getting ready to do that with me? Will they turn me into hot lead? Come on, they don't use hot lead anymore, not even at *The New York Times*. It's all film, they took all the romance out of it. You can't take a kid up to the composing room and have his name set in hot type anymore.

Do you think they really dressed for dinner that last night on the *Titanic*? I mean, did Peggy Guggenheim's father Ben really put on a dinner jacket so he could go down like a gentleman while the band played "Nearer My God to Thee"? I got very drunk one night wearing a dinner jacket at a New Year's Eve party at the golf club but that's not the same thing. The golf club wasn't going to sink; I was the one who was sinking. Besides, we didn't even change into a clean pair of khakis the night the Japanese landed a big troop carrier behind us on the beach at Ormoc where we had landed behind the whole Japanese army on Leyte. We thought sure we were going to die that night but we didn't do anything about our clothes. We were going to die in the same dirty fatigues we'd worn since we left Tacloban two weeks ago. So I don't think men worry much about what they'll be wearing when they're found dead. Women, maybe.

Stephen Dedalus says in *Ulysses* that "history is a nightmare from which I'm trying to recover." You could say that again. But Omar Khayyam was right; you can't change what happened. Red Holtzman, the old Knick coach, says until it has happened, it hasn't happened. But once it has happened you can't wish it away whether it's a dent in the fender of your brand new car or the night you let that good-looking young Random House editor at the cocktail party talk you into drinking stingers before dinner and the next morning you wished to God you hadn't. Omar Khayyam, who was translated by Edward Fitzgerald—which is why I have on my bulletin board a tear sheet from *Publishers Weekly* listing in order *Yogi* by Ed Fitzgerald and Yogi Berra, *The Rubaiyat of Omar Khayyam* translated by Edward Fitzgerald, and *Expo Summer* by Eileen Fitzgerald—said that the moving finger having writ moves on, nor all your piety nor wit can change a word of it, or something like that. Well, if you can't wash it out, maybe St. Mary's knows how to wash it clean.

I feel like going into a church where there's nothing going on. Which church? St. Paul's in London? St. Patrick's on Fifth Avenue? Notre-Dame? Chartres? We once went to an Italian church on North Beach in San Francisco but I don't remember its name. It was beautiful in a homey kind of way and we wondered if Joe DiMaggio had gone there when he was a kid. The churches in Italy had slots into which you could put lira to turn on the floodlights that lit up the paintings on the ceiling. It made you feel like God, or at least St. Michael the Archangel. Such power for fifty lira, which that summer was worth two and a half cents in American money.

Joseph Campbell, the myth man, told Bill Moyers that computers hadn't quite taken over the world yet when General Eisenhower was president and he wasn't all that impressed by them. He walked into a room full of them one day, and when the tour director asked Ike if there was anything he wanted the machines to do for him,

Ike said, "Ask them if there is a God." The man put the question
to the computers and there was a lot of whirring and clicking and
the man came back with a printout that said: "There is now."

The thing I remember best from writing her book with Althea
Gibson, the first black tennis champion, was that she said she used
to heat up a can of Dixie Peach Pomade and stick a curling iron
in it to straighten out her hair before she played a big match. That
and that she called her best friend when she was a kid, her boon
coon. I wonder how that would play with Jesse Jackson. Run, Althea, run.

Run for the roundhouse, Nellie, he can't corner you there. I used
to dream about being lost in a huge brick roundhouse, the trolley
cars lined up in rows waiting to be washed, their poles pulled down
and locked into their sockets. Please. Don't explain it to me. I used
to imagine that they were like the horses in the barns at Empire
City, waiting for their time to cut loose and run again, only the
trolley cars couldn't run on that nice soft dirt at the racetrack, they
had to roll on iron tracks under acres of wire cable that made a
spider web between the old cobblestoned streets and the sky. And
I was in the roundhouse, looking for a safe corner. I was a kid with
a vivid imagination. I wanted everything, especially the clay-court
princess I had seen bending over to pick up the balls she had been
hitting against the garage wall at the end of her tennis court. They
talked about Cyd Charisse's legs. My girl's were better. Sitting with
her on the trolley on a hot summer's night after a movie and an
ice-cream soda was all I'd ever wanted.

What happened between there and here?

I'm tired. I was just thinking about the first night on Guam. We'd
actually done it. We'd climbed down the cargo nets, walked across
the barrier reef, ducked the random rifle fire and the shells from
the Japanese artillery and learned to make jokes about not getting
killed by our own airplanes, and now we were trying to get four
hours sleep before going on guard duty at the edge of the perimeter.
I'd never imagined anything like this. Something fell in my hole
and I reached for my carbine. It was only a toad. I lay back again.
Each of us was alone in these holes we had dug for ourselves under

a navy blue sky as high as it was endless, thickly settled with stars so large and so luminous that each one seemed to have a halo of its own. I thought it must be a curtain lightly drawn in front of the next world, where nobody shot at you and you didn't have to shoot at anybody else. And if something exciting happened, you could celebrate it with a drink. Well, at least a glass of heavenly champagne.

I tried to remember the words to that nostalgic song about Ebbets Field. It took me a while, lying there in this hospital in Minneapolis, Minnesota, not more than half a mile from the Metrodome where the Twins played a kind of Ping-Pong with baseball bats indoors on a rock-hard artificial playing field thirty rows below street level that was nothing at all like the old ball park in Brooklyn where Carl Furillo wouldn't let any visiting ballplayer hit Abe Stark's clothing sign in right field—HIT THIS SIGN AND YOU GET A FREE SUIT—and Jackie Robinson dug his spikes into the real grass and Carl Erskine threw strikes and Peewee Reese made long throws for outs to Gil Hodges. How did it go?

> There used to be a ball park
> where the people played their crazy game
> with a joy I've never seen.
> And the air was such a wonder
> with the hot dogs and the beer
> and there used to be a ball park right here.
>
> And there used to be rock candy,
> and a great big Fourth of July,
> with the fireworks exploding
> all across the summer sky.
> And the people watched in wonder,
> how they laughed and how they cheered,
> And there used to be a ball park right here.

7

How Many Roads
Must a Man Walk Down
Before You Call Him a Man?

Both the stalls were occupied when I walked into the shower room at six o'clock the next morning. But I didn't have to wait long before a big man gone to considerable pot whom I hadn't seen before stepped out of the smaller cubicle and picked up the towel he had left on the bench underneath the mirror. "Good morning," he said, "My name is Tim."

"Good morning," I said. "My name is Ed." It suddenly struck me as pretty funny, so I decided to finish it. "I'm an alcoholic."

"Well," he said, "I don't know if I am but they all tell me I am, so who am I against so many?"

By the time I was out of my shower, he was gone. Before I finished drying off, I discovered that my neighbor in the next shower, the same as yesterday, was Mac. "We could have our first meeting of the day in here," he said cheerfully, "if we could figure out a way to get Denny up this early."

We both knew better. I shaved and dressed, went downstairs and paid thirty-five cents for a copy of the *Minneapolis Star-Tribune*, and took it to the third floor lounge to wait for Mary Scanlan or one of her lieutenants to show up to tell us if we were alive or dead. Mary's good news for me was one thirty-two over one hundred, which sounded a hell of a lot better than yesterday's ridiculous one seventy-two over one thirty although not as good as Dr. Amer's one forty-two over ninety-two. "Don't get carried away," Mary said. "Let's see if it lasts." She was glad that my temperature was right on target at ninety-eight something, and the only thing that bothered her was that my pulse was low.

"How low?" I asked her.

"Would you know the difference?" she asked wisely.

"No, but I thought maybe you'd tell me."

"I would only tell you if it was good," she said, a little smile turning up her unlipsticked morning mouth. "Go eat some breakfast and don't worry."

"You mean don't drink and go to meetings," I teased her. But Mary wasn't about to be teased. "That's right," she said. "Same thing. Both of them are good for your blood pressure."

Denny, the old pro, told me I had to strip my bed and take the old sheets and pillow cases to the linen closet next to the shower room and pick up a new set. Then, because there was no maid service in the Rehab, I had to put the bed back together again. I'd done my share of that in the army before we went overseas and were living in stateside barracks, so I didn't worry about it. But I hadn't counted on a mattress cover that was six inches too tight to fit around the corners of my particular mattress, so, with an ineptitude that would have left Liby totally unsurprised, I spent twenty minutes doing two minutes' worth of work. Then we found out that the morning lecture was on AA.

Instead of Father Martin working at being a Catholic Jackie Mason, the lecturer was a real person, John Emmer, telling us about how the program had just about saved his life and how he owed his present contentment entirely to Bill Wilson and Doctor Bob. (Not our Doctor Bob.) I was glad for him but I wished I didn't have to listen to it. Not even the newest priest fresh from St. Joseph's Seminary, with his ecclesiastical garments still stiff from the box in which they arrived, is quite so agonizingly missionary as the grateful AA convert who feels the only way he can pay off his debt is to spread the word, to go forth and preach to all nations. Whether they like it or not.

Mr. Emmer told us with the loud enthusiasm of a Rotarian that all we had to do was give AA a chance. I wondered briefly if he was deliberately trying to make it sound like "Give Peace a Chance," but after I'd listened to him for a few minutes I realized that back in the sixties he probably would have had my war-protesting kids and their friends locked up. He certainly never tapped his feet to Country Joe McDonald singing "One, two, three . . . what are we fighting for?" or even to Joan Baez singing "Where Have All the Flowers Gone?" Ms. Baez once said that very few AA members are tolerant of society's rebels. I've often wondered how they got to be such good drinkers; didn't they think it was a sin?

The stalwart Emmer did have one good story for us. He talked earnestly about how important it was to find a sponsor with whom you felt comfortable, somebody who could steer you through the difficult first months and who would be there at the other end of the telephone when you needed him. "Well," he said, "him if you're a him. Her if you're a her. The worst thing you can do is cross over for a sponsor. Your sponsor should always be the same sex. I always remember one match-up I knew about where they took a chance on a cross-over. It was a disaster. He spoke all the time for AA and she spoke for Al-Anon, and in the end she stabbed him twenty-seven times."

I was surprised to see my friend from the shower, Tim, sitting in room 355, our group meeting room, when we assembled at nine-thirty, but I was even more surprised after Debbie invited him to tell us something about himself and how he had gotten here. "Well," he said, his bulk spilling over the bridge-table chair he had opti-mistically picked out when he sat down, "I hadn't expected to do this, at least not right away, but I think I may as well tell you all right away that I'm a Catholic priest." He got through that without any difficulty; nobody either groaned or applauded. Ralph said, mildly for him, "Is that so? Now we've got a Presbyterian minister and a Catholic priest. We have an excellent chance of being saved." John had told me at breakfast that Ralph was an Amtrak conductor but he looked more like an engineer in the cab of a Southern Pacific six-eight wheeler.

Father Tim wanted to know who the minister was and Mac admitted his guilt. They shook hands and we all waited for Tim to tell us more. "You asked how I got here," he said, in that ruminative way priests have of leading up to a sore subject instead of confronting it head on. "I guess I had finally had to admit that I'd been drinking a little too much." That sounded familiar. "The Bishop and his assistant had been suggesting to me that I ought to take time off for a rest, and I suppose an evaluation of my situation, and I got tired of resisting them and said I might as well try it. So, here I am."

"You weren't forced to come here?" Debbie asked.

"No, no," Father Tim said dismissively, "nothing like that. There's no question that the bishop thought it would be good for me, but the decision was mine. Nobody made it for me." He told us that his parish was in a little town in South Dakota, near Huron, and that he lived alone, with only a woman housekeeper his own age who had been looking after him for more than twenty years and might criticize his drinking "in the privacy of my own dining room," but would cut off her hand at the wrist before she would make any trouble for him with the Bishop or, even worse, with his flock. So he had all the opportunity in the world to drink. "And I drank," he said. "I admit it." A bit righteously, I thought, I mean, he's not exactly crawling on the floor in sackcloth and ashes. "I hope that I'll be able to accomplish two things there, get back in shape and learn to take better care of myself."

And, seeing a lot of myself as I had been in the way he was, I thought, find the way to look at yourself as you really are and not as you wish you were. But I gave myself two demerits for complacency and I let Father Tim keep the floor. "The only thing I wish," he said, "is that I'd brought more clothes with me. Would you believe these are the only socks I have?" He pointed to the thin clerical silk socks above his sober black shoes. When he pointed, I noticed a large square-cut diamond ring on his left hand. I had thought only cardinals wore rings; well, and maybe bishops. Besides nuns, the brides of Christ. That showed how much I knew about the modern church. I looked at him more closely. If he hadn't put

on so much weight he would be a good-looking man. He had a full
head of graying hair and bold Irish features that lent conviction to
his professionally hearty, reassuring manner. It's like he was consoling us, I thought. But he can't help it; he's in the consoling
business. Actually, if he wasn't so heavy he would look a lot like
Milo O'Shea, who played the drinking priest in *Mass Appeal* on the
stage.

Debbie made a little show of sifting through her notes. "I understood," she said mildly, "that Monsignor Saltzman arranged for you
to come here. In fact, he actually drove you here, didn't he?"

"That's right," Father Tim said agreeably.

"Is that why you didn't bring your clothes with you?" Debbie
wondered. "I mean, he didn't give you a chance to pack, did he?"

For the first time the priest looked uncomfortable. But he was
still almost patronizing to Deb. "That's right," he said. "We just left
from his place and we agreed my things could be sent on from my
parish house. Actually, my secretary will bring them up either today
or tomorrow." His assurance came back quickly. "I guess I still
know how to wash out a pair of socks," he said.

"There's a laundromat on the second floor," Debbie said. "Well,
did you know that Monsignor Saltzman is going to say the masses
at St. Dominic's himself next Sunday?"

"Yes," Tim said. "He told me that."

"And did you know," Debbie asked, "that he has sent a letter to
all of the parishioners telling them that you're here for treatment?"

It was obvious that Father Tim didn't know that. He admitted it.
"No," he said, "he didn't tell me that."

"He gave me a copy of the letter," Deb said. "I'll let you take it
back to your room after the meeting." Clearly she didn't want to
embarrass him by reading the letter out loud or even summarizing
it for us, but Tim fought for his pride. "I don't think it was very
fair of him to do that without telling me," he said. The heartiness
was replaced by defensiveness; instead of consoling us in our time
of common difficulty he was now appealing to our group sense of
fair play. We should see that this was a gravely misunderstood man.
"I assumed he would assign somebody to cover the parish," he said,

"and I told him that my friend Father Behrens, who's retired and who lives there, would be glad to fill in for me. He's done it before."

"Actually," Debbie said, "I understand he's done it quite a few times."

"I suppose so," Tim admitted. "Overall, probably he has."

It was turning out to be not such a dull Friday after all. Debbie turned away from Father Tim and asked Denny if he needed any time this morning. Denny said he didn't. "I don't think there's anything I can do now," he said, "except await the onslaught."

"From Emma, you mean?" Debbie asked.

"Sure. My mama won't give me any heat. She feels bad, but she wants to help. Emma wants to help, too, but she'd like me to be a little more abject. Is that the right word, Ed?"

"If you mean that she wants you to be a little more humble in defeat, more apologetic in your humiliation, I guess that's the right word," I said. "Why, is that what you think she wants?"

"Oh, yeah, she wants me to crawl and beg God for forgiveness," he said. "Well, I ain't gonna do it. I'm sorry as hell . . ."

"That you got caught?" Ralph demanded with a distinct note of truculence in his voice. Ralph wasn't crazy about Denny and, I thought, would like nothing better than to see him forced to crawl a little. I was sure he could hardly wait to see Denny's family get here. Especially Emma. If Emma was going to give Denny a hard time, Ralph would like to have a ringside seat at the circus.

After Debbie had gone around the room and given everybody a chance to talk about anything that might be on their minds, she said it was time for us to say good-bye to Carl and Ken. I hadn't gotten to know either of them enough to work up any strong feeling about their leaving but, just the same, it was my first graduation ceremony, and I was curious. Debbie obviously took it seriously. After the reading of the Thought for the Day, she put a couple of bronze medallions, smaller than Eisenhower silver dollars but bigger than Kennedy half-dollars, on the table next to her chair and said that it was always an important occasion when a group member finished his treatment time and went back home to put his life back together again. "Today we have two of our members leaving us," she said, "and they've been important parts of our group. Neither one of them has had a particularly easy time of it here, if anybody ever has an easy time, but they've both come through wonderfully. Well, I think they have, anyway, and I hope they think so."

As Debbie talked more about the graduating seniors, I began to understand that Mayor Ken, as the others called him, had had his troubles with the administration from the day he arrived at St. Mary's. "I hope, Ken," she said, "you can see now that it wouldn't have done you much good for everybody to stand up and salute every time you complained about something. I think things got pretty well straightened out when you said you would have to leave if you weren't moved out of the room with Carl."

"And you," Ken said, "told me I would just have to leave then. You were right."

"It wasn't just me," Debbie said. "I took your case to staffing, and everybody agreed we had to hold firm or we'd just give away your recovery."

I thought of *The New Yorker* cartoon showing the new man raising his hand at a meeting of the bank directors and asking, "What's a debenture?" But I asked anyway. "What's staffing?"

Debbie understood both my ignorance and my reluctance to have the scene played over my head. "It's a meeting we have of all the people who have anything to do with the patient, to discuss a problem that's important enough to need everybody's opinion. In this case, the vote was unanimous that we had to tell Ken he couldn't take charge of his own treatment."

"You didn't want to put the inmates in charge of the asylum," Ken said.

Debbie never joined in the tendency of the patients to call themselves inmates. She never forgot which side of the street she worked on, which, I decided, was why the patients never forgot it either.

"You're one of the most intelligent, thoughtful people I've ever worked with," Debbie said. "I was sure that if we stuck to our guns you would understand our reasons and come to respect them. And you did." She waited for him to pick up his cue.

"I did," Ken said. He was dressed to go home in a navy blue blazer, white shirt with blue and red rep tie, and gray flannels. I wondered where he was the mayor, but I didn't have to wonder long. It wasn't Sausalito or Scottsdale or Scarsdale but it was a place like them, an enclave of the intellectual affluent. And it turned out that he wasn't a former mayor, it was no honorary title, he was very much the sitting mayor, in office, and he was worried that if the opposition found out about his being here they would use it against him in the next election. "I resented very much being here pretty much against my will. I suppose I could have left the airport and gone somewhere else instead of coming here, so in a sense I came of my own free will, but I knew I would never have done it if my wife and doctor and my best friend hadn't made me, and that was hard to take. I'm not accustomed to having somebody else make my decisions for me. It hurt. I felt diminished."

"That's the same word Ed used to me the first time we talked," Debbie said. "It's hard for men who are used to running things to have somebody else take their lives out of their own hands. But when you've proved that you can't do it yourself, it's what has to be done. Thank God you understood that."

"Finally," Ken said. "It wasn't an overnight revelation."

"You'd been in trouble for a long time," Debbie said. "An overnight cure wouldn't have been for real."

"I think you're right," Ken said. "It took a lot of things. Not just the lectures and the group sessions but all those nights I sat in the room talking things over with Carl, or out walking in the park, or just playing the piano with everybody singing in the lounge. The things we talked about at meals. Gradually getting to understand that as different as we all are we share the same disease. Or weakness. Or whatever it is. I think that's when things began to come together for me, when I could see that it wasn't that I had gone bad or lost all decency but that like everybody else here I had a terrible disease but that it could be arrested and I could have a second chance to make my life what I want it to be. I'll always be grateful to St. Mary's for that, and I'll always be grateful to you, Debbie, for your understanding and your patience."

"Don't forget, I was there once myself," Debbie said. "Now, who do you want to give your medallion to you?"

"My roommate," Ken said unhesitatingly. "I wouldn't have believed I'd ever say that, and whether we ever meet again or not, Carl and I will always disagree on a lot of things, but he helped me get through all this as much as anybody did and I'd like him to give it to me."

"Wonderful," Deb said. "Now, this is how we do it. I'll hand it to Denny here, on Carl's left, and we'll pass it all around the circle and everybody can say whatever they want to say to you, and then when it comes back to Carl he will give it to you."

The people who had been there the longest had the most to say, of course, and I found some of it deeply moving. They weren't speeches, more like memories, fragments of time remembered from weeks of painfully intimate sharing of experiences and emotions. I wondered if all the graduation ceremonies were like this, strong handclasps in words, hugs expressed in awkward gestures, eyes locked in silent friendship. What wasn't said was more touching than what was said. I'd heard a lot of times that you don't really know somebody until you get drunk with them but what I was seeing here was that if you really want to get inside somebody there is no better way to do it than to suffer together in a place like St. Mary's trying to get over being drunks. That strips away all the bullshit.

I was struck by the absence of jokes. This was serious business. There were a few jabs about Mayor Ken's fondness for cashmere sweaters and viyella shirts, and his scorn for what the St. Mary's cooks called a soft-boiled egg—"they only have to put some colored dye on them," Ken interrupted, "and they'll be ready for any child's Easter basket"—but mostly the speakers stuck to his gradual conversion from prisoner to earnest candidate for a degree. It was Denny who said that, and that drew some good-natured sarcasm from Ken. "What do you know about candidates for degrees?" he said. And when Denny protested that he had one, Mayor Ken said with proper disdain, "From the University of Texas? That's worth about as much as a degree in medicine from the University of Grenada."

Carl was shy when he stood up, but he was determined to say what was on his mind. "You all know I'm just a farmer," he said.

"Yes," Ken interrupted, "with a modest spread of three thousand acres and a thousand head of cattle."

"A farmer," Carl repeated undisturbed. "I certainly never expected, when I came here for some tests . . ." This made everybody smile because Carl had never surrendered the fiction that he had come to St. Mary's only for a physical, to make sure all his parts were in working order. He had never admitted for a minute that he had been packed off to the Rehab just like the rest of us, and only Debbie reminded him regularly of the truth. Everybody else let him have his illusion. "I never expected to find myself rooming with a real, live mayor. I didn't blame Ken for being sore about it. Back home we treat our mayors with more respect. We give them quarters of their own even if it's only in jail." He juggled the medallion from one hand to the other. "I don't guess Ken and I said more than a few words to each other the first three or four days. I know that's when he was fussin' with Deb here to get him a room of his own, and like I say, I didn't blame him. But he didn't, and there we were hitched up together whether we liked it or not, so we began to talk. Well, you just know, I didn't know any more about the business of mayoring than Ken knew about being a cattle farmer, so to pass the time we began talking about what we knew and then about how we had begun mixin' working with drinking and how we had gotten here. It got so we liked each other's company so much we would just come back to our room after the nighttime lecture and take off our shoes and talk. I'll tell you, I heard a lot of things about city living that I'd never heard on the radio or seen on the TV. And I suspect Ken heard a couple or three things about life on the farm that he hadn't known about." He held out the medallion to Ken, who was beginning to look as though he might need a Kleenex. "I'm going to miss you, Ken. I know it ain't likely that you'll ever come to Montana to see me, no more than it's likely

I'll get to see you leadin' one of them parades you like so much in your town, but I promise you I'll remember you. I wish you good luck, and stay away from the bottle. You don't need it. You're a good man, Ken."

Mayor Ken was more oratorical but no less personal in his response. "I'm sure," he said firmly, "that I got more out of our enforced togetherness than you did. In the first place I didn't have to start out living with a sorehead the way you did. A spoiled sorehead, at that. And although it's unlikely that you will ever have the opportunity to employ any of the little dodges I revealed to you about the ways in which mayors can fool the people who pay their salaries, it's entirely possible that I might some day find myself living on a farm at least as a guest of one of my affluent constituents, and if that happens, I will know two or three hundred astonishingly secret burrows in which to store bottles against the sudden strike of a hurricane or typhoon or even a hard summer rain. Furthermore, I will remember the way you always bounced back from the assaults of nature, your love of the land and your acute sense of responsibility for it, and your respect for all things that live. I am glad to have known you, Carl, and proud to have you for my friend. Whenever I look at this medallion I will think of how much you helped me to earn it." He turned to Debbie and said, "And, to you, Debbie, I may very well, quite simply, owe my life. Thank you for giving me a chance to save it."

Debbie wrapped her arms around him, reached out for Carl and pulled him into her embrace, too. She kissed each one hard and rubbed her eyes. "You're both wonderful," she said. "God bless you."

"Let's form the wagons in a circle," Denny said, and Mac began, "God grant me the serenity . . ."

When we went out for a walk before lunch, we were quiet for a few blocks, and then Mac asked abruptly, "Do you guys think Tim was fudging about an intervention? It seemed to me that Debbie did everything but outright call him a liar."

"Sure, he was lying," Denny said. "It's obvious they wrapped him up in a package and tied it tight and shipped him here air mail.

Only they didn't trust him to parcel post or even Federal Express, so they had the bishop's prat boy drive him here himself. They were right, too. That man has denial of his denial."

"It will be interesting to see how long he keeps it up," Mac said.

I said I didn't think it would be for long. "Obviously Debbie has the goods on him," I said. "Not just the letter, but whatever the monsignor told her. But my hunch is she's going to work on him to admit that he's an alcoholic. I don't think she gives a damn if he admits he had an intervention or not. That reminds me. I've been meaning to tell you guys that when I was talking to Dr. Amer, I asked him if the intervention patients were harder to work with when they got here than the people who came more or less on their own. And, you know, you've seen him, he's a very unemotional man, real low key, and I got a kick out of the way he said it. He said, 'Well, they're sure angrier.' "

"Wait till he meets Doctor Bob," Denny said. "At least that's one thing that didn't happen to me. But I don't know how much difference it makes. I had to come if I didn't want my ass thrown in jail, that's for sure."

It was the hottest time of the day now, less than half an hour before noon, and without even discussing it we gave up our usual illegitimate walk up South Eighth Street to Twenty-sixth or even Twenty-fifth Avenue and settled for turning right at Twenty-seventh and going back to the Rehab the shortest possible way. "I need a Coke," I said. "It beats me how you can drink so much of that stuff," Denny said. "That's easy," I said, "they won't let me have a gin and tonic." Mac laughed at both of us. "It's a good thing they never run out of coffee," he said. "Oh, for a cold, wet bottle of Lone Star," Denny sighed, but he said it without much passion. He knew he wasn't going to taste a Lone Star until he was back in the state of Texas, or at least on an airplane that was heading for Texas.

They got right on the cafeteria line but I went upstairs first to fix a Coke with ice. If I was lucky they might have a pitcher of iced tea on the salad table but I wasn't taking any chances. It was the way I used to feel about having a martini at the bar when I was meeting a stranger for lunch. You never could tell; he might be a nondrinker and it would be hard to squeeze in more than one drink before the food came. Martini men, and women, like to talk business before they eat, while they're drinking. Coffee persons like to eat fast and then spend an hour talking business. The only way you can beat that is to order wine with your lunch; then you can keep going with the wine while your host is having his coffee. If I was the host, we did it my way. Now I was reduced to making sure I got a Coke.

There wasn't any line for lunch because it was Friday and all the Family Week visitors were on their way back home after getting their last words of advice from the Rehab's justly famous crew of family-counseling tigers on how to live their lives for themselves and not just as slaves to the reformed drunks they were going to get back in a week. "We've got the whole place to ourselves," I said as I dropped my tray of chicken chow mein and rice on the group table. "Yes," Ralph said, "we're going to have to learn to get along without Carl and the mayor." It didn't sound as if he thought that would be hard. I decided to tease him a little. "Carl wasn't so bad," I said. "Carl is all right," he announced fiercely, in his best "the next station stop will be Dubuque" voice. "But it will be just fine with me if I never have to listen to that mayor again. He thinks he's the Prince of Wales on parade."

Nobody was especially cheerful. I wondered if it was always that way when somebody from the group left. It was hard not to think of Ken and Carl sitting down to a real dinner tonight and sleeping in their own beds.

I pampered myself by stopping in the gift shop and buying a Baby Ruth. The conventional wisdom is that alcoholics coming off the stuff substitute sweets for the booze, and who was I to go against the stereotype?

Afternoon group was as draggy as lunch had been. We spent the time rehearsing Denny and John for their family confrontations. Debbie wanted Denny to examine his conscience—I thought she was like a patient priest in the confessional, trying to make sure you had told it all—and was prepared to tell his wife and mother everything there was to tell, and she wanted John to see how important it was to tell his father why he had been afraid of him all these years. She made another pass at Father Tim's impenetrable armor of denial but decided to let him simmer over the weekend. We quit right on the button at three o'clock. Everybody had said enough for the week.

Denny and I saw Debbie hurrying down the hall on her way out and we said we hoped she had a good weekend. "Thank you," our leader said, "I hope you do, too."

"You know," Denny said, looking after her admiringly, "she means it."

"So did we," I said, checking the quarters in my pocket and heading for the soda machine. "I hope she knows somebody who has a swimming pool."

We didn't want to go outside and face that heat again, so Denny followed me into my room. "I'm scared about next week," he said. "I think Emma's gonna have a fit and my poor mother isn't gonna know what hit her."

We sat and talked for about an hour until there was barely time for a quick nap before dinner. Denny adored his mother and loved Emma and didn't want anything to hurt either of them. He didn't want to get hurt, either; he certainly didn't want to lose the love of either of his women. He still didn't quite understand how all this had happened to him when all he had ever wanted was to be nice to people and have a good time.

"It's the good time part that caught up to you," I said. I walked him down to the bulletin board to see what movie they were showing tonight—Denny had told me they always had movies in the lecture hall on Friday and Saturday nights—and when I saw it was Jane Fonda in *The Morning After* I made him promise he would go. He made a deal; he would go to the movie if I would go for the long walk after dinner, heat or no heat. Mac was out because he had a grief group meeting. The movie wasn't until nine o'clock, anyway. We would have plenty of time. We would be able to see the Friday night dinner crowd lining up to board the Showboat on the other side of the river.

The seven o'clock lecture was a video-cassette on the danger of relapse. It was scary. Did anybody really beat this rap? There were a lot of bars in New York City and some of them stayed open very late.

What worried Denny, he told me as we walked out to the fence along the riverbank and down toward the athletic field, was that Debbie was going to try to make him tell Emma about every single thing he'd done while he was doing coke. "I just can't do that," he said. "She knows I had other girls before her, and she may even suspect I've had some since, but she isn't sure and she isn't going to want to hear about it. What good would it do? Why does anybody think Emma's going to be better off if I confess?"

"She isn't," I said unhesitatingly. "That's just taking the guilt off your shoulders and dumping it, or part of it anyway, on hers. No matter what anybody says, don't do it. You don't have to argue about it. Just don't do it. Anyway, I don't believe for a minute that Deb is going to give you a hard time about that. She wants you to face up to the bad things you've done and understand that coke is what made you do them or most of them anyway. She certainly doesn't want to ruin your marriage."

"Yeah, you're probably right about Deb. But I'm not so sure about those women downstairs," Denny said. He was agitated.

"You mean the family counselors?"

"Yeah, them. All they care about, from everything I hear, is stirring up the families, and especially the wives, to make the alcoholics and the druggies eat shit for all the things they done to them. Like they were finally getting their chance to turn the tables. Well, I don't mind them havin' their turn, I just don't see why the counselors think it's goin' to help if they make the patient tell things that's bound to make the wife miserable. But that seems to be what they want. Get it all out, I guess that's what it is. Ken said it was one of the things he had trouble with right up to the end. They wanted him to tell his wife things he admitted he'd done when he was drunk that he said he was goddamned if he would tell her, and they could all just go to hell."

"Don't tell your wife anything you think will hurt her," I said.

"Even one of AA's twelve steps says you should make amends to everybody you've hurt except where it would hurt them to do it. That's like straight from the Sermon on the Mount. Look, stop being afraid of the bogeyman. Nobody can put words in your mouth. If you don't tell Emma, she isn't going to be told."

"I don't trust that sonofabitch Ralph. He heard me tell my story the first time I came into the group and he's dyin' for me to confess it all to Emma. I swear, I think he's one of those what-do-you-call-them voyeur types, you know, who get their kicks out of watching other people do it. He wants to watch Emma suffer and know that he had a hand in it."

"Jesus," I said, "so you fooled around with another woman when you were high, it's not the end of the world."

"I fooled around with a lot of them," Denny said. "And I made the mistake of admitting it and Ralph won't let go of it. You'll see, he's gonna do his best to cause trouble. And the worst of it is I don't even think I actually made it with any of those party women. I was too stoned and so were they."

"He can't make you say what you won't say. Just don't get mad. Say you drank too much and you did the coke and you behaved like a fucking fool, say you're sorry, say you know it wasn't fair to Emma to behave like that behind her back, but never, never say you did it with other women. No matter how many times she says she's forgiven you, she'll never forget it. She doesn't need that and neither do you. Denny, you're not keeping your mouth shut for you, you're keeping it shut for Emma. Forget Ralph. He has no standing in this case."

We were sitting on a park bench looking out across the river through a break in the shrubs and trees. Denny stared at the people going aboard the riverboat. "Every one of those people is going to have a drink in their hands in less than five minutes," he said.

"And we're going to the movies," I said. "I'm going to call up Liby first."

"Emma's probably at the golf club with my folks for dinner," Denny said. "I'll sneak out during the picture and call her then. I want to find out if she's decided to come Sunday night. If she does, you can stand guard outside my room and make sure we have a few minutes alone. Like a half an hour, I mean."

"I don't think they allow that."

"That's why I need you," Denny said. "See you later."

It gave me a good feeling that the U.S. West Communication Co. let the Rehab patients ask the operator to make a credit card call by depositing only a dime, not a quarter, in the slot. The public phone booth in the lobby downstairs required a quarter. Inmates have their privileges.

8

Friday Night at the Bijou

Denny had gotten to the day room refrigerator ahead of me and was making a thick sandwich out of baloney and cheese on white bread with mustard.

"You just ate," I said, not seriously.

"That was three hours ago," he said accurately. "Besides, I never watch a movie without something to eat." He added a generous slab of chocolate brownie to his paper plate, added a cup of coffee and then, as an afterthought, made room for a Goldrush bar which was vanilla ice cream with milk chocolate, caramel, and peanuts. I shook my head in admiration and settled for a North Star vanilla ice cream cup to go with the paper cup of Coke and ice I'd brought with me from my room supply. I'd have to remember to buy a couple more cans of Coke on my way back after the movie. I'd brought the necessary change with me and while I was at it I'd checked my supply. I was down to my last hundred and four quarters. That ought to take care of things for a while.

Denny and I stopped to look at the messages on the two blackboards. Sometimes there were some beauts. These were pretty ordinary:

Beth—Call Aunt Karen
David—Your brother called 8:20 p.m.
John—Marty called, will call you 9:30
Evan—The message is I'm not mad. Call me. Patty

I went into the lecture hall through the door from the day room which left us in the back of the hall. There were only about a dozen people there, at least as many young women as men—it was easy to see why they made movies for the young—and most of them were sprawled out on the floor of the stage, right in front of the lowered screen. The kids had brought their bedclothes with them; they intended to be comfortable. Bedclothes included a sheet as well as a blanket and a couple of pillows. There was a fair amount of cuddling going on but it was all blanket to blanket. "The real action," Denny confided, "will come when they turn out the lights." I thought he was kidding but what did I know? The action right now was with a dozen bags of popcorn the management had supplied for the movie.

Leona came in to start the picture and got a respectful low whistle from the males in the audience.

So did Jane Fonda when the picture began with no titles, only a single frame saying Lorimar Motion Pictures and then a closeup of Jane in bed, looking like the wrath of God. Then the camera switched abruptly to what was obviously a television screen. "It's Eye On L.A.," the voice-over demanded our attention. "Focusing on the new photography combining modeling and pumping iron. Is it, as its promoters claim, a new glorification of the female body in the Ziegfeld manner, or is it a new kind of soft porn? We'll be meeting with the controversial Bobby Korshak, publisher of the successful magazine he calls art and others call obscene. Is he indeed glorifying the female form or is he, as some call him, the King of Sleaze?"

You wondered if somebody had mixed up a television tape with the Fonda movie but then we were back to Jane's head on the pillow. She yawned and grimaced and you knew she had an awful hangover. This was a knowledgeable audience. Jane looked at the man next to her in bed and didn't look any happier. Then she looked at her hand and saw that it was covered with blood. She was appropriately horrified. "What the fuck?" she said, and the gang in the Rehab giggled. This was their kind of language. Then Jane sat up and saw blood all over the bed and even we weren't used to that kind of thing. She pushed the guy next to her and moved the bedclothes off him and suddenly she saw that he had a knife sticking out of his chest and he was extremely dead. Just to be sure, she pushed him hard, and he was still dead. She jumped out of bed, pulled on a short black dress with one bare shoulder and went out of the bedroom into a huge hi-tech-decorated loft. Showing a lot of leg, she walked unsteadily past a Siamese cat sitting on a table straight to the bar where she grabbed a bottle of scotch and poured herself a huge glass of whiskey. She drank down half of it with an eloquent shudder which went collectively through this experienced audience, then carried the glass into the bathroom where she got down on her knees in front of the toilet and threw up helplessly.

This made us all glad we were safe here in St. Mary's, far away from such unreliable medications as Black and White scotch.

Next, Jane washed the blood off her hands and rinsed her haggard face with what I took to be cold water. She stared at that famous face in the mirror and said, "Congratulations." Then she ran to the telephone and called her hairdresser. No, not to make an appointment. Her hairdresser turned out to be Raul Julia, and he's her best friend. She gets him on his car phone while he's tooling through one of the canyons of Beverly Hills like Mulholland or Benedict Canyon or something like that.

"What are you boozing for at ten o'clock in the morning?" Raul wants to know.

"It's the breakfast of champions," Jane says impatiently, as if he ought to know that. "What did I do last night?" This also gets an understanding response from the St. Mary's undergraduates. They know what that's like. "Blackout," some unsophisticated rookie whispered loudly. "No kidding," a more experienced young woman in front of us said bitingly.

The movie was passable but it was the audience that held my attention. Once, Jane flagged down a cab but discovered she had no money and asked the driver to stop at a bar where she knew the bartender and cashed a check for two hundred dollars while she downed a glass of vodka. "Look at all those bottles," somebody said as the camera helpfully panned the shelves behind the bartender. I began to wonder if anybody in charge knew what this picture was about. It might have been better if they had showed us "Debbie Does Dallas" or "Deep Throat" or something like that. It would be easier to get laid than to get a drink in the Rehab.

There was a good response, especially from the high school set on the stage, to some snappy repartee between Fonda and Bridges when he struck out looking for food in her refrigerator. He had already confessed that he was a cop and she wanted to know why he wasn't working at it anymore.

"I got stabbed by a little hooker," he said, "fourteen years of age. She must have hit a nerve. Anyway, I can't draw my weapon anymore." That got a laugh.

Another time, Jane was kissing Bridges. She wrapped her arms around his neck and pulled herself up on him and they kissed a lot. This crew had been away from it for a while and nobody was making any jokes now. The blankets on the stage weren't moving. She pulled his shirt open and he pulled hers off, proving that Fonda not only had legs and an ass but tits, too. This was the first time the sex had gotten as much reaction as the drinking. One deeply appreciative man whistled as Jane athletically braced her knees against Jeff's shoulders while he lifted her bodily off the floor. "See, ladies," he said, "that's what you can do if you follow Jane Fonda's workout tape." One female said, "Chauvinist," but not with a lot of conviction.

This, I thought, was the best audience I'd been to a movie with since we used to see Buck Jones and Hoot Gibson on Saturday afternoon at the Orpheum.

When it was over, we left the kids who'd been eating the popcorn to clean up the floor and went back down the hall to bed. "There's goin' to be a lot of action on the second floor tonight," Denny said.

The second floor was where the kids lived. The nurse on duty must have sneaked in a few times to look at the picture because she looked up as we walked past the station. "See?" she said. "We don't even censor the movies."

"It's a good thing Mac wasn't with us," I said to Denny. "He's a very broadminded minister but this would have stretched him to the limit."

"It stretched me," Denny said ambiguously. "See you at vitals."

9

Saturday Night Is the
Loneliest Night in the Week

Saturday was a long day, with what Denny called a half-ass half-schedule and the rest of the day off with no place to go. At least I achieved a one-fifty over one hundred blood pressure score at the seven o'clock lineup, so I gave in without a struggle to the temptation of sausage patties for breakfast along with the inevitably hardboiled soft-boiled eggs.

"Good going," Denny said. "Fuck the cholesterol."

Mac grinned a little sheepishly as he ate his Cream of Wheat. Doctor Bob compromised with sausage, toast, and coffee, no eggs.

The eight-thirty tape was "Staying Sober, Keeping Straight," which was uninspiring but not quite soporific, either, because all the inmates who were feeling strong enough to look to the future instead of repenting the past were alive to the perils of relapse. When you looked at it as something you were really going to have to deal with, that it was one thing to say you were going to love sitting down to a magnificent steak dinner as soon as you got home but quite another to remind yourself that you were going to have to get the steak down without a Heineken or a bottle of Gevrey-Chambertin, you took it seriously. You might wince a few times at some of the holier-than-thous, but you gave them a chance. What the hell, you're here; you might as well get something out of it.

Denny had explained to Mac and me that because Debbie and the rest of the counselors had the weekend off there were no regular group meetings on Saturday. But we did have to show up in the group's meeting room at nine-thirty for an informal discussion among ourselves. The senior member of the group acted as the chairman of the meeting and this week it was the irascible Mr. Woolard. "Jesus," I said. "Ralph is finally getting his chance to kick the shit out of all of us." "Especially me," Denny said. "He'll be so busy with me he won't have time for anybody else." I didn't have the heart to argue with that premise. It would be Ralph's last chance to force Denny to confess. "If Ralph thinks you've really coughed it all up," I suggested, "maybe he'll let Father Tim give you absolution."

Ralph asserted his command as soon as we all sat down in room 355. "I will read the Thought for the Day," he said challengingly. Nobody argued. "Disillusionment and spiritual confusion mark our age." He looked around the room as though the words he had just read proved beyond any doubt the wisdom of his personal philosophy. "Many of us have cast aside old ideas without acquiring new ones." He paused for a long look at Denny who maintained a placid, even modest, air of full agreement. "Many men and women are creeping through life on their hands and knees, merely because they refuse to rely on any power but themselves. Many of them feel that they are being brave and independent, but actually they are only courting disaster. Anxiety and the inferiority complex have become the greatest of all modern plagues. In AA we have the answer to these ills. Have I ceased to rely on myself only?"

It was exactly the kind of message most likely to make me want to be somewhere else, committing the unforgivable sin of relying on myself instead of on the Holy Eucharist of AA. Denny kicked my ankle gently. We were on the same wavelength.

There was worse to come. Ralph, fully satisfied with the sound of his own voice, the articulation by sacred writ of his own principles, and the knowledge that he was scattering mortar fire on the group members he shrewdly perceived were at best unenthusiastic about the message of the day, went on to let us have the meditation, which was more forthrightly religious. "There is power available to help us to do the right thing," he read. "Therefore we will accept that power. There are miracles of change in people's lives; therefore we will accept those miracles as evidence of God's power."

"For God's sake," I said solemnly, realizing I was being every bit as ambiguous as Denny had been in his double-entendre good night to me after the movie. I wouldn't have done it if Debbie had been there, but Ralph was asking for it. In fact, I felt, he was insisting on it.

Before Ralph could say anything, somebody knocked on the door. When Ralph said, "Come in," a slender, handsome black man in his early thirties walked in the room looking very much at his ease. He was wearing a white golf shirt and a crisply pressed pair of dark red cotton slacks. He looked as if he was on his way to a ten o'clock tee-off time. Ralph, Denny, and John all knew him. They all said hello and they all called him Bobby.

"I thought you'd gone home already," John said.

"I thought I'd *be* home already," Bobby said. He explained to us that the doctors had decided that a back condition that had bothered him since long before he came to St. Mary's cried out for an operation and they were going to do it at Fairview, the sister hospital of St. Mary's at the Riverside Medical Center. "So I've got to wait until they can fit me in," Bobby said, "and they didn't want me hanging around with nothing to do, so they assigned me to Debbie's group. Well, actually, I asked for it. You guys are all right, the ones I know anyway, and Debbie's the best. So here I am. Where do I sign in?"

Ralph was caught in a failure of procedure. "I brought a yellow pad," he said, fumbling in a brown envelope he had rested against the leg of his chair. "I was going to have everybody sign it afterward but we may as well do it right now." He pulled it out, signed it himself, and handed it around. "I have to turn it in to Debbie on Monday," he explained to those of us who didn't know. "It's how she'll know if anybody skipped the meeting."

Father Tim feigned hurt. "She doesn't trust us," he said sadly, scrawling his name.

"Of course she does," Mac said. "She just wants us to know that she cares about what we're doing today, that's all."

"I remember," Ralph said in his best first sergeant manner, "when she really told off the mayor for not bothering to show up. He said he fell asleep and then she blamed the rest of us for not waking him up." I was willing to bet that Ralph was rewriting history to suit himself but what difference did it make? I was honest enough to admit to myself that I didn't like him or any of his works.

Ralph invited anybody who had anything on his mind to feel free. Surprisingly, Sarah spoke up. "I've been talking to my daughter about who should come for Family Week," she said, "and I'm afraid we've got a problem. Denise says she doesn't think we ought to ask my sister to come, just her and my son Ricky, and I don't see how we can do that. Christine, my sister, certainly expects to be asked. After all, she lives right next door to us and she knows everything there is to know."

"Is that the problem?" Mac asked. "Does she know more than Denise thinks she has a right to know?"

Sarah said she thought that was part of it. "Denise hates Christine. Well, I probably shouldn't say she hates her but she sure doesn't like her very much. For one thing, you see, my mother lives with Christine and she owns both the houses. My mother, I mean. They're like on one piece of land that's been in the family forever. So Christine has a hand in running everything because my mother can't do it herself anymore. Christine pays the bills and collects the money that I pay in lieu of rent and all that kind of thing, and I guess my daughter just thinks she has more to do with our family than she has a right to. Anyway, they just bristle at each other, and that's why Denise feels this way. She thinks Christine knows enough about our business already and she doesn't want her sitting here while we talk about why I drink so much."

It was a regular soap opera. Sarah and her sister were the only children, and when their mother, who was in her mideighties, died, they would inherit her estate, presumably on equal terms. There was a will but Sarah's mother's lawyer had it and the mother had never talked about it with the two daughters. As we heard the story

it sounded very much as though young Denise thought it was
entirely possible that Christine, who had constant access to the old
lady, might talk her into making a change in the will that would
leave everything to her and simply trust her to look after Sarah and
her fatherless children. Sarah had been a widow for five years.
Christine had never been married and she had always been considered the smart daughter. She worked for the school board as a
purchasing secretary and she was used to dealing with large sums
of money, so it made sense that she might persuade her mother
that she was the one who ought to be trusted with the estate and
not poor, fumbling Sarah, who on top of everything else had turned
out to be an alcoholic. Sarah never used the word drunk. Not even
about other people, much less herself.

Father Tim suggested that maybe Sarah ought to tell Dinny,
which is what Sarah called her daughter most of the time, that she
thought it should be left up to Debbie. Debbie was conducting this
orchestra, Tim said, and she ought to decide what would be most
helpful. "What about your son?" Tim asked. "Does he think his
aunt ought to be there or not?" Sarah dismissed that as unimpor-
tant. "Ricky doesn't care one way or the other," she said. "He never
does." Tim thought that over. "It sounds," he said in a carefully
nonjudgmental tone, "as though your daughter and your sister fight
because they're so much alike. They both want to be in control,
isn't that right?"

Sarah sighed. "Yes," she said, "that's right."

Denny, Mac, and I all said we thought Tim was right about
leaving it up to Debbie. "In the first place," Mac said, "that gets
you off the hook, Sarah. You won't be the one choosing between
the two."

Sarah liked that, and that was where we left it. Ralph ruled
majestically that it was time to move on to the next subject. Denny
looked ostentatiously at his watch and said, "If we're going to quit
at ten-thirty, which is when we're supposed to, we aren't going to
have much time for another subject."

"We don't have to quit at ten-thirty," Ralph said. "That's just a
suggestion."

"Well, if that's the manufacturer's suggested retail price," Doctor Bob said, "I don't think we ought to mark it up."

We didn't have time to argue about it because a man none of us had seen before walked in the door that Bobby had left open. "I'm sorry to interrupt," he said, "but they told me to come here. My name is Mark Clements, and I've been assigned to Debbie Chapman's group."

I looked around the room. Sarah, Denny, Mac, John, Father Tim, Ralph, Doctor Bob, and me. That was eight. This man would make nine. Our little group wasn't so little anymore. We all introduced ourselves and Ralph invited the new man to tell us something about himself. It was like turning on a faucet. You had the feeling that he had been dammed up for a long time. He was from St. Louis and he was a copywriter for an advertising agency. "You do a lot of drinking when you cover politics," he said apologetically, "and I'm afraid I let it get away from me." He only talked for about ten minutes, but he told us a lot. He had been raised by a foster mother and about a year ago he'd gotten curious about his natural mother and had tracked her down. He found her in a mental institution and ever since he'd been terrified that he and his two sons might be carrying tainted genes. Doctor Bob decided that was in his area. "You shouldn't worry about that," he said. "How old are you, thirty-five, thirty-six?" Mark said he was thirty-eight. "Well," Bob guessed, "if nothing's happened to you by now, it probably isn't going to. The more you worry about it, the worse off you'll be." Nobody argued with that. But Mark said it had certainly contributed to his drinking problem. He talked about how he would wake up in the middle of the night and walk once again through the steel door with one small window that had to be unlocked for him by a uniformed guard when he went to visit his real mother. "I wonder if my wife would have married me if she'd known about her. Carol is pretty proud of her own family background and I always thought it worried her that I'd been a foster child. Something as specifically dangerous as this might really throw her." He didn't say anything for a while, and then, just as the bell rang to tell us it was ten-thirty, he said, "I'm not surprised she's been having an affair."

Maybe he wasn't surprised, but we were. We'd only met him half an hour ago and here he was already telling us that his wife was having an affair. Denny, our most experienced man about town, asked a not-so-dumb question. "With another man?" Mark nodded. "Yes," he said. "A lawyer, as a matter of fact." Denny thought that was convenient. "Maybe he'll give her a special rate," he said, "if she decides to file for a divorce."

"Wait a minute," Ralph said. "Mark is the one who should be asking for a divorce."

"I don't want a divorce," Mark said. "I miss her already. We haven't had relations in months."

Tim thought matters had gone far enough without Debbie. "We'd better save all this for Monday when Debbie is back," he said, and everybody agreed. Even Ralph seemed relieved to call a halt. He stood up and led the Serenity Prayer and our work for the weekend was over except for the wing meeting tonight when we would elect officeholders for such key positions as morning wake up call, dining room table cleanup, television turner-offer (only one of the nurses or assistants could turn it on), and recording secretary for the morning vitals.

Mac and Denny agreed with me that we'd meet outside in ten minutes and go for a long walk before lunch. I used the time to add three more cans of Coca-Cola to my windowsill stock and to fill up on ice cubes for what I expected would be a happy afternoon with Nora. The movie tonight was *Revenge of the Nerds*, which didn't sound like anything I would even understand much less enjoy, so I would write my letters home then.

We had lots to talk about as we made our way counterclockwise around the grounds. Instead of beginning in the park and ending on the street, we did it the other way around. It didn't make it seem longer, just different. We did have to worry a little more that somebody would yell at us as we walked down the illegal block on Twenty-sixth Avenue to South Eighth Street, past the big parking garage, because we were probably more conspicuous walking away from the Rehab than walking toward it. But we needed a little change, and besides, it was Saturday. You could tell it was Saturday because there were more people on the tennis courts and more kids in the swimming pool than we had seen during the week. "Weekends are big around here," Denny said. And that gave him an idea. "Want to go down by the river?" he suggested. "I did it last week with that guy who's always fishing. They finally caught him bringing a couple of fish back and they made him stop but they'll never notice us. We don't have any fishing poles." Now we had a destination; things were looking up. Denny led us across the park past the pool to a break in the trees that turned out to be a neatly worn path. We followed it around clumps of fragrant pine trees and huge boulders to a flight of stone steps that aimed precipitously down toward the river. As we started down we saw that between the steps and the river there was a concrete road with a few cars moving along it at a sedate pace. Right next to the road we came into a picnic grove with half a dozen or more family-size wooden trestle tables, only one of which was occupied. We stood there for a while and watched the practically nonexistent traffic on the river. We stayed there for half an hour and all we saw were two little outboards skimming the surface of the listless Mississippi. "On a Saturday morning in July," I told my friends from Texas and Vermont, "you could walk across Long Island Sound from one boat to another all the way from Sag Harbor to Mystic." We agreed that the river was so narrow here that a five-year-old boy would have no trouble throwing a silver dollar across it. Some Big Muddy. Mark Twain wouldn't even bother to drop a line here; there wasn't enough river to bother with.

We talked about Sarah. "I think the poor woman drinks because between her sister and her daughter she's scared to death," Denny said. Mac thought there was no question that she was the weak vessel caught between a rock and a hard place, and her son was no help because he was just glad the two warrior women picked on her and left him alone. "What we ought to do next week," he said, "is try to find out if the sister is as bad as the daughter says she is. Maybe it's the daughter who ought to be told to back off. Anyway," he finished thoughtfully, "it's a classic case that shows you can't solve the problem by drinking. I heard a man at my last grief meeting say alcoholics drink because they're alcoholics, not because they've got problems. It's just easier for us to blame it on the problems."

Denny was honest about it. "I do coke because I like it," he said. "I like the way it makes me feel. I never blamed anybody else for it."

"I did," I said. "I always liked to drink, but later, when I had problems, I figured I drank more to escape them. You couldn't really escape them. They were still there the next morning. Mostly you'd made them worse. But you sort of got away from them for a while. Maybe I should have tried coke, Denny. At least you had fun."

We all thought the new man, Mark, was just looking for a way to run away from his problems. He didn't look like an alcoholic, and judging from the little he had said, he didn't drink all that much. "All I know," Denny said, "is that if my wife was putting out for somebody else, I'd have a few drinks all right, but only to give me enough nerve to load up my shotgun."

"Who would you shoot?" I asked him, and Denny stopped short. "I don't know," he said honestly. "I'd have to think about that. Both of them, I guess."

"Then," Mac said, "you believe in the double standard, don't you? I mean, you don't think it's so bad for a man to mess around with other women but you don't think a woman has a right to do it."

"That ain't no double standard," Denny said in his best back-country style, "that's the only standard."

We argued about the double standard, and the feminist movement, and what Denny called free love, which he said was as far as he could see never very free anyway because it sure always cost the man a lot, you never heard of a woman paying the bills, did you, all the way back to the Rehab and the weekend quiet of the cafeteria. "Thanks be to God all the families have gone home," Father Tim said as we sat down with our hamburgers and french fries, and Doctor Bob said, "Amen." The hamburger was pretty gristly but at least the ketchup was good and it had the added touch of being sinful because it was all salt and bad for my blood pressure. I reminded myself again that a dry martini has zero cholesterol.

The afternoon was as lazy as I had expected it would be. Denny came by once to ask if I wanted to play some volleyball, and when I said no, I was happy just reading, he stayed around for a while and talked before he dragged himself outside to play. "They need me to do the spiking," he said, and then, more accurately, "there's a real pretty girl on our team who'd miss me if I didn't go."

It was so hot in the afternoon—it got up to 102 at two o'clock, hot enough to drive Denny and his friends in from the volleyball court—that we stayed inside, loafing in the lounge and our rooms and making regular trips to the refrigerator. Thank God the air-conditioning in the Rehab never weakened. In fact, it was so healthy that I kept the control dial in my room set at OFF; I'd have frozen if it were even on LOW. It would have made me want a drink.

Booze was what we ended up talking about watching the Twins play a rare afternoon game in Baltimore. "When does it bother you guys the most, not having a drink?" Denny asked more or less idly. "I mean, I sure wouldn't mind having a long one right now, but I'm not hurtin' for one. On the other hand, I sure could have used one with that hamburger at lunch. There ought to be a law against serving a hamburger without beer."

"It isn't any particular time that gets to me," Mac said. "I suppose any time when I'm feeling bad. It's hard to do a really good job of feeling sorry for yourself without a drink." He grinned at Denny. "I mean a real drink," he said. "I'm not talking about a Lone Star."

"I know what you mean," Denny said. "But when I feel like that I don't want any kind of a drink. What I need is a good hit, a couple of lines I laid out myself, real generous. Then I'm ready to go."

"Go where?" I asked him.

"Anywhere. Any place I want to go, I get there faster with coke."

"But what I don't understand," I said, the reporter in me asking questions now, "is how you can really *do* anything if you're flying on coke. I mean, like playing basketball or having sex. I can see football a little because I suppose anything that keeps you from feeling pain is a help. But what about screwing? Doesn't it make you want more but be able to do less? Like talking a good game before the kickoff and then leaving it in the locker room?"

"Well," Denny said, "in a way. But it works for you as much as it works against you. For one thing, you can hold an erection forever. Well, maybe it's more like half a hard-on, but it's there and you can have an awful lot of fun with it because you can hold it for hours. Of course, you need to because you can't actually do what you've got your eye on, somehow you can't quite connect, and even when you do get it in you can't do what you want to do right away no matter how easy she makes it for you. But what the coke does do is two things. It keeps you hard and it keeps her hungry. If she has to, she'll get down on her hands and knees and crawl for it." Denny was obviously transported to another time and place. "Anyway," he said thoughtfully, "there's ways to enjoy a woman and for her to enjoy you that don't require all that violent physical exercise."

"But isn't it the violent physical exercise that's the most fun?" I protested, proving the relative lack of sophistication of a man born in Manhattan compared to one born in Odessa, Texas.

"*Chacun à son gout,*" Mac said.

"What the hell does that mean?" Denny asked.

"To each their own," I translated into Texas. "The thing that bothers me the most," I said, "is the whole idea of infinity, that I can't *ever* have a drink again. Never mind specifically the martini before lunch and dinner or the wine with the meal, it's thinking about the whole rest of your life that gets me. How can you celebrate anything really important, or for that matter how can you mourn properly, without a drink? I've been trying but I haven't been able to see yet how that can work. What if they called me up and told me Liby had been killed in a car wreck? I'd walk right out of here and get a drink, I know I would. I'd probably get a bottle."

"To mourn," Mac asked, "or to celebrate?"

"I wasn't that mad about her little intervention," I said.

"I was only kidding," Mac said. "Anyway, it's a disease and we've got it and we've got to do what the doctors tell us."

"I think that disease theory is bullshit," Denny said. "I don't have any disease. What I've got is a big fat desire. I don't guess I'm an alcoholic but I think whatever your drug is it's just a lot of candy and they're taking it away from us."

"The problem," I said, "is what are we going to do when nobody's watching us?"

"I'll give up the coke," Denny said. "I know I've got to do that. But there's no way I'm going to give up drinking. No way. No matter what they say, that ain't goin' to hurt me."

"Not if it doesn't get rid of your inhibitions and let you try coke again," I said, knowing I was only repeating what Debbie had been telling him and he wasn't going to listen to me either.

"Not to change the subject," Mac said, "but I'm beginning to get the message at the grief meetings that I wasn't drinking myself to death because my wife died but because I'm an alcoholic. Once I get my head straight about that, once I accept it as a fact and really know it instead of just hearing people preaching it to me—hey, listen to me complaining about preaching—I'll be able to stay away from it because I know it's not just the way to save my life but the only way to make it worth living. Then I'll be able to take off the handcuffs and walk around without a cop watching me every minute." He waited for a reaction. When he didn't get one he said, tentatively, "I think we all will."

"Well," Denny said, "I can tell you right now I'm not going to spend the rest of my life without a drink. I can see the coke is bad, it fucked me up pretty good, and there's no sign that it's ever gonna be legal, so that's out. I'll promise that, and by God, I'll live up to it. No more coke, ever. But I'm only thirty-four years old and I've still got a lot of livin' to do and I sure as hell ain't gonna do it on Coca-Cola and Dr Pepper. No way. Emma ain't gonna like it but she's just gonna have to get used to it. I'm gonna have my martinis before dinner and wine with it and a beer whenever I'm thirsty. Only at night and on weekends, though. I'll be a Boy Scout while I'm workin', but the rest of the time I'm gonna have a little fun."

"I'm different," I said. "I'm sixty-eight years old and I've already had my share. I don't like it but I can see that if I started drinking again I'd be dead in nothing flat. So if I can manage to stay away from it, I will. Like I said, maybe when I need something, I ought to try coke. I could just trade habits with you, Denny."

"You can't do that," Denny said. "If it's a disease you have to catch it first, like the clap."

"Don't worry," I said. "The last thing in the world I want to do is fool around with that messy shit."

"After some of the pictures we've seen," Mac said, "I don't see how anybody can do it. Talk about cutting off your own nose."

"On the other hand," I said, "there are few prettier sights than a crystal clear martini, powder dry and bitter cold, in a big old-fashioned glass with a handful of ice cubes floating in it like little sailboats on Cape Cod Bay."

They thought I was crazy, but what the hell, so did I. What was the use of writing passionate love letters to a beautiful woman you will never see again?

Back in my room, I thought about what a strange couple of best friends Denny and I made. It was an unlikely pairing not only because he was, at thirty-four, exactly half my age, but he was even a young thirty-four. He had been successfully running his father's trucking business, the biggest in the county back home in Odessa, for the last five or six years, and he liked to work. You would expect him to be good at the sales side; he loved traveling and meeting people and schmoozing them into signing more contracts than they had planned to. But he even liked the administrative side, worrying about purchasing and insurance and billing and building maintenance and all the rest of the things his father used to take care of until he decided he had worked long enough and it was Denny's turn. The only thing was, when Dennison Cravath, Jr. stopped working and started playing, he didn't relax. He just switched interests. He played just as hard as he worked, and he was as much the prince off duty as he was on the job. He expected everybody to do what he told them to do and to approve of everything he did. That was how it always had been.

Both sides of Denny's hot-blooded character appealed to me. I admired the competent workman who wanted to make his own mark on his grandfather's business, and prove to his mother and father and wife that he was worth something, and I enjoyed the country club playboy who got a kick out of proving that everything was just as up-to-date in Odessa as it was in Kansas City. "We don't have the big buildings you got in New York," he said, "but when it comes to creature comforts, if you got the money, you can have it. Airplanes and trucks and trains go from east to west, and from west to east for that matter, and if you can eat it or drink it or smoke it or stick it into yourself with a needle, you can bet your ass we've got it in Odessa."

I knew his wife was beautiful even before I met her because he told me she was and I believed him. She had a plain name, Emma, but, I remembered, so did Lord Nelson's lady. Denny said she was a wonderful lover, as passionate as she was expert, but that the same genes that made her great in bed made her a lioness when she was mad. "Lately," he said, "I been making her hot the wrong way."

Emma might have put up with Denny's escapades longer and more patiently if she hadn't brought two young daughters to their marriage. They had known each other in college, at the University of Texas, but she had been pinned by a big man on campus who married her as soon as they got their diplomas. At the time, Denny didn't want to marry anybody. He wanted, first, to have a good time, and then to go back home when he was ready, learn how to take over the business, and then work hard and keep right on having a good time. He knew Emma would be a good wife for a successful businessman in Odessa but he wasn't ready for that much settling down yet. Once Emma made it clear that with her it was all built around an exchange of wedding rings, Denny was satisfied to admire her from a distance and play the rest of the field for fun. At Texas, the field was big and it was classy. There were women of all kinds, for all tastes, and they weren't all as fussy as Emma. "I was in hog heaven," he said, "and it wasn't all that much worse when I got back home. There are plenty of good-looking women in Odessa, and as long as you ain't married, they all think they've got a chance and they don't mind showing you what they've got that you're going to get. There are even a lot who are married and intend to stay married but who need a change once in a while."

He'd been home working for a few years, doing a lot of selling and modernizing the business while he was doing it, proving to his father that computers weren't just expensive toys for college classrooms or priceless tools for huge businesses like Texaco or American Airlines, when he ran into Emma at their tenth class reunion in Austin. "She was better looking than she ever was, I swear," he said, "and she told me right away that she was getting divorced. The first night of the weekend she was a lot of fun to drink with and dance with, and do some pot with, although she wouldn't do any coke with me when I tried to get her to, and the second night was sensational in bed. We only went out for a couple of hours at a time, then we'd head back to the hotel for some more loving. I told her when she had that divorce in her pocket she ought to come to Odessa for a visit. She said she would, and by God, she did."

Denny fell head over heels in love. He even loved Emma's two little girls, Margo and Sally, who were eight and six, and they liked him. Back in Denny's hometown, Emma was right up front about what she wanted. She wanted to get married again and have a man to help her make a home for her two kids and to help her forget the bad part of her marriage. Her husband hadn't been much fun to live with and she was ready to try it the other way. She didn't deny Denny the pleasures of their well-matched bodies but she told him flat out that it wasn't going to last forever if he didn't intend to make it legal. Denny dragged his feet as much as he could but he finally came to the big choice. He could take on the same kind of responsibility at home he had in the office, and have Emma for cocktails and dessert every night, or he could keep his free-lance status and do without the Emma he craved. He didn't kid himself that she was going to be easy to replace. He had had a hundred women and she was the best he had ever had. He needed her, even more than the cocaine he had begun to snort every weekend instead of just once or twice a month. He had a feeling she would help him keep everything under control, so he gave in and said yes. He thought he could be happy if he had her all the time.

Well, most of the time, anyway. "The rest of the time," he said,

"I thought I could go on little business trips and drink some and do some coke and loosen up a little if that was what I needed." He thought it would work.

Emma had set a deadline of Easter for them to be married. If the resurrection of our lord Jesus Christ came and went without Emma getting a new ring and a new name, Denny would have to forget those little happinesses she had brought him and find somebody else who knew how to do the things he liked. The trouble was, the more Denny experimented, the more he realized what a good thing he had in Emma. So he waited almost to the last minute, but he didn't take any chances. By the time Margo and Sally walked to the church in their Easter bonnets and their new dresses from Neiman-Marcus, their mama was Mrs. Dennison Cravath, Jr. and she had told them that they would never have to worry about anything ever again.

They didn't, for a long time. Denny and Emma picked out a beautiful old house only a few hundred yards from the country club, close enough for the girls to be able to walk to the swimming pool and the tennis courts if they had to. The three new Cravath women, cherished and spoiled as much by Denny's parents as by him, had only to want something and they had it. Once they had transferred from their Austin school to a private academy in Odessa, and had made some new friends, the girls were blissfully happy. Emma already had four or five good old girl friends from the university living in Odessa, and she made more new friends at the club and settled in to enjoy her position as the wife of one of the reigning princes of the city, which made her a princess of the realm. It was all she could ask for. Well, it would have been nice if Denny stayed home with her a little more, but, after all, he had to make a living for them. She would be the last one to complain about that. She did wish, though, that he wouldn't drink quite as much as he did. A big martini at home while they were getting dressed to go out, two or three at the bar before dinner, another one at the table, and a bottle of wine with dinner, and a couple of brandies after dinner. Emma never saw anybody have one brandy. It was no wonder she asked herself sometimes why she bothered to take the pill every day. Her lusty husband didn't have much lust these days.

She had no idea that he was having high old times with something more deadly than booze, and unfortunately not only a dangerous and expensive pleasure but an illegal one.

Neither did Denny's mother, Tracy (that was her maiden name). Mama took a relaxed, philosophical—even, you might say, prideful—view of his drinking. "He's my boy," she said, "and we all do it." But she was about to learn that the world had changed since she was a girl and that there were worse terrors loose in Texas than getting drunk or pregnant or both.

We were all about to learn a lot. The holocaust of Family Week was about to fall on Denny and John but the rest of us were going to be part of it, too, and then we would all have our turns. Tim gave me a couple of good night chocolates and a blessing when he walked me to my room after I'd given up on television and was heading back to Nora. I told him I appreciated the blessing because it came from him but that I liked the chocolates even better. They had been brought to him by one of his parishioners and they were Godivas. He told me he was going to say Mass in the chapel at nine o'clock in the morning and I was welcome if I wanted to come. I said no, thanks, I had given it up for good. Tim said I should remember what Debbie preaches and refrain from projecting. "You never know what's going to happen," he said. "Didn't you say that about that basketball coach?" "You're right," I said. "Until it has happened, it hasn't happened."

"Anyway," Tim said, "if I can't get you on Sunday morning, maybe I can get you some Saturday night. We can say Mass then, too, you know. We've done that to make it more convenient for people like you who don't want their Sunday morning golf games interfered with."

"You do it," I said, "for your constituents who use birth control and who go to communion once a month anyway by telling the priest they won't do it again until the next time, which is supposed to be a firm purpose of amendment. Now your marketing people have decided that Saturday night Mass will keep those fine upstanding citizens coming to church because they can go to confession Saturday afternoon, go to Mass at five o'clock and take communion, then go out for a big Saturday night dinner, go home and screw their brains out, and either sleep late Sunday morning or get up early and play golf before the priests get there."

"Edward, Edward . . ." Tim said, shaking his head. "I fear for your immortal soul."

"So do I, Tim," I said. "So do I."

10

Sunday, Bloody Sunday

There was no getting around it, whether you had religion or not, Sunday was the worst day of the week. There was nothing at all on the patient's schedule except an AA meeting at seven-fifteen P.M. which was widely advertised as REQUIRED. I thought it spoke poorly for the management's confidence in the inmates' interest in attending, but after I went I understood why they gave you no choice.

The day began with a huge ache where the Sunday *Times* ought to be. I didn't feel any better after I wasted a dollar and a quarter on the Sunday *Star-Tribune* but at least the group had a television program for the whole week.

We didn't even have the morning vitals on Sunday but things began to look up with a change for breakfast. A strange nurse at the third floor station told us that breakfast would be served only in the main hospital cafeteria which almost everybody seemed to feel was a superior place. Having been there a lot last summer I thought that was partly because it had carpet on the floor instead of a bare floor like the Rehab and partly because the doctors and nurses and staff people ate there so it had to be better. The truth was that the food was exactly the same in both places; it was all cooked in the Fairview Hospital kitchen and trucked over. The hospital did have an ice-cream machine, a Coca-Cola dispenser, and an ice machine, and for a non-coffee drinker like me, the Coke was a big deal. The manufactured orange juice I wouldn't drink was even worse than the stuff you got back home at Nedick's or Orange Julius.

Actually, the breakfast wasn't bad. Thick slices of ham and scrambled eggs with raisin toast on the side. When we went outside to walk it off, the heat had let up a little and we did the long walk with just enough cheating added to keep us out almost an hour. We even stood at the front door for a while with the smokers, appreciating the good-looking young women in their cut-off jeans, before we headed for our rooms. "I have to admit," I said as we climbed up the two flights of stairs instead of waiting for the one elevator that was running, "I would like to have a drink. Absolut on the rocks, with a little soda. As Red Smith used to say, no lime, thank you."

Alone in 349, I told myself that if all I wanted was a vodka and soda I must be in pretty good shape. A month ago I would have wanted half a bottle of Absolut. Now I was more interested in the whole setting, a long wooden bar like the one at the 21 Club, a friendly bartender who knew just how I liked my drink made, and a comfortable stool to sit on while I reviewed the state of the world. I wanted to talk to Peter Kriendler about how things weren't like they used to be but it wasn't true that they never were. When Jack Kriendler and Charlie Berns had started their speakeasy, New York was a more civilized place to live in than it is now. I missed Peter Kriendler. I missed New York. The St. Mary's Rehabilitation Center on South Seventh Street in Minneapolis, Minnesota was a long way from 21 West Fifty-second Street.

It was just as well that Denny came in to tell me that he was too restless to read. "You can't blame me," he said. "Lovin' tonight."

"How are you going to manage it?" I asked, curious but not at all disbelieving. I had respect for Denny's resourcefulness. "I know Emma and your mother are coming, but how are you going to get out?"

"I don't have to get out," Denny said. "Mama won't hang around

long. She hates hospitals. And anyway she'll want to get back to
the hotel so she can have a couple of drinks before dinner. She
knows Emma won't drink while she's out here, they tell them not
to, and besides, she says she was giving in to the devil when she
drank with me and she ain't gonna do it anymore. So that'll leave
Emma here alone with me. I don't imagine any nurse would walk
into a man's room when he's alone with his wife after they haven't
seen each other for two weeks, do you?"

"I don't suppose she would. If she knew his wife was in there.
But what if she just walked in to say hello and you were . . ."

"Screwing? Well, my back would be to her. I wouldn't be looking
at her. So Emma would be the one who would have to say hello."
Then Denny got serious. "Come on," he said, "she'd get the hell
out of there so fast she wouldn't even be sure what she'd seen.
Anyway, like I said, you could hang out in the hall for a little bit
after my mother leaves, maybe talk to Mac or Tim or somebody,
and keep an eye on the door. I'll only need about five minutes," he
said. "I'll settle for one time." Denny was so disarming you couldn't
say no to him.

When Emma showed up with her lively mother-in-law around
four o'clock, she was every centimeter the Texas belle Denny had
promised. Tall and fashionably slim, she was wearing black de-
signer slacks and a green silk blouse disarmingly opened down to
the third button. She looked as if she were on her way to lunch at
the golf club. Her face was taut alabaster with picture perfect features dramatized by impossibly high cheekbones, a Michelle Pfeif-
fer mouth and dark blue eyes that searched confidently for your
reaction to the way she looked. I don't know how she affected
women but she knew as well as we did how she affected men and
it was plain that she enjoyed it. Her eyes were alive with interest
even when she was amused; I could imagine what they looked like
when she was aroused.

Denny's mother was perfectly cast for her part, attractively
younger looking than you might have guessed and casually dressed
in Neiman-Marcus's best. She stayed just long enough to show
that she cared and left just soon enough to "let the young people

have a chance to catch up." I thought Mama had no doubt what they were going to catch up on and I approved of her attitude. The Rehab could use a little loving.

I didn't have to stand guard long, which was a good thing because neither Mac nor Tim was around. I assumed the clergy kept Sunday differently from the rest of us. When the door to Denny's room opened, you couldn't see a hair mussed on Emma, but I thought her eyes studied me like a coconspirator as they headed out for a walk. "I know it's hot," Emma said in her marvelous southwestern drawl with a question mark at the end of the sentence, "but you can call a cab for me, honey, and we can get a little fresh air while we're waiting for it?"

Just before I went into my room I saw Sarah talking in the lounge with two young people, one male and one female, whom I guessed were her children. The girl seemed to be doing most of the talking and it looked very much as if our group guess was right on target. We hadn't seen sister Christine yet but there didn't seem to be much doubt that the daughter could hold her own when it came to holding the floor. Poor Sarah.

At dinner, our table was more subdued than usual. Neither Sarah nor Denny had half the animation they'd shown at lunch and I wondered if they both had had family arguments. I decided it would be more tactful to talk to John and at least he was forthright. He said he was pretty nervous about the week coming up but he was glad that he didn't have to face his father tomorrow. "They'll be busy all day with the family counselors," he said with relief. I told him I was rooting for him. I could afford to; I had a week of grace before Liby and Kevin got here. Liby had told me the last time we talked that Eileen wouldn't be able to come. She had her one-year-old baby to worry about. Kevin probably wished he had a good reason to skip it, too. Who didn't?

After we had gone through the dishwashing line, Denny said he wanted to talk, so we braved the heat and walked over to the statue of St. Mary and stood looking out at the river just before it turned right to sweep past the Metrodome and downtown Minneapolis. We were surprised to see a freshly painted tugboat steaming placidly down the river from the city. It wasn't tugging anything but it was a novelty to see any substantial boat out there. "She's gonna be tough," Denny said, and I knew he wasn't talking about the tugboat. "She's comin' down real hard on the idea of me ever takin' a drink again. She makes a martini sound like pure fire and brimstone. She says God will take his revenge on me if I do."

"I'm sorry," I said. "You know that's bullshit but it's tough to have to live with."

"Yeah," he said. "Worse than that, she says my mother is still in a state of shock over my getting arrested and thinks it was some kind of a fluke thing I got into with some bad people. She hasn't any idea I've been doin' drugs since I was a kid. Emma says it's going to shock her right out of her pants and it's going to hurt her a lot." He was talking slowly. "The worst of it is," he said, "that even Emma doesn't know the half of it. I mean the stuff I've told Debbie and the group is going to blow her mind, too. But I got to tell it. I can't say it was only for the group to hear. They don't let you get away with that here and sure as hell Debbie ain't gonna let me get away with it. That's what Family Week is all about, a clean breast and all that shit. Everything out in the open. A fresh start." He made a rude noise. "Yeah, and with us hung out on the clothesline for the crows to pick on."

"Your mother and Emma aren't crows," I said.

"No," he said, "but I feel like bait."

We decided it was too hot to stay out, and besides, we'd better take a rest before suffering through the required AA meeting.

"I wish I could get a sick pass," I said.

"It's got to be better than Family Week," he said.

It wasn't much better. It was a little less of an assault on the mind than the tent revival meeting I'd wandered into once when we were on maneuvers in West Virginia, but only a little. God took over the saving of the speaker's soul in the first minute of the story of his life and His guidance was offered to us secondhand for forty-four more minutes of excruciatingly banal testimony that jarred Denny's Texas sensibilities as much as my Manhattan ones.

The speaker was a young man in his thirties who was accom-

panied by a respectfully adoring wife who looked as satisfied as if
she had just found the gold egg in her Easter basket. He said that
he had let his chances to succeed in a big company slip away
because he had put drinking and having a good time first. "He
probably worked up to three beers a day," Denny whispered. When
he began missing appointments and forgetting what he had said
to people when he did remember to meet them, he knew he was
in deep trouble. So he began to drink even more. "Now," Denny
said, "he started having a beer at lunch." He began neglecting his
wife. "Now," Denny said, "that's serious. She ain't bad looking."
So he tried to stop, he knew the people who were telling him he
should stop were right, but he couldn't. He was powerless. But at
least he knew he was powerless before the devil of alcohol—"Oh,
God," Denny said, "Emma should be here"—and he knew he didn't
have much time left before he lost his job and his wife and everything he held dear. So when a good friend at work told him he had
had the same kind of toboggan ride downhill and had been saved
by AA, he decided to give it a chance. He might not have done it
except that God, in His mysterious way, made it happen. He got
fired. "I had to go home and tell my sweet wife that I had lost my
job," he said, "and I had to get drunk before I could tell her. So I
was ready to listen when my friend said he wanted to take me to
an AA meeting, and I went. I was uncomfortable, just the way
many of you are tonight"—"he doesn't know the half of it," Denny
said—"but I stuck it out and I heard a message that changed my
life. 'Turn it over,' is what the speaker said that night. 'Admit you
can't do it yourself and put your life in the hands of the Higher
Power. Why not? Have you done such a good job on your own?'
Well, I decided to try it, and I did. I turned everything over to my
Higher Power, whom I call God, and I stopped drinking because
they told me that was the key to everything, and I made up my
mind I would follow His way. I struck out on my own as a real-
estate salesman and I worked hard. I put all the energy I used to
dissipate in drinking and high times into my work, and I began
gradually to succeed. I kept letting go and letting God, and it
worked. I took a few chances and they turned out well for me. Now

I have my own agency with two people working for me, and I feel good, I'm healthy, and I've got my pride back."

"And he's gettin' laid regular again," Denny said.

"And I've got my wife back," the young man finished triumphantly. "You can do it, too, if you'll just surrender your pride, stop worshipping the devil through alcohol, and turn yourself over to the program and to God."

"I wonder if that was what Jim and Tammy did," I said irreverently. Denny said, "They didn't have time. They were too busy counting money."

As we walked out of the cafeteria we wondered how long we would last if we stopped depending on our own willpower and turned everything over to God. How long would it take for Him to let us find a taxi for the ride downtown to the best bar in town? Hell, we could walk to the Viking Grill on Riverside in less than five minutes. We decided we weren't ready to be Born Again. We were still having trouble straightening out our first lives.

At least my eight o'clock blood pressure reading was better. Marjorie Noonsong said it was one fifty-four over ninety. Not bad.

In the hall, outside our rooms, Denny said he was glad he was going to have a chance to practice telling his story all in one piece to the group tomorrow before he had to face his mother and Emma on Tuesday. "You guys will help me get it together," he said. "At least I know you're on my side. Debbie, too. She wants me to come clean, but she doesn't want to put my skin on a lampshade and she doesn't want to see our marriage busted up. I'm lucky I've got you guys."

"Okay," I said, trying to think of some way to cheer him up. "But don't forget the Tommy Lasorda rule."

"The Dodger manager? What's his rule?"

"Never tell your troubles to your friends. Eighty percent of them don't care, and the other twenty percent are glad." We shook hands and said good night.

A little later, Mac stopped by to say good night and to tell me his grief meeting had been a little better. "Now," he said, "it's time for some private grieving."

After Mac left, the hall was quieter than I could remember it being for a long time. It made me think of the night before the battle of Agincourt in *Henry V*. I began to try to recite the St. Crispin's Day speech, and I fell asleep thinking we could use a little touch of Harry in the night around here.

11

Confess Yourself to Heaven

The cubicle that I liked best was occupied when I walked into the shower room at five minutes to six Monday morning. I guessed the early bird was either Mac or Father Tim and I told myself I wasn't getting up early enough. I made do with the lesser shower, which helpfully provided me a leftover piece of soap so I didn't have to unwrap the one I'd brought with me—little things matter in the Rehab—and when I got out Father Tim was standing there drying off his massive body with one of the hospital's skimpy towels. "I should have asked my secretary to bring me some towels along with my clothes," he grumbled. "I've got some real good ones from hotels in Florida. Winter vacations, you know."

Mac, just walking in, heard that. "I'm surprised at you, Father. Stealing towels. I hope you confessed that."

"Indeed I did not," Tim said. "I considered that I had paid for them several times over. And not, as Edward here did, off the expense account. I paid for them with my own hard-earned money. Good morning, Reverend Mac."

It was the first time I had heard anybody in the group give Mac a title. I had wondered why everybody called Tim by the title Father and nobody called Mac anything except Mac. I had decided it was another manifestation of the mystique of the One True Church.

I was also struck by the fact that I was the only sinner who was always up betimes with the clergy. Maybe I had missed my calling.

My morning blood pressure was a disappointing one fifty-four over one hundred; I had thought the bottom number would surely drop down from last night's ninety and instead here it was up again. That put me in enough of a "to hell with it" mood to support my leaning toward bacon and buttered toast for breakfast. I more or less salved my conscience with a dish of Del Monte fruit salad, which I've loved since I was a kid.

Mary Verkennes, one of the sweetest and most caring of the nurses, stopped me on my way out of the cafeteria; she was on watch duty at the table by the entrance, making sure everybody wore his I.D. badge. The inmates were always forgetting their badges, and Clark, the otherwise officious tyrant of the serving counter, hated to be the enforcer. He didn't want to be the one to send the offender back upstairs for his badge. The truth was that Mary would probably fry an egg for you herself rather than let you go hungry. But even St. Mary's has to behave like the infantry once in a while. Mary told me she had heard somebody say that I had asked Bobby to bring me a *Times* every morning from the hospital lobby and she just wanted to say that when Bobby went in for his operation she would be glad to take over the job. "I have to go over there every morning anyway," she said, "and I'll be glad to do it." She did, too, for the last two weeks I was there, and that's not the kind of service they promise in the Rehab brochure.

Ironically, the morning lecture was by David Hiers, the Rehab's director of operations, number two man to the boss, Jay Hauge. David wanted the troops to do a better job of keeping the place clean and to pay attention to the other rules, too, like no using alcohol and drugs and no sexual activity with fellow patients. "He didn't say anything about the nurses," Denny said as we went back to our rooms. "I've still got my eye on those nurses."

"You don't have to worry about Hiers," I told him. "You'd better worry about Emma."

There was another new face in room 355 when we reported there at nine-thirty. I thought that was a good thing; it might take some of the heat off Denny and John who looked as nervous as a couple of investment bankers accused of insider trading waiting for the jury to speak its verdict. The new man said his name was Paul, he was from Bloomington, right next door to Minneapolis, and he was a member of the International Union of Operating Engineers and made good money working on big construction projects like apartment buildings, office buildings and malls. You wouldn't call him self-assured; cocky would be more like it. "I think," Doctor Bob said to me, "he thinks he's a better drunk than we are." Debbie seemed to think he was holding back something. She knew that he had been sent here by a judge, and she asked him how his case stood. Paul said, "It's pretty much all over. The judge said he's going to put me on probation." But Debbie persisted. "What about your wife?" she asked. "I understand she has a charge against you. Assault, right?" Paul seemed a little uncomfortable about that. He was a big man, over six feet and husky, and clearly he didn't want the group to think he was the kind of man who would beat up a woman. "That was a misunderstanding," he said. "We had a big argument and I pushed her, and when she got hysterical I held her against the wall to keep her quiet. Then, when I let her go, she called the cops. But she explained later that she had over-reacted. The trouble was, the cops had me on disorderly conduct, and that's still on the sheet. The judge said coming here would count in my favor, so I'm pretty sure he'll dismiss the charge." He sounded convincing.

Debbie was persistent. "Your wife isn't pressing charges, then?"

Paul evaded the question. "Well," he said, "of course she was the one who started the whole thing by calling the cops." He finally looked straight at Debbie. "It won't take much," he said, "to straighten it out."

Debbie asked John to read the Thought for Today and Denny kept his eyes on me while John read the part about how "we in Alcoholics Anonymous have renewed our faith in a Higher Power" and went on to "We believe that faith is always close at hand, waiting for those who will listen to the heartbeat of the spirit." It sounded to me like a Chevrolet commercial. I wished there was some way St. Mary's could get me sober without trying to cleanse me in the blood of the lamb or whatever it is they do. I felt a little better about the end of the thought, which John read in a firm but expressionless voice: "We believe there is a force for good in the universe and that if we link up with this force, we are carried onward to a new life." It made me think of the movie *Star Wars* and the usher in the lobby who told everybody as they walked out, "May the Force be with you."

The first order of business was for John to go over the entire history he was going to tell his parents. Debbie wanted particularly to have him promise he would tell his father that the reason why he hadn't asked him for help when he'd been arrested was because he would rather spend six months in jail than face him.

"What did you think he would do to you?" Debbie asked.

"It was just his anger," John said. "He could get very mad. I'd always been afraid of him."

"But you said he never hit you," Debbie reminded him. "What did he ever do that made you so afraid of him?"

John was embarrassed. It was as if he was afraid of looking childish. "It's kind of hard to say," he said. "I guess it was the way he looked, so fierce, and you always had the feeling he would do whatever he thought he had to do to get you to do what he wanted. He was always very controlled but that just made you nervous about what he'd be like if he ever lost control. What it came down to was that my brother and I never wanted to do anything to make him mad. If we were in some kind of little trouble, like at school or something, we'd try to work through my mom. She could always deal with him better than we could."

"Okay, John," Debbie said, "now it's your turn."

Denny's run-through took longer because Ralph had made up his mind that he was going to be a pain in the ass about making sure that Denny didn't leave any sin unconfessed, mortal or venial. When we talked about it later, on our walk, Mac and I tried to calm Denny down. He was ready to go right up to Ralph on the sidewalk outside the Rehab and punch him in the mouth. "Cigarette and all," he said grimly. "That sonofabitch ain't gonna rest until he gets

Emma to take off her wedding ring and throw it at me. What did
I ever do to him?"

"You didn't do anything to him," Mac said. "His wife did."

Doctor Bob had a late bulletin for us when we got on the chow
line which was painfully long on account of all the Family Week
visitors. It reached all the way through the lobby corridor and down
the hall on the other side almost to the beauty shop where the little
old ladies from the fifth floor hospice went to have their white hair
rinsed blue. "Hey," Bob said, "I think something is happening with
the new man, Paul. I think Debbie threw him out of the group."

"Can she do that?" Denny was interested. Maybe he was worried
that she might throw him out if Ralph convinced her that Denny
was holding out on her and the group. Not to mention Emma and
his mother.

"Sure, she can," Bob said. "The counselor has the power to expel
anybody she thinks is hurting the group. And don't think Debbie
wouldn't do it. In this case I think she's got some cause. Paul came
into my room right after group and asked if he could talk to me for
a minute. He said he knew I was a doctor and he needed to know
if it made any sense for him to be charged with criminal activity
for trying to have relations with his wife when she was pregnant.
I said I was a doctor, not a lawyer, but I could tell him that lots of
people kept on having sex right up until a few weeks before the
baby was born. I said there was no reason not to if she isn't having
any trouble carrying the baby and if they're careful. I told him the
best position is with the wife on her side and one leg over the man
so he can approach her without disturbing her pelvis." Bob dropped
his voice even lower. "He said that was his trouble. She hadn't
wanted to do it at all and he sort of forced her to let him. Makes
you wonder if Debbie isn't right to keep asking him if his wife
hasn't got a serious charge against him."

That was interesting but not as fascinating as the conversation
I overheard between a couple of patients' wives on the line in front
of me. "I can't wait for a chance to stick it to him good," one of
them said. "I swear, I'll shove it all the way in and twist it."

"I know how you feel," the other one said. "I'm really torn about it. Half of me wants to defend him and the other half wants to kick the shit out of him."

They strengthened us for the afternoon with hot roast beef sandwiches with gravy but I thought Denny and John needed it just to get through lunch. The inmates aren't supposed to have any private contact with their family members until group on Tuesday, so all the guys could do was wave at their people sitting at separate tables on the other side of the room. They were still eating when we walked past them on our way to the dishwashing line. Denny waved wistfully at Emma. John didn't even wave at his parents; he just nodded his head. It all seemed silly, but, as Sarah said, you had to figure they knew what they were doing. Every now and then I thought bitterly about the man in administration who wouldn't let me move away from my pot-smoking, twenty-one-year-old roommate when I was an outpatient last summer, but I kept my mouth shut. I hadn't spent four years in the infantry for nothing.

"You'll notice Paul isn't with us," Debbie told us at the beginning of the afternoon meeting. "He's gone back to his probation officer for reassignment."

Before he actually left the building, Paul admitted to Doctor Bob that he had not only punched his wife but, despite her condition, even kicked her in the body, and she was charging him with both assault and rape. It wasn't, a few of us observed, just your run-of-the-mill family fight. "They couldn't keep him here," Bob said, "after he had lied to the group like that." Nobody disagreed. We all felt a little sick. He had seemed like such a nice guy. Could booze make that much of a difference?

Debbie asked me to meet her in her office after group. She wanted to talk about my Family Week. Mostly, it turned out, she wanted to be sure I wasn't going to hold anything back. "Liby is going to say what she feels," she said, "and that's what you've got to do." Kevin had said the same thing in a letter. I wasn't so sure. The last thing I was interested in was causing more trouble. It didn't make a whole lot of sense to me to start running a home movie of our past. Experience had taught me that all that would come of that would be a Molotov cocktail of recriminations and regrets. I had learned that the worst thing I could do was to use self-pity as an excuse to drink.

Debbie asked me when my drinking had gone out of control, what I thought had caused it, and what I thought might be done about it, but I didn't have any answers for her. I didn't even have any answers for me except that I knew I was through feeling sorry for myself.

Probably to put me in a mood to trade hopes and fears with her, Debbie told me a lot about herself. Most of it came out all at once, and because I was so interested in finding out all I could about this woman who had become so important to me, I didn't interrupt her. There was going to be plenty of time to talk about me.

Deborah Schroeder had had an unhappy childhood. She was born in Wausau, Wisconsin, and grew up in the small Wisconsin town of Stevens Point. Her mother died when Debbie was twelve and her father was a frequent drinker who got even worse after he married again, to a woman who had been divorced seven times. "He told me about her," she said, "in a phone call from Florida where they had gone on a honeymoon. All I could hear was the tinkle of ice cubes in the background." When her father came back with his new wife, who everybody called Sam, and her seven-year-old adopted son, who was actually her sister's son, Debbie's life was turned upside down. Her stepmother wanted to live in California, so they moved to La Jolla where life was one long tall drink after another. "I'd been there with them for three months," Debbie said, "with Dad drinking steadily through the days and nights, and my stepmother constantly taking me to Schwab's Drugstore hoping I would be 'discovered' like Lana Turner, when my brother Rob called and offered me a room in his house in Sheboygan. I jumped at it. My stepmother kept screaming that my leaving would kill my father, but I didn't believe a word of it and I was on the first plane I could get out of San Diego. All I knew was that they were killing me."

Debbie's new life was like the little girl with the curl; when it was good it was very good and when it was bad it was horrid. Rob was a teacher in the high school where Debbie became a student, and he was slowly but steadily following in his father's footsteps as a drinker. His moods changed with bewildering speed. "He would be the best brother a girl could ask for all day long," she said, "and I was always proud to tell people he was my brother. But after he'd had a few beers at night, he would go to work on me. He accused me of being a loudmouth and a 'prick-tease' at school and he told me I was an embarrassment to him. He said I was stupid and the way I was going I'd end up having to get married, probably to a ditchdigger, and I would never amount to anything. Then, in the morning, after he had slept it off, he would be all sweetness again and I'd wonder if last night's tirade had really happened or if I'd just had a nightmare. But as my high school years went on, those nights got worse, not only for me but for his wife, and I began to understand that he was just as much of an alcoholic as my father was."

Searching for something to build her own life on, Debbie took up theatrics. She was good at it and she became involved in all of the school's productions. But her brother didn't like it. He thought it was more of her showing off. "One night," she remembered, "our rehearsal lasted until after ten, and my brother, who had promised to pick me up, walked in drunk. He bawled out the director for keeping us kids up so late—I was a senior then, eighteen years old, and a lot more than a kid—and he called me names all the way home. Bimbo was his favorite, and prick-tease was always part of it. He went on and on about how I was headed for trouble and would never amount to anything. No wonder I was interested when the next day's paper had a big story about a Miss Sheboygan Scholarship Pageant being organized. I was interested not only in being Miss Sheboygan, which I thought would show my brother something, but I wanted that scholarship. I needed a way out of all this. Maybe this was my chance not only to escape but also to prove I wasn't the born loser Rob kept telling me I was. I entered the contest.

"An actress from the community theater agreed to coach me," Debbie said. "We chose for my performance piece a three-minute segment from *Romeo and Juliet* where Juliet takes the poison. We worked on it for two months straight, and I've always thought it was as much because of my performance as because of my legs or anything else that I won."

Debbie was wryly funny about the next step on her show business ladder. "I didn't do as well in the state pageant," she said. "For one thing I didn't have the same compulsion to show my brother how wrong he was, and for another, I was scared to death. I did win the 'Miss Congeniality' prize. You know, the consolation prize they give to the girl who couldn't possibly win anything else."

But Debbie was determined. She used her scholarship to put herself through Lakeland College where she majored in public speaking and theater with education courses so she could be a teacher. Then she fell in love, got married, and had a baby son, Christopher. She and her husband both drank but he was no alcoholic. "Actually," Debbie said, "he couldn't drink worth a damn." They were never happy in the marriage and they agreed to a divorce in 1977. Debbie, who had worked as a cocktail waitress and a secretary while she was in college, got a job as a substitute teacher in the Sheboygan schools and then became a customer service coordinator ("that means secretary," she says) for the Georgia Pacific Corporation. She was drinking steadily now, mostly scotch, and had begun to rely on Valium to calm her nerves. When money was tight she switched to beer. "I had a twelve-pack-a-day habit, in addition to the twenty mgs of Valium," she said, shaking her head. "My life was getting to be a mess. Then I lost my job because a friend didn't cover for me when I was sick, and I went to a therapist who asked me if I had a drinking problem. I said, no, I didn't, but I certainly had a job problem."

She also had a drinking and a drug problem but she was denying it even to herself. She was making ten thousand dollars a year and spending most of it on booze and drugs. "I functioned all day on Valium and Extra-Strength Tylenol," she said, "drank lunch if I went to lunch at all, had a few more drinks before I fixed dinner for the baby and me, then went out later, usually to a dingy bar called The Harbour Lights where I wouldn't have to look nice or impress anybody, just sit in front of the television and drink scotch until I couldn't see straight. I drank even more on the weekends and I used the Valium instead of liquor in the morning so I could kid myself that I wasn't an alcoholic.

"When I got sick the doctor gave me a gross cough syrup that I hated and some big antibiotic pills that I called horse pills. I decided it would be dangerous to mix the medicine and the antibiotics with alcohol and Valium so I tried giving up the good stuff for a while and I promptly went into withdrawal and got really sick. My brother Rob had been to Hazelden for six weeks, and his psychiatrist, who had been seeing me, too, had taken him off Valium, so I got off it, too, partly because I had lost my source of supply. I was a mess. Then my sister, Anne Hansen, who was a chemical dependency counselor, encouraged me to go to Parkview, outside Minneapolis, a treatment center that's gone now. She took care of Christopher for me while I was in there for five and a half weeks, and the people at Parkview changed my life. In more ways than one, because one of them thought I might make a good counselor some day and encouraged me to try for their training program. I was accepted by the director, Tom Chapman, who became my father-in-law after I married his son, Dustin, who was also a counselor there. I was almost through my second year of training, the internship part, when Al Piekarski, one of the counselors, recommended me to his wife, Maureen Dudley, who was the supervisor of counselors at St. Mary's. Maureen hired me, and my life began all over again.

"It still had one more painful twist to take, though. My father-in-law became the executive director of a new treatment center, Maryville, on the old Hubert Humphrey estate on Lake Waverly, Minnesota. Both Dustin and I took jobs on the staff and were given the estate's beautiful guest house, right on the lake, a dream house of a log cabin with three bedrooms and a huge fireplace in the living room, to live in. It was all too good to be true. 'I just hope you know what you're doing, Deb,' my boss Maureen told me. 'This could be a huge mistake.' Thank God she also told me she hated to lose me, and I remembered that. Well, it was all too good to be true, all right, and our dream world fell apart, house and all. Maryville came under new management, and I was unhappy and I left. As I always tell everybody, I crawled back to St. Mary's.

"What happened, and I was lucky, was that Maureen was able to give me an 'on call' job with no guarantee of hours and no benefits, but with the probability of steady work. I told her I would sweep the floors and clean the toilets for her if I had to, and two years later I was back on the staff full-time, my life healed at last. Maureen gave me the full-time job even though I was seven months pregnant with my second baby, my first with Dustin, a wonderful little boy we named Patrick. I love St. Mary's, and I have Maureen to thank for seeing me through the full circle from unpaid intern at Parkview to counselor at St. Mary's to senior counselor at Maryville to unemployed and finally senior counselor at St. Mary's."

Debbie's first regular assignment at St. Mary's was with juniors, and then, in an astonishing switch, Maureen perceptively put her in charge of the seniors, including outpatient me, in the summer of 1987.

I'd felt close to Debbie before this heart to heart but I would have had to be blind not to see that she had told me her own story to show me that I hadn't invented any of these problems and certainly wasn't entitled to take out a patent on drinking as a cure for self-pity. I remembered what Mac had said about learning slowly that he didn't drink because his wife had died, he drank because he liked to drink.

Debbie didn't fight with me about AA or about God. She wanted me to stop drinking and to feel good about life sober. She had chosen to give me this much of herself because she wanted to be sure I would be wide open to the collisions that were about to happen among the Cravaths and the Terranovas. She didn't want me to miss anything their stories, wildly dissimilar but eerily alike, would tell me about the way families can be ripped apart by the terrible drug dependency of one member. She was hoping I would see that just as surely as families can split their wholeness they can solder their circles back together again. She thought if I could understand what they had done to each other I might see the universality of why they had done it and learn what it would take to set them free and make them families again.

I skipped dinner that night. I made myself a ham and cheese sandwich out of the day room refrigerator and ate it with a Coke in my room. I wanted to be alone for a while. It was the first time I'd been alone without the comforting license to drink that I'd had in my pocket as long as I could remember. I was uneasy. It had been a long time since I had considered any of it, even the littlest bit, might be my fault. Up to now, the worst time had been the three or four hours in the Yonkers City Jail, when I thought I had gone down as far as I could go. But even then I still had my justification. It wasn't my fault; I just hadn't been strong enough to deal with all the trouble I'd known.

I sat there for a long time before Denny and Mac dragged me out for a walk. I was thinking about a song, Edith Piaf singing "*Je ne regrette rien.*" Maybe the Little Sparrow didn't regret anything, but I regretted everything.

12

Every Unhappy Family
Is Unhappy in its Own Way

It was like a court martial in room 355 when Family Week finally got under way in earnest the next afternoon, except that it was hard to tell who was the defendant, who was a witness, and who was on the jury. Debbie looked like the judge but we already knew that all she was going to do was let the opposing sides fight it out. She wasn't even going to stop the fight just because somebody got hurt. Pain always hung over the Rehab like tear gas but this was where the wounds were swabbed out with raw alcohol and it wasn't the kind you could drink.

Debbie didn't waste time on small talk. She had already given us some of her ideas on Family Week during morning group, while the visitors were having their own therapy meetings with the family-counselor agitators, as Bobby Moore called them. Deb heard him say that once and she shot him down with one burst from her deck guns. "That's enough of that smartass talk, Bobby," she told him. "I don't need that kind of help from you." She had said that she thought this week was going well. "I always figure that if there's good preparation on Monday, you get the big breakthroughs on Tuesday, which is what I'm hoping for this afternoon, and then you can mop up any last-ditch resistance on Wednesday. If there's anybody who hasn't made real progress by Thursday, there's no sense in keeping that patient for a fourth week. You might as well send him home." Then she said, with a tablespoonful of the old Deborah optimism, "we aren't going to have that kind of a problem."

After Sarah read the Thought for the Day, which began with the announcement that "Today is ours," causing Denny to aim an ostentatious wink at Mac and me, Debbie called the meeting to order. She didn't give the edgy family members time to sit around and get nervous. "We'll start with Denny and his family," she said, and she had Emma and Tracy Cravath introduce themselves. Mama was up for the occasion, perky, unashamedly curious. Emma was tense, her fine features held regally calm by sheer force of will. She looked like Marie Antoinette in the *Conciergerie*, waiting for the peasants to come for her with the tumbril.

Debbie said, "We usually have the family members speak first, without interruption by the patient. The idea is to give them a chance to get everything off their minds and to make it possible to have a full discussion after the patient says what he wants to say. But Denny's case is different because you don't know his drug history. The group does, but you don't. So I want to begin by having Denny tell you what he has been doing with drugs ever since he began using them."

It was an extraordinary scene. Denny's wife and mother had lived through the shock of his arrest, the discovery that he had been using cocaine for a long time, and the realization that their unhappiness with the amount of drinking he had been doing was trivial, just incidental to the real story.

Denny was ready. He had been over it so many times that he was able to go through it step by step, from sniffing glue in grammar school to smoking pot in the sixth grade, then graduating to injections of speed and occasional LSD and heroin trips in high school, mixing heroin and cocaine in speedballs, and finally settling down with cocaine in college and ever since.

His mother was the first to speak. "I never had any idea," she said. "So that's why you always needed money so bad. And I thought you were just spending it on girls and having a good time."

"I'm sorry, Ma," Denny said, and he looked sorry. Emma just

stared at him. Denny went on with his recital. He told about apartments rented in the college town for parties that always included liquor and women but that were mostly for the guys to get knocked out on coke. He told about using it in bathrooms at restaurants, at the country club, and even in the toilets on airplanes if the flight was long enough to make him need it.

"I can't believe," Emma said, "that you stuffed that powder up your nose the way we saw it in those disgusting movies yesterday. Is that what you did?"

Denny hung his head a little but he told the truth. "Yes, I did."

"Would you do it again?" Ralph demanded, taking over as the judge. "Would you do it now if you could?"

I could see Denny's knuckles squeeze tight, and I knew what he would like to do with them. "I sure would," he said, "but I hope when I leave here I won't want to anymore." He looked at Emma and his mother. "Right now, this is the hardest thing I've ever done. I'm really sorry, Ma, and Emma, for hurtin' you like this."

Ralph wasn't going to let go. It was hard to see why it was so important to him to make Denny suffer but he was like one of those English pit bulls. "What about the things you did when you were using cocaine?" he persisted.

Emma spoke up for herself. "I don't think I need to know every stupid thing he did."

Denny knew he wasn't going to get away scot free. "What Ralph is talking about," he said, "is that I told the group there were some pretty wild parties with both sexes, and I'm not proud of everything I did at them." He spoke directly to Emma. "But I never went all the way with any of those women, never. I was there for the coke and the other stuff just happened."

"What about the time you came home at six o'clock in the morning without your underwear?" Emma asked in a flat voice. Then, as if she had just wanted him to know she wasn't stupid, she changed the subject. "Why didn't you ever think about me when you were doing that stuff? What about that night when you had the golf team from the university sleep over at our house after you took them out to the club for dinner, and they were running all over the place stoned out of their minds? I've got two daughters livin' in that house. And me, what about me? I had to throw one of them out of my bedroom. I could have been raped."

Emma said it like "ryped" but there was nothing funny about it. She was crying, rubbing her eyes with Kleenex, unable to stop the deep sobs. Her mother-in-law reached out to hold her hand.

Debbie didn't throw Denny a life preserver; she let him sit there and take it. His mother took over. "You're going to have to figure out a way to pay back your father the money you borrowed from him," she said. "It wouldn't be fair to the others if you didn't."

"I know, Ma," Denny said. "I promise you I'll work my ass off when I get home. I'll do whatever you and Daddy think is the right thing." He waited, careful not to mix up the two things. "And I'll make it up to you, Emma," he said, "I swear I will."

"But if you don't stop drinking, and if you start using drugs again," Emma said, "I'm through. I'm tellin' you now I'm never goin' to go through this again. I just can't. You're goin' to have to choose. It's either them or me."

Tracy Cravath made her declaration, too. "Son," she said, "I want you to know that if you can't stay straight and Emma throws you out, I won't take you in."

"I understand, Ma," Denny said. He looked as though he really did.

Emma wanted to get some things off her own chest. "I blame myself some," she said. "I've been thinkin' about it a lot. I would get so mad at him for drinkin' so much that I just kind of tuned everything else out. If I'd had a half an eye I should have seen he was doin' somethin' else. I don't see now how I didn't." She took a deep breath. "I know Denny thinks I don't love him as much as I did my first husband, my little girls' father. And there's truth in that. I don't think a woman can fall in love that way twice. You just don't have it in you. I gave that man everything I had to give, and it wasn't enough, and I'm just not goin' to do that ever again. I've got to save something for myself. But that doesn't mean I'm not anxious to be the best wife I can be to Denny. I love him a lot."

"Speak right to him," Debbie urged, "and look right at him when you talk to him."

Emma looked right at him and her voice rose and became firmer. "I'll do everything I can to make you happy," she said, "but you've got to meet me halfway. I know you think you can drink without it being a problem, but what worries me, and what they told us downstairs, is that it will lead you back to the cocaine. Sure as God made little green apples, you're goin' to drink too much some night, and one of those no-good friends of yours is goin' to say, let's do it, and you'll be too drunk to say no. The people downstairs . . ."

"The hell with the people downstairs," Denny interrupted. "They're just tryin' to scare you to death, that's all."

"Well, wait just a minute," Emma said. "What I wanted to say is that they say we have to change our lives completely, that we can't go to the country club anymore because that was such a big part of our old life and we've got to have a new life without it, but I know that's not possible for us and I'm not goin' to ask you to do that."

"I should hope not," Denny grumbled. "God, that's only about all of our social life, that's all. Are we supposed to go into a monastery or something?"

"I'm tryin' to tell you, I know that wouldn't work for us," Emma said patiently. "It's all tied up with your family and with the business and everything. So I'm not askin' for that. But you've got to stop drinkin' or everything is going to fall apart again. You ought to be able to see that, Denny."

"No, I don't see that," Denny said. "I'll give up the coke. I promise you that. Nothin', not ever again. But I can't give up everything. Let's just see how it goes when we get home. We don't have to fight the whole Civil War here."

Mac and I had warned Denny against taking on the whole St. Mary's establishment on their home ground. "Just promise to be good," I told him, "and wait till you get home to make a contract with Emma. Show her you're going to change. Put in time with no drinking during the week, only on weekends, and even then only with meals. Don't just ask her to take everything on faith. Let her see what you intend to do. Give her a chance to believe it."

Ralph picked up his ax again. "You oughtn't to let him off the hook that easy," he said. "If he goes home and starts drinking again, he'll be right back where he was in no time."

"That's pretty judgmental of you," I said. "This young woman is fighting for her marriage. I don't think we ought to discourage her. Or Denny either. He's going to have to change his life drastically. I think he ought to be encouraged, and if Emma's willing to give him a chance, so should we."

Debbie decided it was her turn. "Denny," she said, "the thing that worries me is the whole business of alcohol breaking down your inhibitions and making it easy for you to do what you know you shouldn't do. And there's another thing. You may be right that you're not an alcoholic now. I'll go along with that. But if you go home and just trade alcohol for your cocaine habit, you're probably going to become an alcoholic before you even know where you are."

"But, Debbie," Denny said stubbornly, "I am not going to spend the next fifty years or however many it turns out to be of my life dyin' for a drink and not havin' it just because everybody's afraid I'll start doin' coke again. I am not goin' to do coke, I know I can't do it, and I agree I have got to give it up. But I am not goin' to give up drinking, and that's that. I'll be careful, and I won't drink except when I don't have to work and it's perfectly safe, but . . . ."

Debbie was blunt. "It's never safe," she said.

Tracy Cravath sympathized with Denny. "I know it's hard to think about giving it up," she said. "I mean, what's there to do at five o'clock except have a drink?" Then she went on to talk some more about money, about how much Denny's father had loaned him and how that would have to come out of the shares of his two sisters if he didn't pay it back, and Denny agreed that he would.

Emma didn't say anything more about Denny's wild parties but she did say that she had been a faithful wife and would always be one. Denny didn't pick up that ball at all. He let the session end with the promise that he would do everything he could to make up for all the trouble he had caused, and in a grave, old-fashioned

Texas way he told Mama and Emma that he loved them both very much.

Debbie was satisfied to let it go at that for now. She turned to the Terranovas.

There had been so much charged electricity in the room that I hadn't paid that much attention to John's parents. The famous Hawk, who had introduced himself as John's father, Dan, looked even younger than I had expected from John's admiring description; there wasn't an ounce of fat on his body and not a wrinkle on his face. I guessed he was about five ten and weighed about one hundred sixty pounds. He looked fit for a fight or a marathon. Mrs. Terranova, who said we should call her Midge which was what everybody called her because her real name was Philomena, "and that's too long to say, and I don't like Fanny," had a smile that lit up the whole room. She wasn't conventionally pretty, her features were too irregular for that, but she was nice looking and she had the figure of a twenty-year-old. She wore tight jeans that either were pre-washed or had been washed a hundred times, and they clutched her slender legs like a pair of pliers. She wore her University of Minnesota T-shirt just a shade less tight. She looked as though she was on her way to a football game.

This time Debbie went by the book and gave the floor to the parents. Midge let her husband take it.

"I want to say right away," Dan Terranova told his son, "that the thing I don't understand the most, and that's been driving me crazy ever since all this came to our attention, is why in the world you let them put you through a trial and send you to jail for six months without ever once getting in touch with us. I just don't get it. You knew we would help. All you had to do was make that one telephone call they have to let you make, and I would have been there in a minute. Now, you knew that, John, didn't you?"

I stole a look at Debbie. She looked so satisfied with this beginning that I wondered if she had orchestrated it.

John said, "Yeah," and that was all he said.

"And as bad as the jail thing was," his father said, "the stabbing was even harder to understand." He fixed the intensity of his hypnotic eyes on his son. "It's simply incredible to me that, after all the years we lived together and all the things we did together, good and bad, you could lie in a hospital half dead from knife wounds and not even let us know what had happened to you, much less give us a chance to help." There wasn't a sound in the room. It was clearly John's time to speak, but he didn't say a word and his father didn't push him. When nobody said anything for a minute, Debbie asked Dan to talk about why he thought John had left home the way he had, almost in the middle of the night, without even going to his high school graduation, and never gone back until now. Dan said, "I honestly don't know. We argued with the kids, John and his brother Andy, to shape up the way we wanted them to, but I never thought we gave them an especially hard time. Neither did Midge." Midge didn't say anything but she nodded in agreement. Dan was trying hard. "It was partly the times," he said. "Their friends were doing the popular things, smoking dope, I'm sure, talking against everything decent and straight, and I wasn't going to let my kids slide into that kind of an attitude without putting up a fight. I put up a fight, all right, and what happened was that the boys left home. John first, Andy next. John was gone for the longest time, and with the least contact with us, just a postcard once every few months and that was all. We didn't even hear from him last Christmas and we had no idea why until we found out he'd been in jail." He shook his head. "It didn't make a father feel very good," he said.

Midge spoke up. "Or a mother," she said, her mouth two tight lines. I was rooting for her not to cry because it was painfully clear she didn't want to.

Dan traced the sources of the family's divisions. "John was always smart," he said. "You could tell it in a million ways. He paid attention to things, he reacted to them. He had opinions and he had ideas. But he wouldn't work in school. It was as though he thought if he did he would be giving in to the system and he wasn't about to do that. I always blamed those friends of his. Some of them were really bad and it mattered a lot more to him to be accepted by them than it did to please us. So, what happened was bound to happen. I kept

after him to stay away from those kids and to work harder and do
better in school, and he kept getting angrier and more distant. Then,
when he just barely had the marks to graduate, he skipped out of
the house while it was still dark and didn't even wait to get his
diploma."

John spoke up. "There was all the business about Virginia, too,"
he said.

"Well, I should think that would have made you want to stick
around," his father said. He explained. "John had a crush on this
pretty blonde girl right down the street from us," he said, "and she
dropped him for another boy. He was going to go to the university
and she liked that. John must have told her he was just going to
go out on his own and do the road thing and work when he felt
like it and I guess she didn't think there was much of a future in
that for a girl. Right, John?"

John said, "Right." He didn't elaborate. We hadn't heard anything
about Virginia before, and I wondered if her rejection had cut
deeper than his disagreement with his father. Midge shed some
light on that. "Virginia came to see me the week John left," she
began.

"Speak right to him," Debbie said, just as she had instructed
Emma. "Don't talk about him. And look right at him, please."

"She was real sorry about breaking up with him," Midge went
on. "She told me she had hoped if she did it might make him think
more about what he was giving up." She did what Debbie had said
and looked right at her son. "I got the feeling," she said, "that you
two had been doing a little more than holding hands."

"Yeah," John, ever loquacious, said, "we had."

"Mostly she wanted to know, that first time, if I knew how she
could get in touch with you. But I didn't, and it hurt me to have
to tell her that, but I told her, and she only asked me one more
time." She waited, in case John wanted to say something, and then
she finished. "We both figured," she said, "that you didn't want us
to know where you were, and that was your choice." This time she
reached for a Kleenex but what crying she did she did without
making a sound. Midge had her pride.

Debbie led the three of them through a reconstruction of John's time in high school. She kept asking questions about how much they knew about John's drug use but all they knew was that they had found marijuana around the house once. Dan had confronted John with it and raised such hell that it never happened again. They had never known or suspected that he had used anything else until Dan had gotten Peggy's letter and had gone to bring him back home.

Debbie's first charge to John was to tell them his whole drug history, just as Denny had done. The slowly awakening surprise, and then shock, that this produced was at least as profound as the Cravaths' had been. John had used even more varieties of stimulants than Denny had, probably because he and his friends had had less money and had been more willing to try anything that promised to deliver a kick. They used prescription drugs, street drugs, over-the-counter drugs and homemade drugs. One night it was heroin, the next speed, the next cocaine, then LSD, mescaline, hash, morphine, Demerol, Seconal, whatever. And always marijuana. They smoked pot the way straight people smoked cigarettes and thought nothing more of it than that. Their only problem was getting their hands on the money they needed to buy the stuff.

"I never stole," John said. "I never wanted anything bad enough to rob houses for it." He told his mother and father what he had already told us about his time with Peggy; he even told them about siphoning the gas out of the pickup and how maybe that was just enough to convince the judge to send him to jail. He took a long time working his way up to saying what he had to say, and his father didn't help him. "I know it's hard for you to understand," John said, "but I was scared to call you. I'm just beginning to understand it myself. Debbie's helped, and so have the rest of the people in the group. I guess they could see before I could that I've been afraid of making you mad for so long that it's a habit. I just made up my mind I'd rather stick it out by myself than face up to you. I know it was wrong." That came slowly, but it came, and you could see The Hawk's face lighten a shade when John said it.

"So you came home," his father said, "and we got you in here, and from what you say and from what Debbie tells me, it's been working. What I want to know is, if it was to happen now, and you were in bad trouble, would you call us and let us help?"

John didn't think it over. He didn't waste any time. He didn't consider it. "Yes," he said. "Yes. I would."

Watching him, I thought about the obscure word anomie. That was John all over. When the meeting was over, and we had all said the Serenity Prayer together, I looked it up to be sure I was remembering it right. "Rootless," the dictionary said. "The breakdown or absence of social norms and values." Right on; that was John.

You could see, much more clearly than when he had been talking just to the group, how hard John was struggling to tell nothing but the truth and yet not hurt anybody any more than he had to. I thought he was really reaching deep for it when he said, tensely, "All I wanted was to be free, and that's why I ran away, and then I found out that the drugs made me feel even more free. I didn't know enough to know they were only making me a different kind of a prisoner. That's what I've been finding out here." His lean face was like a death mask. "I'll tell you," he said, "it feels good just to be hungry again."

A lot of us knew what he meant.

Dr. Amer was at the nurses' station after the meeting and he stopped me for a blood pressure reading. He also told me that Kirby Puckett was due for a hot streak and the Twins, who had fallen out of first place by a game and a half, would be back up there in a couple of days. I told him I thought Puckett had a hitch in his swing but he was hell of a hitter anyway. I teased him by saying Ducky Medwick had always hit with his foot in the bucket and it never bothered him, but he had never heard of Ducky Medwick and it just confirmed his general impression that I was too old to be drinking so much. He liked my blood pressure, though, one thirty-two over eighty-six, and he told Connie Krantz she could take me off the Ativan now. I was going to tell her she could give the Ativan to Denny, who needed it more than I did, but I decided nobody would laugh.

Denny and Mac were waiting when the doctor finished with me and we headed downstairs to go outside for the long walk. We passed a couple of young women standing on the second floor landing talking about their inmate husbands. "I don't know," one of them was saying, "if I'm ready to listen to his list of resentments."

Father Tim was coming out of the gift shop clutching a couple of contraband Hershey bars in his hand and he walked right up to us, his buddies, two unbelievers and a member of the fallen away clergy. "Have you heard," he began without preamble, "about the priest who was looking for a seat in the dining car and the only one he could find was at a table with two nuns. So when he sat down he introduced himself and said he was going to have a drink before dinner and he wished they would have one with him. But they got all flustered and said, no, they couldn't, it would look terrible, a couple of nuns drinking in public, and with a priest no less, but thanks just the same. Now, naturally, he would have none of that, so he told the waiter 'We'll all have a dry martini on the rocks, only tell the bartender to put the sisters' drinks in coffee cups, thank you very much.' Well, they were sitting toward the end of the car not far from the galley, and they could hear the waiter give the order, including the whole business about the coffee cups, and then they heard the bartender saying, in a loud voice, 'Are those two nuns still in the dining car?' "

Tim had a million of them, most of them about nuns and not many of them as clean as that one. It was easy to picture him back at the parish, having lunch with the boys from the Rotary Club or the Chamber of Commerce, breaking them up with his pre-absolved humor. I noticed that while he was telling us the story he managed to slip the chocolate bars into his pants pocket.

We never did get to take our walk because Eileen Zierman, the unit assistant who chaperoned the store walks that were scheduled three or four times a week, asked us if we wanted to go on the four o'clock walk, and that reminded Denny and me that we wanted to take our dirty clothes over to the combination laundry and dry cleaner's across the street from the supermarket that was the walk's principal destination along with the drug store. We told Eileen, yes, we were in, and we went back upstairs to pack up our underwear, socks, and golf shirts to be washed and a couple of pairs of slacks to be dry cleaned. For Denny, who had only a week to go, it was the last time he would have to do it. I figured I could manage with just one more trip in a week or so. Mac thought we were both crazy, or, more to the point, as lazy as sin. He did his own laundry with half a package of detergent Carl Bruhl had given him when he left and a handful of quarters.

We had a half hour to kill before the walk so we went over to pay a visit to St. Mary. She was as calm as the river, and as everlasting. We hoped some of her peace would rub off on us.

Dinner was pretty good, a choice between baked chicken with cranberries and ham loaf with horseradish and cream sauce. I ate some of the ham loaf and every mouthful of the escalloped potatoes that went with it. I could hear one of the young women at the next table saying in despair, "Diet or die tomorrow. My God, I've never been so corpulent in my life." She was a nineteen-year-old kid whose face was still black and blue and swollen from the beating her father had given her the day she came in. She probably weighed about ninety pounds.

I went back upstairs to rest before the seven o'clock lecture and read some more about Nora Joyce, who hardly ever had enough to eat, and her husband, who never had enough to drink.

The last thing Denny said to me before we said good night was that he had been asking around and had decided to take the girls to a place called Anthony's Wharf for dinner on Thursday night, the Family Week night when the patient gets a pass from three o'clock to nine. "It's on the river," he said, "and it's one of those sort of restorations, I guess. Anyway, I hear it's nice, and there's something to look at, so maybe it'll take my mind off having a drink."

"Well," I said, "you sure won't have to worry about Emma having a drink. It sounds like she's going to go dry to her heavenly condominium."

"Yeah," Denny said, "but you can bet Mama will have one. She hasn't sat down to dinner without a martini since she had pneumonia when I was ten years old."

There were some times the next morning when I wasn't so sure the two women were going to let Denny take them anywhere. They had obviously spent the night before drawing up their lists of grievances and then had had their weapons cleaned and polished at the morning meetings downstairs. Bobby Moore's assessment of what happened when the family counselors counseled the families might not make Debbie feel happy but it looked to me as though it constituted Pulitzer Prize-winning reporting.

Ralph got his wish when Emma started off letting Denny have it with both barrels for his treatment of her. She began to cry early on. "You never cared whether I went with you or not," she said. "In fact, I think you probably arranged a lot of those parties so they'd be hard for me to get to because you didn't want me there. Then you could do your cocaine and whatever else you did, and with women, too, and I wasn't there to call you on it. How do I know you aren't goin' to go right back to doin' like that if you start drinkin' again when you get home? I don't think I can trust you."

"That's why I think you've got to make a full confession and then turn over a whole new leaf," Ralph said righteously. I thought even Debbie would like to stuff a carrot in his mouth. It was too much for Denny. "Why don't you just shut the fuck up?" Denny said. "It doesn't look to me like you're really trying to help. Debbie didn't even ask for any feedback yet. Why don't you just let Emma speak for herself? She's doin' all right."

Emma didn't have to carry the ball alone; Mama was primed, too. She had had time to think about Denny's revelations about using drugs from his grade school days, and she was about as angry as it was possible for her to get with her beloved son, with whom mostly she was well pleased. "You're just doin' your best to waste your opportunities," she said. "It's obvious to everybody that you're the right person to carry on the family business, and I agree that you've done a good job of bringing it back from some bad times, but you're not goin' to be able to look after it if you keep on like this. And we've got more than sixty people dependin' on it. That means they're dependin' on you. And here you are filling yourself up with drugs. I'm ashamed, Denny, I'm just ashamed to tears."

She wasn't crying, though, and she didn't cry. Mama was pioneer stuff.

The two women made an interesting study. Their relationship with Denny and with each other was sharply illuminated as the morning wore on, with Mac and me holding a lot of important clues from things Denny had told us on our walks.

It was clear that Tracy liked her daughter-in-law, Emma, even if she had had the poor taste to marry another man first and have two children with him. But she loved Denny. Nobody had any confusion about that. For instance, Tracy was tolerant of Emma's strict Baptist attitudes but she was relieved that the same woman who thought you ought to spend a lot of time on your knees praying for salvation also thought it was okay to regularly spend time letting your husband enjoy the body you worked so hard to keep in the best possible shape. Mama wouldn't want Denny to have to do without. Not to worry. When she swam in a meet, Emma swam for herself, not for Jesus, and she liked to exercise the same slender legs making love. But she plainly had the feeling that her loving ought to be handed out like a reward; she thought her man ought to earn it by paying his dues to the Lord. And that was where Denny failed the course.

Except, what's a girl to do? A born controller, Emma was still trying to figure out a way to win this one. If she kicked him out of her bed he would just shrug his shoulders and amiably shuffle off with a clear conscience to accept the favors of an endless pool of good-looking young women standing in line waiting their turn to make him happy and incidentally to share his coke with him. Neither Mama nor Emma wanted that.

You could safely conclude, from what Mama said, that Denny came by his drinking honestly. His father, Ham, the name he had been called since he was christened Dennison Hamilton Cravath, Jr. after his own father and was called Ham to keep them apart, thought everybody drank martinis for serious drinking and bourbon and branch water for day-long sieges. He didn't know anything about these new-fangled drugs, and if you asked him about them, he would have said that was big-city stuff, mostly the niggers anyway. White boys drank.

Denny was a white boy and he did everything, especially, in the last few years, cocaine. The women of the family had come all the way to Minneapolis from Odessa to see what they could do about putting a stop to that.

Denny had the last word. "I know it's not enough just to say you don't have to worry," he said, "but I'm not goin' to do coke, or any other drugs for that matter, anymore and you'll see that I mean it."

"I'm not sure I will," Emma said. "I didn't know you were doin' it when you were doin' it."

"What you got to do, Denny," Debbie said, "is keep remembering that slogan Nancy Reagan uses: 'Just say no.' "

"Wait a minute," my outraged Democratic soul protested. "Let's not put our hopes on anything the Republicans say. It's entirely possible that that coke Denny got in trouble buying was flown up here on one of Ollie North's government airplanes. That's the way they said no, flying the stuff in on airplanes we were paying for."

Debbie got rid of me gracefully by turning the meeting over to the Terranovas. They took it over without a moment of hesitation; it was as if they had so much to say they were afraid that there might not be enough time. The star of the afternoon was The Hawk. Dan Terranova, who could have been believably cast as the field commander of the Minneapolis Bureau of the DEA, said right away that he was prepared to do whatever the people at St. Mary's thought he ought to do. It didn't matter what it cost. What mattered was that it was the right thing. He did what Debbie had told everybody to do, looked right at John while he talked. "The one thing I think I shouldn't do," he said, "is bring you into the company. I don't think that would be good for you. Andy's going to have to leave, too. It just doesn't work out for the boss's son to be part of a work gang. It's different for Denny here. He's helping his father run the company, and when he's the only one of them there, he's the boss. But you'd be one of the crew and the other guys would resent it. Anyway, the people downstairs think the first thing you ought to do is go to a halfway house, and I agree. That way you can get back into it gradually. You can get a job because it's important for you to be working, and I'll make up whatever other money you need. Okay?"

John said, "Okay."

"And you can come to see us whenever you feel like it," his mother said with a hint of wistfulness. "I mean, we won't bug you, just when you feel like it."

"I'll come," John said. He gave his mother a warm look. "I'll feel like it."

The contentiousness of yesterday's first confrontations was all gone. Debbie looked like the director of the high school play when everybody had gotten through it without missing a cue or stumbling over a line.

The Serenity Prayer sounded to me like the ancient litany of the approaching communion: "Receive the Holy Spirit: whose sins you shall forgive, they are forgiven them; and whose sins you shall retain, they are retained."

They all seemed to be forgiven.

The group had a quiet day on Thursday while the family members were off doing their own things, like learning how to talk to each other. "Sometimes," Denny said at breakfast, "I think we could do with a lot less talking." But he was just being contrary. John didn't seem to think it was such a bad idea. "At least the old man is trying," he said. Then they had an afternoon lecture on what to expect after treatment. Denny didn't have anything to say about that but John said, "That's the sixty-four dollar question." Neither of them made any jokes about it.

There wasn't much for me to do except be glad for Denny that he was hoping to be in bed with Emma this very afternoon. Mama had already told him that she would stay at the hotel while he took Emma out to dinner. "I can't drink comfortably in front of her while she's the way she is now," Mama had said. "And I don't want to be in the way." Denny had reserved a Hertz car and was going to drive out into the lake country for a look at some open spaces, and

Mama said she would like to go along for the ride. But after that she planned to eat a room service dinner while they painted the town at St. Anthony's Wharf.

Mac and I agreed, on our afternoon walk, that we were getting a preview of what life at the Rehab would be like without Denny.

"Dull," Mac said. Five or ten minutes later he added, "Present company excepted."

Two things happened that made the early evening memorable. The first was one of the great lines of the lecture series, delivered by a St. Mary's graduate who told us the horrifying story of his fall to the bottom—he was a doctor who had lost his license and almost his life in a terrible auto crash—so we would know that you can come back from the very jaws of hell. He told us about something inspiring that Billy Graham had said on a recent television broadcast, and he threw in a quick apology. "I don't usually watch Billy Graham," he said, "but he came on right after the 'Wheel of Fortune.' "

The other was the noisy arrival on our floor of a female inmate in her late forties whose face was swollen from crying and disfigured by a round purple bruise the size of a quarter on her right cheek. Her name was Delia, she said, Dilly for short, and she and her husband ran a motel with a little restaurant on the outskirts of St. Paul. They had put her in the room next to Mac's, just across the hall from Denny's and mine, and she had gotten restless and wandered into the lounge where I was sitting eating ice cream with Mac and Father Tim. We were worried about her appearance but she said they had done everything they could for her and had told her all she had to do now was rest, but she was too nervous to rest. "I want to go home," she said.

Tim identified himself as a priest and she said she was a Catholic—"even if a damn poor one," she said—and that she was glad to know he was there.

"There is no such thing as a poor Catholic," Tim said. "Not even Edward here, although the good Lord knows he tries hard enough. There are only some who are in a state of grace and others who have to get back in it."

That didn't seem to encourage Dilly very much. "What I need," she said, "is to get my husband in a state of grace." She pressed two of her fingers against the bruise on her cheek. "Sometimes," she said, "I think maybe my husband is just trying to get rid of me. But it's my house, too, and the business is more mine than his. It was my father's, and he sold it to Michael for practically nothing just so he could be sure I'd be taken care of."

"Is your name on the business, too?" Mac asked.

"No," Dilly said. "Just his." I couldn't hear any bitterness in the way she said it. It seemed to her to be right and proper that it should belong to her husband.

"Did you have a fight?" Tim asked her.

She shrugged impatiently. "No," she said. "I mean, he caught me with a glass of gin, that's all, and I'm not supposed to drink while I'm working the cash in the restaurant." She pushed down the shoulders of her low-necked sweater, careless that she was exposing much of the cleavage of her big breasts. "Look at my arms," she said. You could see a scattering of yellow and purple bruises there, too. She seemed almost proud of them. She pulled her sweater back up. "He punches my boobs, too, but I don't want to embarrass the Father."

I thought Dilly was getting herself together when we persuaded her to go to dinner with us. She didn't eat much of the dinner but she did talk with a little more confidence and she stopped trying to cover up the mark on her face with her free hand. And it was a good sign that she ate a whole piece of chocolate cream pie with whipped cream. Afterward, she went outside with the smokers and pulled a pack of Camels out of her bag and lit one up with ferocity. An old-fashioned girl, I thought; Camels, yet. What interested me even more was the intent way she studied every car that pulled up anywhere near the Rehab entrance. It was as if she was waiting for somebody to come for her, like John Dillinger in the Cook County Jail.

It all was a lot clearer a little after nine o'clock when Denny stopped by my room, looking like the proverbial cat after a canary dinner. "Everything is going to be all right," he said dreamily.

"Booze definitely takes second place to pussy." But Denny had only been there a few minutes when Mac came in. "Dilly left," he reported. "The night nurse just told me she went in to see how she was and she was gone. She left a note on the desk saying she had to go home."

Denny stretched. "Well," he said, "maybe they'll make up. Makin' up is better than fightin'. Hell, it's even better than drinkin'."

"Which means," Mac said, leaving with Denny, "drinking and making up must be the best of all possible worlds. It's too bad some of us don't have either."

13

Is It Any Wonder I Drink?

There was no way of knowing how much making up Dilly had done the night before but she was back at the breakfast table in the morning and it didn't take Dr. Amer or Mary Scanlan to see that she had done a lot of drinking. Her bruise had faded a little, so at least she hadn't been banged around anymore last night, but her eyes looked terrible, her voice was ragged and hoarse, and her hands trembled badly whenever she lifted up her coffee cup. She was the star of our morning group.

Nobody read the Thought for the Day quite so slowly as Sarah did. I was never sure whether it was because she needed glasses and was too vain to wear them or because she had trouble grasping the meaning of the words she was reading and tried to do it as she went along, but she read the words out as though each one came straight from the Mount. We all kept sneaking surreptitious looks at Dilly to see how she was taking it because, depending on your point of view, the message seemed either singularly appropriate or monstrously inept:

"After we had sobered up through the AA program, we gradually began to get a peace of mind and serenity which we never thought were possible. This peace of mind is based on a feeling that fundamentally all is well. That does not mean that all is well on the surface of things. Little things can keep going wrong and big things can keep on upsetting us. But deep down in our hearts we know that eventually everything is going to be all right. . . ."

Did we now?

Dilly told the group more or less what she had told Tim, Mac, and me the night before, but with more details. She and her husband had met when she was a senior in high school and he was driving a truck for Anheuser Busch. They started going steady after she graduated and he began working for her father doing odd jobs around the motel and the restaurant. "It's really more of a bar than a restaurant," she said. "The only food we serve is sandwiches that are already made up. We don't even fry hamburgers." When they got married, her father suggested that Michael come into the business and learn how to run it so he could retire and take his fishing tackle to Florida. Michael was glad to say yes. "I can always keep my Teamsters card," he said.

Dilly said she would have been better off if he had just kept driving his truck. "Then he would have been out of the house all day," she said, "and I wouldn't have had him looking over my shoulder every minute."

"You mean you were already drinking when you got married?" Debbie asked. "It wasn't something that started because you were having trouble with your husband?"

"No, I've been drinking since I was fifteen," Dilly said. "Michael drinks, too, but he doesn't need it the way I do, and he blows his top when I drink on the job. He says we'll lose our shirts if we drink the stuff while we're supposed to be selling it. I know he's right, and I keep promising him I won't, but I just can't sit there watching everybody else having a good time and not have a little myself."

"What's a little?" Debbie wanted to know.

"I don't measure it," Dilly said, immediately on the defensive. "How could I? He doesn't let me drink civilized like the rest of them. I have to sneak it. So I just pour some in a glass whenever I get a chance."

"Well," Debbie persisted. "Two shots worth? Three? Do you add ice?"

"I only add ice when I know he isn't going to be around for a while," Dilly said. "That's a treat then. But mostly I just pour some fast in a glass like the ones we use for water. I have to drink it fast, too. He doesn't care if he gives me the back of his hand right in the bar. He stands in front of me so nobody can see what he's doing. Of course, he can't do too much to me there. It's when we get home that I really get it."

"Your son must know he abuses you," Debbie said. "I'm surprised he hasn't said anything about it to us."

"He takes his father's side," Dilly said. She was sullen now, the misunderstood wife. "He knows he has to keep in good with him."

"Do you think you drink a pint of vodka a day?" Debbie asked.

Dilly thought about that for a while, then made up her mind to be defiant. "More," she said. "If I'm home alone, and he's working or on a trip, I'll get through a quart." Then she was contrite. "I know I drink too much," she said, "but, my God, I have good cause." Debbie was getting ready to ask another question but Dilly interrupted her. "I didn't even tell you the worst part," she said. "Michael has other women in the motel. I do the books so I can tell when he's letting a woman stay overnight free. He marks the book paid but the money isn't there. He used to say he borrowed it when I'd catch him at it but now he just tells me to mind my own business."

"Have you ever caught him with another woman?" Debbie asked.

"No," Dilly said. "I don't try to. I wouldn't want to see it. But I know he does it. Is it any wonder I drink?"

There was no sign of Dilly at lunchtime. She didn't show up at the table and we didn't see her outside. "Maybe she's sleeping it off," Denny said. He knew he had to say good-bye to Tracy and Emma today, so he was entitled to be a little acerbic. His only company tonight would be Mac and me. The door to Dilly's room was closed, so the first we knew about what had happened to her was when we assembled in 355 at one-thirty. Debbie had been in touch with both her husband and her son, separately. "She just got in a cab and went back home," Debbie said, "but first she bought a bottle and got drunk. She said she sat in the stands at the Augsburg College football stadium until it was all gone. Then she went out on the street and got a cab to take her home. Her husband found her there after I talked to him. He swore she got that bruise on her face when she fell down drunk on the coffee table in their living room and he said any bruises on her arms she probably got from him holding on to her to keep her from going out of the house drunk. Her son says he knows his father has never hit her. He says she lies about it to everybody because it makes people feel sorry for her and think it's not surprising that she drinks. Finally, I called her parish priest and he told me he's investigated the family exhaustively and he's convinced that she's lying. He said he thinks Michael used to get aggravated enough to slap her in the face but since he's seen the way she uses that against him he doesn't even do that anymore. She makes up the whole thing, the priest said. He agreed with me, and so did her husband, that the best thing for her now is a sanitarium where she can have twenty-four-hour nursing care. They think she'll agree to go in as a voluntary patient, but her husband said if he has to he'll have her committed. The priest said he would help."

We went back to work on our own problems. It was hard for a while to get our hearts into it but Sarah, Doctor Bob, and I used up the time that was left going over what we thought were the main problems we had to discuss during Family Week. I said I thought mine was my stubborn feeling that I wouldn't drink so much if everybody would just leave me alone to drink out in the open when it was an appropriate time for a drink. The trouble was, thinking about Dilly took away a lot of the conviction I had that it might work out that way for me. "I'm afraid," I said, "that Dilly's trouble is the best illustration I could ask for of how stupid it is to think like that."

Inside, I was beginning to think for the first time that maybe my carefully protected conviction that there were good reasons why I drank was just another justification, like Dilly's. Her voice was beginning to be mixed in with mine:

"Is it any wonder I drink?"

No wonder so many writers are alcoholics. It takes a good writer to keep up with the need for excuses. But the truth is, for a writer, an extra drink is like an extra adjective. The sentence is bound to be better without it.

Before group ended, Debbie picked up a piece of paper, read off my name, Sarah's, Mac's, Doctor Bob's, and Mark's and said we were all to report to the cafeteria at four o'clock to take the MMPI test. I had done the test, an interminable 566-question true or false exercise in stupidity, last summer, but I knew it wouldn't do any good to try to talk them out of it. I'd have to suffer through it, even though I knew you had to pay seventy-five dollars for it. I teased Eileen Zierman, who was in charge of the operation, about not telling us that we had to pay for it, but she was untroubled. "It goes with the territory," she said.

I suppose it's the same tenacious grip on my pride that makes me dislike both AA and blatant assaults on your intelligence like the MMPI. (Minnesota Multiphasic Personality Inventory. How could you take seriously anything with a name like that?) but I sat through it, silently racing Mac to see who could finish faster. The questions ranged from inane to vacuous, and if you tried conscientiously to be scrupulously honest, from puzzling to unanswerable.

How can you answer True or False to these questions?

There seems to be a lump in my throat much of the time.
No one seems to understand me.
I have had very peculiar and strange experiences.
My soul sometimes leaves my body.
Sometimes when I am not feeling well I am cross.
Everything tastes the same.
I dislike having people about me.
Once in a while I think of things too bad to talk about.
Peculiar odors come to me at times.
Most of the time I wish I were dead.

I certainly would have wished I were dead if I'd had to take anymore tests like that. Anyway, so far as the little man sitting behind a black curtain behind the computer was concerned, I might not have been ready to be listed as dead but I was certainly missing in action. "Mr. Fitzgerald," he said in his report, "completed an invalid profile psychometrically." I looked up psychometrics; it means "the measurement of mental traits." I must admit I was even more amused by the definition of the word psychometry: "the *alleged* art or faculty of divining facts concerning a person or object by contact with or proximity to the object." The test examiner, in the best Soviet tradition reaching his conclusion without bothering to talk to me, went on to say, "He appears to have taken an extreme stance of presenting himself in the best possible light, minimizing adjustment difficulties. He uses both sophisticated rationalizing and intellectualizing and to some degree a more naive denial mechanism, leading him to attribute personal qualities to himself which apply to virtually no one."

I especially liked the accusation that "Mr. Fitzgerald portrays himself as unusually oriented towards aesthetic, artistic, and intellectual pursuits."

No wonder all prisoners learn that it's best to lie to your captors, to just say fuck it and tell them what they want to hear. Telling the truth only gets you into trouble.

Along with everybody else in the Rehab, I thought the unidentified hero who made up the widely circulated parody of the MMPI deserved a lot more credit than the genius who did the real thing. Some of the parodist's best efforts included:

I salivate at the sight of mittens.
Spinach makes me feel alone.
Dirty stories make me think about sex.
I often repeat myself.
I often repeat myself.
Recently I have been getting shorter.
Constantly losing my underwear doesn't bother me.

Weeping brings tears to my eyes.
I never seem to finish whatever I

· Except for the underwear line, which seemed to have been thrown in specifically for Denny and made me mistrust the whole thing, I thought the parody won hands down over the actual test. At least some real thought went into it. Let's face it, the MMPI is just a step above a fortune cookie.

As if all that, plus roast beef for dinner, wasn't enough for one day, we had a replacement for Dilly before the television set was turned on at eight o'clock. We had barely had time to walk off our dinner when the night nurse introduced us to the new occupant of the room Dilly had just left. This woman had been beaten up by somebody who was genuinely enthusiastic about his work. Her face was a patchwork of ugly bruises in shocking discolorations of green, blue, yellow, purple, and red, most of them thickly swollen. Her mouth was puffed out like a peeled orange, no longer tightly held together, and the bottom lip still had a jagged line of dried blood on it. I had never seen a human being so brutally beaten up outside of the prize ring, and I had never seen a woman anywhere so grievously battered.

Her name was Betty-Louise, she said we should call her Betty-Lou, and she had come with a policeman friend from Marshalltown, Iowa, a city of thirty thousand people not far from Des Moines. She was attractively roly-poly, with the sexiest figure in the place. "No cellulite there," Denny decided, adding that, "Back home we would say she was built like a Coca-Cola bottle." Betty-Lou was the new star of the Rehab and it touched your heart that she was so eager to please. You had the feeling that somebody had scared her to death.

She blurted a lot of it out right away when Debbie invited her to tell us something about herself and how she had gotten here. She was the office manager for the town clerk back home in Iowa, she said, and it was a good job that she'd gotten after she had worked for the town for fifteen years ever since she got out of business school. She owned her own house, only two bedrooms but a real nice bungalow, she said, and she'd been married once but had been divorced for five years. "He was a bum," she said. "He drank all the time, never worked, and just wanted to live off me. I got rid of him. Then, about six months ago, I met this man in the bar and grill where I go a lot for drinks and dinner. He was new in town and he was a handsome man and he made a big play for me and I wasn't hard to get. I'd been alone a long time."

But Betty-Lou had traded the devil for the deep blue sea, or maybe it was the other way around. The new man was much worse than her first husband. If she did anything to displease him, he simply hit her. He didn't bother to hit her where the marks wouldn't show, either. He broke her nose twice, fractured her jaw once, and gave her "more black eyes than I could honestly count." It got so that she missed so many days at work, and invented so many suspicious stories to account for the bruises on her face, that her boss became suspicious and she finally told him the truth. Betty-Lou told it to us with her pretty round face working, trying to keep from crying. "He deliberately hurt me in all three of my orifices," she said, "usually on the same night when he was really mad at me. He used his male thing on me like a weapon. The worst was, when he really wanted to hurt me, he would give it to me in the ass. I don't mean doggy-style screwing. I mean right in the ass, and without any preparation, no vaseline or KY or anything like that. He just ripped into me. He liked it if he made me bleed. And even after he did that, he'd still hit me. He kicked me with his shoes on. Once he knocked out two of my front teeth." She touched her teeth. "These two are fake," she said. Then she began to cry. "I never knew what I had done wrong," she said, "but I guess he was showing me that he owned me." He wanted money from her all the time, and if she didn't give it to him fast enough, drawing it out of the bank, turning stocks into cash, even selling her jewelry, he would hit her. She didn't say how much money he had taken from her but she didn't have to tell us how far he had been willing to go to get it.

Her boss, the town clerk, had made her promise that she would call 911 the next time he beat her up or hurt her with sex, but when she tried to do that he caught her and knocked her unconscious. When she didn't show up for work the next morning, her boss went to her house with a policeman and made the man let them see her. The chief of police arrested him and decided to send Betty-Lou to St. Mary's because he thought she had been trying to drink herself to death and because he thought she would be safe there. Then the chief traded Betty-Lou's promise not to press charges against him for the man's promise to get out of town and never come back. All Betty-Lou had to do now was get sober and go back to the job that was waiting for her and the house that had had all of its locks changed.

As bad as she felt, Betty-Lou sat down at the table and had dinner with us. Well, she had a bowl of chicken soup and a dish of rice pudding. The way she looked, it must have hurt to have eaten even that much food. She talked mostly to Sarah, who was sitting across the table from her, but she spoke clearly enough for the rest of us to hear.

The thing that worried her the most was that she was afraid her husband would follow her here. He had said he would when the cops came to the house after her boss had called them and asked them to see if she was all right. Her husband, who had the incongruously beautiful name of Dion, had threatened her with even worse punishment when she left with the cops. He said she was his wife and she had no right to just walk off like that, and he would find her no matter where she went. The sergeant told him that they were going to ask the judge to issue a writ of protection for her, and that he could be arrested if he knowingly went within five hundred yards of her, but he had insisted that wouldn't stop him. His last words to the cops were, "Anyway, I need to go to the hospital as much as she does." No wonder Betty-Lou was nervous.

I didn't see her anymore that night but the next morning at breakfast she said that Dion had shown up at midnight but that the admissions people, who had been warned, had refused to admit him and had had the security guards walk him out of the building. She hoped and prayed that she would never see him again.

"What will you do when you get out of here?" Sarah asked her.

"I'll be okay back home," Betty-Lou said. "The cop who brought me here told me they won't let him bother me even if they have to watch my house night and day. They're pretty mad at him for beating me up like that." Her sore mouth didn't even quiver. You couldn't help liking Betty-Louise. Later, on the path somewhere between the volleyball court and the swimming pool, the three of us agreed that she was going to be good for the group. She had already done something we wouldn't have believed was possible; she had made us ashamed of feeling sorry for ourselves.

I was sorry that Denny and John kept missing chunks of our introduction to her but they were gone for the rest of the morning for a last time together with their families before they went home. There was a meeting in the chapel to talk about how to improve their communication with each other and then the awarding of the family members' medallions.

"I don't know what I have to go to any of this for," Denny complained to Mac and me. "All I have to do to improve communication is to take the plugs out of my ears and let it all come through right while she's yelling at me instead of making her repeat it later, and I could buy her a medal in any army and navy store."

Later, at lunch, he had mellowed some. "Thank God that's over," he said, adding a few additional stirs to his plate of tiny stir-fried shrimp. "Although," he admitted with one of those impish grins, "I have to admit I'll miss old Emma. It'll be a whole week."

Everything was back to normal except for the sight of Betty-Lou chewing on one side of her mouth because the other side still hurt too much. "I think," she said to Sarah, "I'll buy a gun when I get home."

Sarah's response was uncharacteristically tart. "You'd be better off," she said, "if you'd just stay out of those bars."

If Betty-Lou's arrival was the harshest note of the weekend, Sunday morning provided easily the sweetest. We had come back from a hot walk and were hanging around the lobby by the gift shop wondering what we were going to do with the rest of the day. We might have gone straight upstairs to take showers and lie down in the cool of our rooms if we hadn't been transfixed by one of those utterly candid overheard conversations that tell you more about the Rehab than any lecture.

She was a good-looking young woman in her late thirties with sculpted features and a full figure.

He was in his late twenties, carelessly lean in his workingman's K Marts.

Whenever he thought she wasn't going to catch him at it, he stared at her body as if he was trying to guess her weight, and whenever she thought he wasn't going to catch her at it, she checked him out as though she was trying to decide if he was carrying a gun.

"If you live around here," he said, "have you ever been to Jimmy's?"

"Oh, sure," she said, every inch the knowledgeable older woman.

"You get three for one there on Saturday night," he said wistfully.

"I was up to two quarts of scotch a day before I came in," she said. "I'd start out with a drink first thing in the morning, before I brushed my teeth. But I still might have made it if I hadn't started dipping coke." She looked across the room at a fat young woman struggling toward the door with a heavy suitcase. "Go help her," she said. After he did, she said, "Do you know her?"

"She claims she's a lady wrestler. Some of the guys wondered if it was any different with a wrestler."

"Too bad she isn't Chinese," she said.

"What?"

"Never mind. You know, I did four grams the night before I came in."

He shook his head. "Wow. You must have been as high as a kite."

"I know I didn't sleep all night."

"I couldn't do that much," he said. "Anyway, I couldn't afford it. I was buying quarters and halves. How could you afford all that?"

"I have a good job," she said, "and I do a little hooking on the side."

Denny pushed me toward the gift shop. "Come on, come on," he said. In the store he said, "I hope she doesn't expect to charge for it here." He never mentioned her again, and when we went back out into the lounge, she was gone. But we were just in time to see The Hawk push open the noisy front door and walk in with two baseball bats in one strong hand and a couple of gloves hanging from the other. In a gleaming white T-shirt innocent of advertising or slogans, and stone-washed jeans, he made every other male in the lobby look like a slob. The Hawk had obviously come to play.

After we talked with him and found out that he wasn't simply going to deliver the equipment to John but fully intended to play himself, we promised we would see him later at the ball field. When we did, we forgot all about Betty-Lou's troubles, and, for a while, even our own. It was a scene straight out of "Our Town," or maybe a *Saturday Evening Post* cover by Norman Rockwell. Not the sophisticated interpretations of the sport by Leroy Neiman like the ones hanging in the Rehab tunnel, all squiggles and slants and dramatic shadows, but All-American yellow bantam corn with honest faces running wet with sweat and emotion. It was ruthlessly hot on the dusty ball field with the great curve of I-94 for a backdrop, but that didn't stop The Hawk from volunteering to be the steady pitcher when they chose up sides in the time-honored manner, best players picked first, worst players picked last. John, who was one of the two men doing the picking, warned him that he was asking for trouble, it was too hot. "As long as I don't sit down," his old man said, "I'll be all right. I need a good workout."

"You're going to get it," John said, and there wasn't a touch of sarcasm in the way he said it, only sneaking admiration. This was the father he had told us about, only here he was trying to do it John's way, not his. We hung around for a couple of innings and were glad to see John trot out between innings with a can of Coke for the old man, but we never saw him sit down once. When we left to finish our walk, The Hawk's light-colored jeans were dark with sweat.

"Score one for Family Week," Denny said.

"It's doing it the hard way," Mac said, "but it gets done. Maybe the hard way is the only way it can work when you're as far gone as we were."

"Remember," I said, "when Maureen Dudley gave the talk about how she had put together the first Family Week here? And we made all those jokes about was she bragging she'd invented it or confessing that she'd done it? Anyway, one thing she said was that the patient had to understand that he didn't have a corner on the pain. I'm beginning to see what she meant."

I saw even more of what she meant when the speaker in my room told me, a few minutes after four, that I had visitors at the nurses' station. It was Liby and Kevin. I kissed Liby and shook hands with Kevin and said they should have taken a rest before they shlepped out here to the hospital. "We can rest later," Liby said. "We wanted to take advantage of the visitors' hours." Kevin just shook hands with me. He was on his way to Seattle for HBO, where they were making a movie, and he would only be able to stay until Wednesday morning.

Liby wore a skirt and blouse and Kevin wore basic golf slacks and shirt. It might be an even hundred out but they weren't going to show up at my hospital looking like a bag lady and a bottle scavenger.

Meeting your wife and son in a Rehab for alcoholics and drug addicts is an uncertain proposition. They're not surprised to find you here because they put you here. You're not proud to be here but at least you're still here, you haven't escaped.

It was just as well that the posted visiting hours were almost over; we wouldn't have known what to do with it if we'd had more than the three quarters of an hour or so we had to kill. I was lucky that Denny and Mac were in the lounge. I'd told Liby so much about them in my letters and phone calls that she probably felt as if she was meeting a couple of men from my company, which she'd been doing ever since my company was Service Co., 307th Infantry, 77th Infantry Division, Army of the United States. Just as she knew the difference between the Literary Guild and the Book-of-the-Month Club, Liby knew that A.U.S. meant the draft army and

U.S.A. meant the regular army. We had been married a long time.

Mac told Liby she was meeting the whole group all at once. "Our group, I mean," he said.

"I know," she said. "I think you're lucky, the three of you being so comfortable with each other. From what Fitz tells me, you never have any trouble finding things to talk about."

"Our only problem," Denny said, "is whose turn it is to talk."

After the lounge, I showed Liby and Kevin the day room with the telephones, the Coke machine and the refrigerator, which activated the inspector in her because she never believes me when I tell her there is food available, she always thinks I make it up to appease her. The Rehab passed; there was even a fresh sheet of brownies sitting there waiting for the evening noshers. Then I showed them the lecture hall and pointed out Debbie's name on the wall and the two rows of chairs next to it that belonged to our group. "This one," I said, pointing to the chair against the wall in the first of our two rows, "is where Father Tim sits, right behind the prettiest girl in the place, Murphy, so he can check to make sure she gets in on time."

Denny had come in behind us. "So he can check to see if she's wearing a proper bra, you mean," he said. "Hey," he said, "excuse me, Liby, but Mary said I should tell you that you left a package on the desk and you shouldn't forget it." The package was a box of Godiva chocolates for me, and we didn't forget it.

After we had safely stowed the candy in my room, I walked them down to the second floor and showed them the chapel. We sat there for a while and tried to talk as though the circumstances weren't as strange as they were. Kevin reminded me that he could only stay Monday and Tuesday, which the counselors had told Liby were the crucial days, and would have to leave at the crack of dawn Wednesday morning for the movie set in Seattle. Movie is a word from my generation; Kevin calls them films.

I already knew that they had told Liby they would like her to stay through Wednesday but that she didn't have to stay for the Thursday and Friday ceremonies which she had already done last summer. I would be glad to be out of the Family Week spotlight and back offstage in our group's private life as soon as possible. I knew I had to go through with it, just as everybody else had to go through it, including Liby and Kevin, but that didn't mean I liked it. The first patient who says he does like it will be awarded the Maureen Dudley Medal, a profile of a man hitting himself over the head with a ball peen hammer.

Downstairs, Liby called the hotel and asked the van to come for them. We went outside to wait for it but the heat drove us back into the lobby and we stayed there until the transportation arrived. We were all glad when it did; nobody knew what to say. We knew we would be seeing each other tomorrow.

I hoped Liby would have, as Denny's mother had had, a powder dry, bitter cold martini before dinner. After all, it wasn't her fault she had married an alcoholic.

Neither life nor love stays the same forever. When you sit on the runway at La Guardia and look across the field at the buildings of Manhattan and wonder why it is you have such a fierce affection for the Empire State and Chrysler Buildings and such simmering anger about the World Trade Center and the Pan Am Building, you know you're getting old. And when the airplane powers up over the Whitestone and the Throgg's Neck Bridges, which weren't there when you were a boy, and gives you a happy look at Yankee Stadium, which was built when you were three years old, you know that nostalgia, like cabbage, can be sweet and sour. The subways, you remember, used to be safe and clean—well, safer and cleaner— and you could buy a little package of two Chiclets for a penny in a machine on the platform, your choice of Dentyne or Spearmint. You could walk with your girl in Central Park at night and you could take her out to dinner and have a drink with her for five bucks. When we went to the theater we used to have two drinks before dinner at Dinty Moore's on West Forty-sixth Street, and then, if we still had time to kill before an eight-thirty curtain, walk across the street to the Circus Bar at the Hotel Piccadilly and have a brandy to add a touch of splendor to what probably was a twenty dollar night out. Times change. So do people. Grand Central Terminal looked better without the Pan Am Building on top of it and I looked better without this plastic hospital bracelet on my wrist.

Denny took me for a walk around the block before dinner. "You've got to remember," he said, "that they're just as nervous as you are. They're sure they did the right thing but they aren't sure you know it and they're not going to breathe easy until you say you do. Take it easy. It's all gonna work out."

I liked the way the day ended. We were sent over to the main hospital cafeteria for dinner, which was fine with me because I could have iced tea to drink with my dinner, which turned out to be a tuna fish casserole on English muffins just like in the Campbell's Soup recipes, and then have a Coke with my dessert. When I made my second trip through the line with a piece of chocolate pie with whipped cream, and the Coke, I asked the woman at the cash register if I owed her anything for the soda.

"You sure don't, honey," she said. "As long as you have that badge on, you don't have to pay for anything in here."

Those motherly types always get to you. I wondered if I could get her to come over Friday morning and make my bed.

14

Calvary

Two of the ubiquitous wives got my Tuesday morning, the day we were to confront our families, off to an appropriate Rehab start. They were standing by the newspaper boxes when we walked toward the door after breakfast. We had left the cafeteria quickly because all I could do was wave at Liby and Kevin anyway and I didn't want to prolong the agony of looking at them across the room pretending to be interested in the scenes of Italy hanging on the walls. The two grass widows looked glum.

"I hadn't seen him since the day we put him in," one of them was saying, "and I'd made up my mind I was going to be every bit as polite and careful as I figured he would be. But then I walked in his room and he had me flat on my back on the bed before he even said hello."

"Jesus," I said when we got outside, "did either of you see Lily Tomlin's one-woman show about the search for signs of intelligent life in the universe? She had a great line in there about what if Andy Warhol was right and everybody will be famous for fifteen minutes, how will there ever be room for us all at Betty Ford's? Now I know the answer. All the leftovers will come to St. Mary's."

This, like D-Day on Guam or the first time I had to present a five-year plan to the Time Inc. board of directors, was one of the days of my years when I had to earn my keep. Except that it was harder than that; it was exposure.

Debbie stayed away from the scheduled Family Week targets in the morning and let Betty-Lou, Mark, and Father Tim talk about their histories. Father Tim kept wanting to pray for Betty-Lou, who was willing to take all the help she could get, and to give Mark absolution despite the fact that as far as the rest of us could see he was more sinned against than a sinner. We all kept hoping we'd hear more about his wife's running around but he was more interested in talking about his fears that his genes were contaminated by a bad seed. It was all diverting enough to kill the morning easily. Then, with the last preliminary over, it was time for the main event.

We arranged ourselves in the lounge opposite our usual meeting room, which Debbie had traded with her friend Charlie Bloss for the occasion because we had so many people. Besides Liby and Kevin, the visitors included Sarah's sister Christine and her two kids, Denise and Ricky, and Doctor Bob's considerable contingent, his wife Casey, two of his daughters, Eleanor and Molly, and Eleanor's husband Garry. So we had nine extras to go with our nine regulars plus Debbie and Bobby Moore, who showed up at the last minute apologizing that they still hadn't assigned him a room for his operation.

I thanked him for the *Times* he brought me and Debbie warned him briefly that she would kill him if he opened his mouth at the wrong time, and to show his good intentions Bobby carried twice as many extra chairs from the bedrooms as anybody else did. Finally, all twenty of us sat down in a large, loose semicircle. It was definitely not the cozy little campfire klatsch you would have chosen for a public confession. But it was the way it was. There was no place to hide. I thought about the townspeople throwing stones at the adulteress in *Zorba*.

When Debbie asked for a volunteer, Doctor Bob said he would read the Thought for the Day. I was sure he had already read it. He gave every word its full measure.

"Two things can spoil group unity—gossip and criticism. To avoid these divisive things, we must realize that we're all in the same boat. We're like a group of people in a lifeboat after the steamer has sunk. If we're going to be saved, we've got to pull together. It's a matter of life or death for us. Gossip and criticism are sure ways of disrupting any AA group. We're all in AA to keep sober ourselves and to help each other to keep sober. And neither gossip nor criticism helps anyone to stay sober."

Maybe that wasn't a threat but it would do, I thought, until one came along. I stole a look at Casey Sommerfield, Doctor Bob's wife, and she looked to me as though she had read him loud and clear and couldn't care less what he thought the rules ought to be. Casey, like Emma Cravath, was holding herself tightly together, but she was more defiant than Emma had been. It was as though she knew there was going to be a war, nothing she might do would stop it, and she didn't intend to lose it. She was dressed in her Sunday best, jewelry and all, and you could see that when Doctor Bob married her she must have been exactly what he had told us she was, the prettiest girl on the block. The young people in the family were dressed for Saturday afternoon shopping and clearly were going to let Mama take the field against the irascible doctor. They were afraid of him; they hardly looked at him.

Sarah's sister Christine was like a class mother at the school picnic. She worried about having enough chairs, about water glasses for everybody who wanted one, and about a sweater for Sarah because the air-conditioning was up pretty high. She didn't complain about anything; she just wanted to help. The son, Ricky, didn't say anything, and the daughter, who looked more like a Denise than a Dinny, held herself stiffly apart from her aunt's ministrations, ready to strike back if she was touched.

Thank God, Liby and Kevin looked about as calm as it's possible to be in such a situation. Denny helped by trading jokes with Kevin, treating him like a card-carrying equal.

Bobby Moore had pushed a small chair into a corner behind Debbie's back.

Now that the play is about to begin, I thought, all the characters assembled onstage and the curtain up, we need a bit of action, a sudden noise or a surprise entrance, something to shatter the tension and make a bold beginning, like a butcher knife slicing the first chop off a roast. I hoped I wasn't going to be the first chop.

"The way we're going to do this," Debbie said, "is for everybody to introduce themselves, and then for each family group to say what they feel about the patient and the events that led to the patient's being here. The patients won't say anything this morning. They'll just listen. Then this afternoon, after lunch, they'll have their chance to say what they think, and after they finish, one family group at a time, we'll have both the patients and the family members ask questions and talk about anything that's on their minds. Tomorrow afternoon and Wednesday afternoon, when you family members will be back here again, we'll try to concentrate on what's going to happen after treatment, on Plan A for the patient's aftercare program and Plan B which will be the fallback if Plan A doesn't work. Now, let's start with the Sommerfield family. Who wants to go first?"

Casey took charge right away. "I'll wait for last," she said. "Why don't you go first, Eleanor? Tell Daddy how we decided to do the intervention."

"Why don't you let her tell me what she wants to tell me?" Doctor Bob broke in. Casey didn't say anything and Eleanor began to talk quickly, like a referee breaking up a clinch. There was nothing rehearsed about her narrative. Her voice carried through the room but never lost a quaver that you felt sure wasn't normal. She was a slender, small young woman and she seemed nervous about being in the same room with her father even with her husband next to her while she told all these strangers the reasons why she had agreed to help kidnap him to St. Mary's. "Because that's what it was," she said, "a kidnapping. There's no use saying it was no different from calling an ambulance in an emergency because it was different. The difference was that he wouldn't have tolerated it and we all knew it. So we were doing it against his will, and I'd never done anything like that before in my whole life."

"Look right at your father," Debbie coached. Eleanor did, but only briefly. As soon as she started to talk again, she looked down at her hands in her lap. "I'm sure that if he'd had a gun in his hands when they were taking him out of the house, he'd have turned it on us right then, right in the living room," she said hoarsely.

"Goddamn right I would," Doctor Bob said.

"Bob," Debbie cautioned.

"Anyway," Eleanor said, "I guess it was the guns that made me willing to go along. I was afraid that you"—this time she shifted in her chair enough to look right at him—"might finally use one of those things like you were always threatening to do. If you got drunk enough, I mean. I knew you would never do it if you were sober, no matter how angry you got, but you were hardly ever sober anymore. It seemed to me it was worse than when you were taking all those pills a couple of years ago. You had less control. So I was afraid you would shoot Mama, or one of us, and then you'd be dreadfully sorry, only it would be too late if somebody was dead or even hurt bad. So I thought this was better." In a final show of spirit, she said, straightening up, "I still think so, Daddy."

"Thank you, baby," Doctor Bob said. "I'm sorry I caused you so much unhappiness."

"Daddy," Molly said, "I think that's all any of us want to hear, that you are sorry and that you know we had reason to be upset and scared. I wish you would forgive us for the intervention. We did it for you as much as for us. Will you forgive us, Daddy?"

"No," Bob said. "I will certainly never forgive Casey. She doesn't believe me, but some day, so help me God, I will get even."

Molly watched as her sister began to cry. She held out until she tried to speak again, and then she began to cry, too. "I think there are a lot of things you ought to be sorry for," she said. "Some of those parties you used to have at the summer place were pretty hard on us when we were getting bigger. I don't think you ever stopped to consider how much we hated having all those stewed friends of yours running around our house every night at dinner-time. I remember once we were all swimming in the pool and that doctor friend of yours you'd brought up from the hospital was all over me in the pool like white on rice. I was scared, but I was even more scared of complaining about it to you. Having a good time with your friends was more important to you than worrying about us." She reached for more Kleenex. "I still love you, Daddy," she said, "but you've got to stop drinking like that."

Casey began by looking at the rest of us before she looked at her husband, but she included him in her general statement. "Please excuse me," she said, "if I don't cry." Her recitation was dry of tone as well as of eye. It wasn't exactly memorized but it had certainly been carefully thought out. She traced their times together from college days on, she blamed herself equally for liking to drink more than was good for them, and she said she was convinced they would never have had a chance to put things back together if they hadn't done the intervention. "The night we had to call the cops was the last straw for me," she said. She explained to the rest of us what had happened. "Eleanor and Garry had been home with me for most of the afternoon," she said, "when Molly came in and asked if she could borrow my car to go to a couple of stores. Molly doesn't live with us; she has her own apartment. I said my car was in the garage for some work. Eleanor and Garry said she could have their car if she knew she would be back soon, because they had to leave in half an hour or so, but Molly said she would use Daddy's car if it was here. I said it was, he was upstairs watching television or reading, so Molly took the keys off the table in the hall and went out. Bob came down an hour or so later, after Eleanor and Garry had gone, and had a fit when he found out Molly had taken his car. He didn't even want to go out, he was just mad that she'd taken it without asking him. He went back upstairs about as mad as I'd ever seen him. Then, when Molly came back, he came rushing downstairs with a shotgun in his arms and pointed it right at the two of us. I thought he was going to kill us both right then and there."

"I should have," Bob said.

Casey stared him down. "You don't mean that," she said.

"No, I don't," he said. "I wanted to do exactly what I did do, scare the pants off all of you. But you had to go and call the cops."

The cops had taken Doctor Bob off to the station and had kept
him in a cell overnight. The longer they kept him there, the angrier
he got, and then they were afraid to let him out. So he stayed there
until morning when Casey finally came and got him. She let him
off at the house, where his car was standing in the driveway, and
then drove off and spent the day with some friends. When she
finally went back home, she found him in his den, dead drunk.
"He stayed drunk until we did the intervention," she said, clear-
eyed to the last.

Sarah's family, diametrically opposite, told a story of sadness, the
patient as victim instead of villain, the drinking seen as a narcotic
taken to dull her own pain and not as a one-woman carnival or a
virago's revenge. Sarah was a worm that had turned with a silent
strike to the heart of the family's complacency, a complacency
which she felt was built on her submissiveness and at her expense.
It was clear, as she talked slowly but passionately when Debbie
suggested she explain how it had started, that she had begun to
see herself as the household drudge taken for granted by everybody
and never considered as a person with her own wants and needs.
  "Nobody really needed me," she said softly. "They just needed
things done, and I was the one who did them. Even my mother
didn't need me except to sit and watch the soaps with her in the
afternoon and bring her a cup of tea when she wanted it. So I began
to drink some of the wine I kept in the house for cooking, and I
liked it, so then I started buying wine for drinking. I liked that
even better, and I hid a half gallon of it in the broom closet behind
the brooms and mops that nobody ever went near except me, anyway, and I put a regular bottle of it in the cupboard right next to
the cooking wine and just replaced it whenever it got low. After a
while I decided it would be a good idea to have another half gallon
in the basement, so it was never hard for me to get to some if I felt
like it.
  "How did you drink it?" Debbie asked. "Right out of the bottle?"
  "Oh, no," Sarah said. "I kept a juice glass in the pocket of my
apron and I'd use that for a glassful when I was moving around

the house. When I was in the kitchen I just drank it out of my water glass."

"How much wine do you think you were drinking?" Debbie asked.

"I don't know," Sarah said. "I only replaced one of the half gallons once a week, hardly ever more than that, but I probably bought two or even three of the smaller bottles." She seemed almost proud. "I drank quite a lot of it," she said. "I pretty much stopped drinking water."

She had looked so bad when we first saw her that the group had always had trouble believing that she hadn't been drinking anything except wine. Doctor Bob asked the question we'd all wondered about. "Are you sure," he asked, "you didn't have a bottle of vodka stashed somewhere?"

"Oh, my goodness, no," Sarah said. "Wine was all I ever drank. I liked the taste of it."

"Well, didn't any of the rest of you notice that she was acting different?" Denny asked.

Denise spoke up defensively. "I've asked myself that a million times," she said, "but I know I didn't. She might have seemed a little slower about everything, but you don't think about that when it's happening except maybe to wonder if Mama isn't extra tired lately. You don't suddenly, after all those years, ask yourself if she isn't drinking too much."

All of them, sister Christine and the two kids, said Sarah had never been known to drink more than her share at any of the family outings or holiday dinners. She would always have a glass or two of wine but she never reached for more or asked why didn't they get another bottle or anything like that. They simply were unprepared for this sudden switch to steady drinking.

"The reason you family members didn't notice anything," Debbie said, "was undoubtedly because Sarah stayed at the same level of drunkenness all the time. She got herself into a sustaining mode and she just kept drinking enough to stay there pretty much all the time."

Sarah giggled. "I even used to put some of that rosé wine in my water pitcher when I went over to sit with Mama in the afternoon," she said, "so by the time I went back home to start cooking dinner I had a nice buzz on."

She had really put one over on all of them.

Until the morning she fell out of bed. That was when the balloon blew up. "I didn't feel too good when I went to bed," Sarah said, "and I got up once to see if I had to throw up. The room was moving, and I felt weak. But nothing came up, so I went back to bed. Then the next thing I knew I had hit the floor and there was a lot of noise and the lights came on and Dinny was trying to lift me up. My back hurt. My head, too. And I was very sick to my stomach."

"I couldn't even get her to the bathroom in time," Denise said. "I was scared to death because she was as white as a sheet of paper and she wasn't making a sound. I thought she was either dead or dying. I called the ambulance on 911 and just started to pray. Thank God, they got there fast."

"I never knew anything about it," Christine said, "until the ambulance came. I would have been glad to go to the hospital with Sarah, but Denise didn't want me to. She said it would be better if I stayed home with Mama."

"I had everything under control," Denise said. "After all, I do work in the hospital. I see things like this every day."

"Well, you're never going to see me like that again," Sarah said fervently. "Never. I'm so grateful for this place I don't know how to tell it. But when I get home I'm not even going to keep a bottle of cooking wine in the house. I'm never going to go through this again. It's all over."

"It may be all over for you, Mother," Denise said, "but it will never be over for me."

That turned it over to the Fitzgeralds. I noticed with relief that it was a few minutes past two-thirty, and even if Debbie let the meeting run on a little later than three, the chances were I'd get away with less time devoted to me than either Doctor Bob or Sarah had

had. That might not have been the proper attitude but it was the attitude I had. Let's get it over with.

Liby began to cry almost as soon as she began to talk. She apologized, she said she had sworn she wouldn't, but there it was. She told our history as she knew it and felt it, all the long years of marriage, the traveling, the jobs with lavish entertainment, the splendid restaurants, the day-in-and-day-out drinking. "I like to drink, too," she said, "but Fitz is different. It's as though he has to drink or he can't function. Then, when he drinks too much, he can't function anyway. One trouble is, he never eats. I mean, he eats like a bird. Meanwhile, he's drinking everything in sight and there's no food in him to help keep him going. When he got older, it just all came apart. Somehow, when he was younger, he could get by. But now he just can't do it anymore. But he tries to. And if you tell him not to drink, or to try to drink less, he gets mad. It's been worse since he retired. I suppose he feels left out, not needed anymore, he misses all the excitement of his wonderful job. Anyway, for the last four or five years, he's been getting steadily worse." Liby made a dent in the Kleenex box but she was going to get it all said no matter what. I wished she didn't have to do it. This was not what she was best at.

"He always drank too much," she said, "but so did just about everybody else he worked with. The sportswriters all drank all the time, and it was so easy for them, people were always giving it to them. The press box and the press room and the complimentary tables at race tracks and restaurants were all part of the business. Then it wasn't much different in the book business, when he changed jobs. There were lunches and parties all the time. Drinking was part of the life. It wasn't so bad when he was younger. He seemed to be able to stand it better. And he worked hard, and he was successful, so it was hard to tell him he couldn't drink so much. But I remember way back in the fifties he fell down a flight of stairs when we were leaving a theater and he didn't wake up until he found himself on the floor of the men's room where somebody had carried him. I didn't even know where he was for a long time. I

was frantic. Then I had to take him home in a taxi and take care
of him like he was a baby.

"God knows what happened when I wasn't with him. But he got
drunk lots of times when I was with him. He'd fall asleep right at
the table. I can remember twice he did it at New Year's Eve parties,
black-tie dinners, and I could have died with embarrassment. I was
so ashamed for him.

"He was usually pretty good at dinners where he was working.
He would wait until after to drink all he wanted. Then I would have
to look after him. I can't think how many dinners I had to drive
home from because even he knew he was in no condition to drive.
Considering the number of nights he did drive us home from the
city after he'd been drinking at lunch and at dinner, it's a miracle
nothing terrible ever happened.

"Things began to get worse when the doctor told him, a couple
of years before he retired, that his liver was getting bad. First, he
made him stop drinking for thirty days. Then, when it got better,
Fitz went right back to drinking as much as ever. Then it got bad
again, and he had to stop again. This time he was supposed to stop,
period. But instead he began to hide it and lie about it. I hated that.
He never used to lie to me about anything and now he was lying
all the time. And the drinking was worse. I'm sure that hiding it,
and drinking straight out of the bottle, or gulping down a few quick
drinks at a bar when he could grab the chance, he drank more
than he ever had. And his body couldn't take it anymore. It made
me feel very sad.

"Then there was the DWI, when Kevin and I had to go pick him
up at the jail because they had taken his license and he couldn't
drive his car home, and there were two five-day detoxes in a hospital
in Port Chester, and finally last year coming here. Now, here again.

"I don't know what else to say," Liby said, crying freely now,
"except what I've already told him. If it doesn't change, if he doesn't
stop, I can't live with him anymore. One of us is going to have to
leave home."

Kevin cried, too. He didn't finish the first sentence before his
voice broke. "I didn't want to come," he said, "but I didn't want

not to come even more. It's hard to see Dad like this, although it's easier than it was to see him the way he was at home before he came here. I don't know what to say except that I always looked up to him, I always respected him, this was the man who could make anything happen, and then it all changed when he began to drink so much.

"I was told to think of some specific examples of bad times," Kevin said.

"Look at your father," Debbie said. "Talk right to him."

"So I tried to remember some," Kevin told me, "and I thought right away about that dinner we had before Christmas last year at the Cafe Argenteuil, you and Mom and Linda and me. You came in a little late and it was obvious that you'd been drinking. Mom said she wasn't sure but your speech patterns were off and your words were a little slurred and you were more intense about everything than you would have been if you'd been sober. Later, after we'd eaten, it was even more obvious that you'd been drinking. You were tired, and your eyes were blinking a lot, and everybody was so worried about you it wasn't much of a Merry Christmas dinner.

"But the worst was Christmas itself. You kept disappearing into the garage and coming back without anything in your hands, no wood for the fireplace or anything at all that I could see, so I went out and took a look and found an empty vodka bottle in the trash basket. By the time we sat down to dinner it didn't make any difference that all you had at your place was a glass of Coke, you were pretty drunk already. It made me feel terrible for you, first that you had to do it, and second that you had to sneak it. It's hard to keep your respect for your father under those conditions." I thought he was finished but then he said, "And now I've got something else to worry about, maybe it's hereditary."

Kevin wasn't crying anymore but I felt like crying. I sat there wondering how I had managed to get myself into this disaster. It was beginning to feel as though I hadn't had a Lost Weekend, I'd had a Lost Decade. I remembered Eileen saying, the day I told her I'd begun to drink again and I didn't see any reason why I shouldn't, that she wouldn't be able to leave me alone with her little baby girl anymore. I put that together with what Kevin had just finished saying and I didn't want to be alone with me either.

I saw them for a minute in the lobby afterward, waiting for the van to take them back to the hotel. Denny and Mac and I were on our way out for a walk. We didn't say much. I hoped they would have a good dinner and I said that because Kevin was going on to the Coast early Wednesday morning, and we wouldn't be able to have the regular Family Week dinner together on Thursday night, they ought to ask Debbie if we could go out tomorrow night instead. Liby said she would ask her. Kevin said he would like that, and Debbie came through with a pass for me before she went home.

We didn't do a whole lot of talking on our walk. Mac said he wasn't looking forward to his confrontation with his son next week. "They really know how to hurt you," he said. And Denny wanted to make me feel better but didn't know how. "What it all comes down to," I said, "is that I can't drink anymore. I wish I could say I would only drink a little bit, but I know I can't. It's easier for me if I don't drink at all. Drinking one drink just makes me want more. So that's how it's got to be when I get home. No booze, ever. Period."

That was easier to decide than the question of whether or not Liby should drink. The counselors had told her to clean out all the liquor in the house and to stop drinking herself, and that was pretty much all she thought about while she and Kevin were going to their meetings Tuesday morning. We could talk about it tonight. I was free from five o'clock until nine and that was plenty of time to get around to everything I wanted to talk about, which pretty much came down to how I wanted to say I was sorry. I thought about the old song, "What can I do to prove it to you I'm sorry?" Not much, I had to admit. Nothing a drinker promises means anything except a day of not drinking, and then another day of not drinking, and then the hope of another day and still more days to come.

I had taken Liby to a fine old Minneapolis downtown restaurant, Murray's, last summer, so I thought we would try something different this time and I made a reservation for the three of us at the place Denny had gone with Emma, Anthony's Wharf, in St. Anthony's Main, a Ghirardhelli Square-South Street Seaport kind of restoration on the riverfront. I took a taxi from the Rehab to the hotel and had a Coke with them there while we watched the CBS News in Liby's room, and then we took another cab to the restaurant. A friendly young woman gave us a table by a window looking out over the Mississippi, even narrower there than it is behind the hospital, and we had as pleasant a dinner as a family could hope to have with an inmate on a four-hour pass.

I was glad that Liby had a glass of white wine before dinner. I would rather she had ordered a martini but at least the white wine seemed to be saying that she hadn't bought the Rehab's argument that she should quit entirely. We talked about it for a while because Kevin said quietly that he thought she ought to stop. He said he thought it was going to be too hard on me if she drank every night before dinner while I was trying to stick to Coke. I said it was exactly the other way around. I felt I had caused enough trouble already, and if I had to be responsible for her not drinking, too, I'd just be more miserable. It wouldn't help, I said, it would hurt. Kevin didn't make a federal case out of it; he had said what he wanted to say. So had I, and Liby said she would go along with what I wanted, which was not only that she should drink whatever she wanted to whenever she wanted to but also that we would keep right on serving drinks to our friends just as we always had. Then we talked about Kevin's trip and about the work he was doing on his house and about how lucky I had been to fall among Denny and Mac, not to mention Debbie, and what a great place St. Mary's is—and this fish isn't bad, either.

We didn't see a single boat on the river, nor any kids flying kites on the riverbank. But we ignored our cholesterol and calorie problems and had ice cream for dessert, and then we took a cab back to the Holiday Inn. I kept the cab, because there wasn't any point in going upstairs for fifteen minutes, and I said good night to them there. The last time I had done it was probably when he was two years old but I put my arm around Kevin and kissed him on the cheek.

All three of us knew it was a promise.

Arlene Larson took my blood pressure when I walked past the

station at a quarter of nine. It was one fourteen over seventy-four. I slept well. The last thing I remember is hitting a five iron over the water on the ninth hole and watching the ball hit the bank safely and roll halfway up to the green. It wasn't on, but it was close. A wee chip and a putt was all I needed. It was a good time to fall asleep.

15

The Hardest One to
Forgive Is Yourself

St. Mary must have been looking out for me despite my long-standing condition of dues nonpayment because the morning lecture was Helen Griffith's justly famous talk on spirituality, which was just what I needed. Helen is a handsomely weathered, gray-haired former nun with a birdlike quickness to her movements and a motherly personality that warmly embraces everybody she's talking to. I wondered what she was going to do with the big tape deck she carefully placed on the stage and I quietly applauded the folksiness with which she sat herself down next to it, arranging her skirt underneath her for comfort and looking out at us like a Campfire Girl Leader getting ready for a sing-along. But her voice was serious and her message intense. She talked first about religion, which is almost always certain to turn me off and make me resentful of this invasion of my privacy, but Helen was easy to listen to and, in spite of myself, I decided to give her a chance. I could always tune her out and think about something else if things got tough.

"I remember being cracked over the knuckles with the steel edge of a metal ruler when I was a kid in grammar school," she said, "by a nun who was angry at me for not knowing what nine times nine was. But I've learned since that you can't use an instance like that to put down all religion or religious people. Acts like that, no matter how well intentioned, have nothing to do with religion or with spirituality.

"Religion is the belief in God as a supernatural being, and the formal worship of God as a supernatural being.

"Spirituality has to do with a person's soul. Spirituality has to do with a person's spirit. It has to do with my relationship with myself, with other people, and with the God of my understanding."

Helen said that when alcoholism begins to chisel and chip away at you, it works first on the spiritual side. She said spirituality is the first thing to go and the last thing to return. The first clues you get, before the tremors and the swollen livers and the other physical manifestations, are the behavioral changes in the addict. He or she isn't the same person anymore. So the first need is to rebuild that person's spirituality. There is a lot more involved than just removing the chemicals.

"If one word can be wrapped like a blanket around the whole recovery process," she said, "it would be surrender. Surrender is the key. I know to most people, including most people in this room, surrender has a negative aspect. It implies giving up, quitting, sometimes even imprisonment, but that's not the kind of surrender I'm talking about. I mean surrender in a positive sense. There needs to be a surrender to powerlessness and unmanageability. First you deny it, then you're angry about it, and finally you give up, you surrender."

That reminded me of Polly McCall, my counselor at Freedom Institute, telling me that nobody goes to the treatment center voluntarily, they go because they've finally realized that the jig is up, there's no place else to go, nothing else to do. One thing is sure, you've proved that you can't do it by yourself.

Helen said that she tells the families of the patients that they have to accept the fact that they cannot control what the patient is going to do about drinking alcohol, shooting up, popping pills, smoking dope, or whatever it is they do. You tried as hard as you could to get them to stop, and you failed. You've learned that the Serenity Prayer is right; you must accept the things you cannot change.

"I tell them that doesn't take anything away from their love," Helen said, "but it puts the responsibility back on the patient and it frees them to do what they have to do to take care of themselves. Last year six people I worked with closely returned to using, and died. If that should happen to your families, at least they'll be free to do what they need to do for themselves. They must surrender to their powerlessness to manage the dependent person's life. You, the recovering dependents, have to do that for yourselves."

Helen really got to me when she said that you can't erase anything you did or said in the terrible times of the struggle against dependency, everything happened exactly the way it happened. But you can forgive yourself, and it is absolutely crucial that you do. You've got to stop running from the pain, the shame, the guilt, and the ugliness. You have to admit it, accept it, and forgive it.

"The hardest thing I've ever had to do in my life," she said, hugging her knees tightly, "was to admit that I, Helen, good, kind, gentle Helen, when I was drunk, was capable of anything. I had to deal with that. Self-forgiveness is absolutely crucial. It's the key to all the rest of it."

Wasn't that what Mac had been talking about? He had to find a way to forgive himself for what he had done to his wife because she wasn't here anymore to forgive him herself.

"It frees me," Helen said, "to accept the forgiveness of others, and it frees me to forgive others. You can't carry the past around like a great big boulder on your back." She made the sensible point that forgiving is not forgetting. "You probably will never be able to forget all the bad things you did when you were drinking or using drugs but you can forgive yourself and you have to do it." She went back to the point that the family members were not responsible for their person's chemical use. "Maybe," she said, "some of them have found out here that they're a candidate for the Gold Star Enabler of the Year Award, but they are not responsible for what the user did. They did the very best they could."

I thought that must be a comforting message to the family members struggling downstairs with their own guilt and their own despair, but it's an important message for us up here, too. As tempting as it is to blame somebody else for what we did, we're the ones who did it.

I was less attentive when Helen talked about how much AA had meant to her, but I liked what she said about how important the fellowship was to her, and it reinforced my belief that for people who are more gregarious than I am, more comfortable talking in groups, it's probably a great help. "AA," Helen said, "is a tool, an important tool that you can use to help make things work and grow for you. It will help you cultivate the kind of sobriety that will be deep and lasting."

I was as eager as everybody else to applaud when she finished by asking herself, "What kind of God will take me the way I am right now? The God of Love, of Mercy, of Understanding, the God who will give me the strength to live this day without drinking."

She turned to the tape recorder and told us that she wanted to play for us a song she had heard on her car radio the first day she went back to work after her time in the treatment center. "I said to myself, 'My God, this is the story of my life, this is what happened to me.'" And she turned up the volume to let us hear Judy Collins' rich, powerful folksinger's voice wash over us like falling rain:

> "Amazing grace, how sweet the sound
> That saved a wretch like me.
> I once was lost but now I'm found,
> Was blind, but now I see."

I took Judy's voice to group with me. It was a good way to begin the last day of my Family Week. I felt I was ready for whatever it might bring.

Luckily, the first thing it brought Mac and me when we walked around the building after Helen's lecture was a good laugh contributed by two women talking together on the sidewalk in front of the Rehab. "Well," the first one said, "you know what my mother said in the group meeting yesterday? She said I had no right to complain about her taking so many pills. 'I'm entitled to those pills,' she said. 'I'm under a doctor's care.' I said, 'Mother, you're under three doctors' care. Do they know about each other?' "

Another day in the Rehab. Kevin was gone, flying off to the West Coast, and there was only one round to go in my painfully public struggle over what to do with the rest of my life. Tomorrow, Liby would be gone, too. In fact, the last I would see of her would be at group this afternoon. Then, the day after tomorrow, Denny would be gone, and Mac and I would have to make it together the rest of the way. But first there was the rest of today to get through.

It turned out to be easier than I had thought. Debbie had had to make a major change in our Family Week schedules because Father Tim's twin sister, a prominent Catholic educator named Sister Mary Carlotta, had shown up unexpectedly and had to be fitted into our plans right now. That, Father Tim had insisted, meant that his best friend, Father Hugh Behrens, also had to be invited into the center ring of the coliseum. Debbie figured she could get them started this morning and finish with them tomorrow, when Liby would be gone. So our morning Group was completely taken up by an exquisitely polite but uncompromisingly determined unpeeling, layer by artichoke layer, of the lifelong hostility between Tim and his sister. I had said that St. Mary's was a gold mine of material for a writer but when I said it I hadn't known about these two. Father Tim versus Sister Mary Carlotta was an extra added attraction, an unadvertised preview. Whether it was a preview of heaven, hell, or the nothingness that I was convinced was all that there was, I didn't know. But I was captivated by the correct bitterness of this Roman ballet, a pas de deux performed with wine that had been kept in the decanter so long it had turned to vinegar.

"I'm grateful for this opportunity to get to know my brother better," Sister Mary Carlotta said when Debbie asked her if she had anything she wanted to say.

"I'm glad you are," Father Tim said.

"Oh, stop it, Tim," Debbie said. "You just think you have to play the curmudgeon. But you don't. You're among friends."

"Well, I know I feel that I am," Sister Mary Carlotta said brightly. "It's such a lucky thing I had come to see some people in Minneapolis, and was planning to go see Tim while I was here. That's how I found out where he was. If I was back home, I probably never would have known."

"That would have been a shame," Tim said. Debbie glared at him but he looked perfectly comfortable with the way things were going.

Debbie conducted a brief reconstruction of the histories of the two protagonists. Father Tim had been a parish priest all of his adult life, and his sister, who was a twin but not identical, had been as much of a success story as a Catholic nun could dream of. She had begun as a grammar school teacher, had quickly risen to principal of the school, and then moved on to the administration levels of the city's parochial school system. She had been the superintendent of schools for twelve years before reaching the mandatory retirement age of sixty-five. Then, the week after her retirement dinner, only last month, she had been offered and had quickly accepted the job of supervisor of curricula for the parochial schools of the third largest city west of the Arkansas River. She was too good to lose, and to Father Tim, who had never won, that carried the taste of gall. Her presence among his inquisitors at this show trial of his failures as man and priest was a lash he had not expected to be asked to bear.

"Nobody has even bothered to tell me how you got here," Father Tim complained. You could see that he hated to appear childish but he wasn't going to lend his imprimatur to her unwanted presence, either.

"I invited her," Debbie said. "Monsignor Saltzman told me Sister was in Minneapolis. She had called the rectory and found out you had left, so she called him to ask how she could get in touch with you. I called her and asked if she would be willing to come for Family Week."

"You might have asked me," Father Tim said. "It may not be my week but it is my family."

"You would only have said no," Debbie said. "I decided Sister Mary Carlotta might be able to help us see your problems more clearly and work through them. You asked your friend Father Beh-

rens to come, and I asked Sister Mary Carlotta to come. We're even."
Debbie gave him her warmest we're-all-in-this-together smile. Father Tim didn't smile back.

Father Behrens decided it was time to get into the game. He was a retired priest whose parish had been twenty miles from Tim's and who had been his frequent dinner, traveling, and drinking companion. After he retired he had moved into a condominium in Tim's parish, and their friendship had deepened. When Tim was sick, or went on a trip, Father Behrens filled in for him. It made Tim's life easier that he didn't have to apply to the diocesan office, specifically to Monsignor Saltzman, the bishop's right-hand man, for a substitute when he couldn't say Mass himself.

"With all due respect, Father Behrens," Sister Mary Carlotta said, "you were an enabler. It didn't do my brother any good to know that any time he was too sick to say Mass you would take over without any fuss. It would have been better for him if he hadn't been able to hide from the bishop's office the fact that he couldn't perform his duties. If they had known about it, they might have done something a lot sooner than they did."

"There you go," Father Tim said, "making judgments from a thousand miles away. What does a nun know about a priest's duties and obligations anyway?"

Now we were getting somewhere. Father Tim thought nuns should be seen, preferably working, and not heard. He thought Vatican Council II and the women's movement were both abominations and that the assertive, pushy nun was the epitome of both. Tim, who stood ready to defend his church's traditional stations of the cross against all the modernists who wanted to get rid of them along with the Latin ordinary of the Mass, would gladly have created a new station to accommodate the suffering of the modern nun, street clothes, Coach bag and all.

Nothing pleased Tim more than the knowledge that the most successful nun, embodied by his sister, complete with expensive clothes paid for by her respectful order and all the badges of office awarded her by church and state alike, had no money in that genuine leather bag hanging stylishly from her shoulder. "They don't let them accumulate money, you know," he had told me with no noticeable sadness. "Whenever they want something that costs money, they have to get somebody else to pay for it. That's why I don't invite my sister as often as she would like me to. I would have to pay for it."

Sister Mary Carlotta wasn't ready to forgive Tim for not inviting her to the twenty-fifth anniversary of his ordination. "I really felt left out," she said. "I didn't see how you could invite a church full of strangers and not invite your own sister. And me a nun, part of the church myself."

It was painfully obvious that Sister Mary Carlotta had provided the answer to her own question. It was exactly because she was a nun that Father Tim hadn't invited her. There was such a thing as knowing your place.

Maybe, I thought, if she had volunteered to supervise the catering and serving of the luncheon that followed the anniversary Mass, Tim would have been glad to have had her do it.

Sister did not do a lot of suffering in silence. She even complained that, when she was a guest in his rectory, and he made drinks for them, he would pour less than half as much whiskey into her glass as he did into his. That was too much for Tim. "Oh, for heaven's sake," he said, "all you had to do was say you wanted more. Now, you know that. Talk about a no-win situation. First, I'm too free with the whiskey, now I'm too stingy with it."

"My point," Sister said, "is that you were always afraid you wouldn't get enough."

That reminded me of Tim's story about the nun who, as the principal of the high school, was invited by the bishop to accompany him to the annual diocesan awards dinner. She was terrified that she would make a fool of herself by doing the wrong thing but her friends counseled her to just follow the bishop's lead and do whatever he did. So, she drank martinis before dinner when the bishop did, drank wine with dinner when he did, and had a brandy after dinner when he did. When they offered the bishop a second brandy, he declined politely. "No, thank you," he said, "if I have another one I'll feel it." When they offered the nun another, she also declined. "No," she said, "thank you, but if I have another one, I'll let him."

It's too bad, I thought, that Father Tim can't see Sister Mary Carlotta, or whatever her real name is, as his sister instead of as Sister. Nuns just don't get very far inside Father Tim's door unless they're carrying food and drink for him and his friends or mops and brooms to clean up afterward.

"They don't work the way they used to," he said, making a general observation about the nuns in his parish convent. "They used to take care of the altar and the vestments and all that kind of thing, but no more. They stopped that when they put on the short skirts."

"All they do now is teach?" I asked.

"Even that is questionable much of the time," he said.

"You see how terrible he is?" Sister said, almost fondly. "Thank God for Family Week. If it hadn't been for this, I would never have been heard."

Tim never conceded that he drank himself into a lazy stupor every day. He began by saying that he probably drank more than he ought to, and ended up by admitting that he had gotten to the point where he would be annoyed if somebody wanted him to do something right after Mass when he had planned to take his ease in his living room with a bottle of good scotch whiskey. He had denial in capital letters.

I asked him how he had managed to buy all the liquor he needed in such a small town without attracting unwelcome attention, but he said he didn't buy much there. "I used to drive out in the country and buy it by the case," he said. "I hardly ever bought it in the same place more than once or twice a year. And a few of my parishioners who knew what I liked to drink would give me a case at Christmas or something like that."

"Like the Fourth of July?" I suggested.

Father Tim wasn't offended. "Or Groundhog Day," he said.

The morning went a lot faster than the afternoon did, but even that wasn't so bad. We talked about plans for after-care, and both Debbie and her boss Maureen Dudley, who sat in on that discussion, were satisfied with my promise that I would do whatever

Freedom Institute asked me to do. "As long," I said, "as it doesn't involve more than one AA meeting a week."

"But if they ask you to do one," Debbie said, pressing the point, "you'll do it."

"I'll do it," I said.

"I don't know how much good it will do you," Maureen said, "if your mind is made up in advance that you're going to hate it."

"I don't either," I said. "I'm just promising to do what I'm told. I'm not promising to like it."

Maureen said she thought my biggest problem was that I was bored. My life, she said, had been so interesting when I was working that I didn't know what to do now except drink. It was the only part of my old life that I could still have. Now it was up to me to make a new life. I couldn't just avoid life the way some people do, by sleeping all the time, or watching one soap opera after another or one football or basketball or baseball game after another. And I was probably the wrong sex to go shopping all the time. So, if I couldn't avoid reality, I had to make a new reality that I could be happy with. If I didn't, I might think myself into a state of depression and drink myself to death out of despair. It seemed to me that she was telling me I had better find some work to do.

I'd had a lot of respect for Maureen ever since I first heard her in the lecture hall. I thought she had had a lot of guts to tell the largely hostile audience of nervous inmates that the Family Week they were dreading was her idea. When the St. Mary's program first began they used to have the family members in one day a week, on Tuesday. "Terrible Tuesday, we called it," Maureen said. "If there were ten members in the group and they all had one or two family members come in on Tuesday, it was a zoo. Nobody got to say much of anything. Then I saw a Family Week program working at Heart View in Mandan, South Dakota, and I borrowed the idea lock, stock, and barrel. It had shown me how bad ours was, and I wanted the best. Being a teacher, I thought I could do it even better than they did. I talked one of our senior counselors into working with me on it right from the beginning, when we had only two families a week. Now it involves everybody, and it works. It isn't easy for anybody, neither the patient nor the families, but they become aware of how they've hurt each other, it all gets laid out, and you can't change what you're not aware of."

Hazelden, Maureen said, does it differently. "Their family program doesn't provide any interaction between patient and family member. Maybe they think by keeping them apart they're keeping them from killing each other, I don't know. All I know is that ours is painful, but it works. Probably because, as I like to keep saying, it shows the patient that he hasn't got a corner on the pain. There's plenty to go around."

Bringing it back to me, and maybe to Mac, Maureen said that Family Week shows there is more despair among the older patients than among the younger. "It's harder," she said, "to heal the accumulation of so many years of pain and suffering." That's why they wait until the third week to bring the warring parties together. At first, the older patient just wants peace and quiet. That's why he drank, I thought.

"But when they leave," she said with her tough confidence, "they have new expectations." I thought she was telling me I'd better have them, or else. I liked her. She made me reach back and take out and examine some of the new strength Debbie had been building in me. I told her what I had told Deb; I would get back to work and I would do whatever Freedom Institute told me to do.

I liked her last words. "Don't be too penitent or too obedient," she said. "Be yourself."

I decided that if Jay Hauge was the Lou Holtz of St. Mary's, Maureen was the Bobby Knight.

Liby was glad that I was willing to put myself in Freedom Institute's hands. She knew I trusted Connie Murray, the director, as implicitly as she did, and she was willing to quit while she was ahead. I think we both knew that afternoon that the time at St. Mary's had come to an end. She was quiet; she didn't have anything more to say. When a family counselor sat in for a while toward the end of the afternoon, she said to Liby, out of the blue, "You're really afraid of him, aren't you?" Liby said yes and let it go at that. I didn't. When I saw the counselor later I said, "You've got it all wrong. She doesn't placate me. I'm the one who placates her." The counselor looked like a UN negotiator who has been unfairly accused of tilting toward Israel. It took me a couple of months to understand that I had missed the point. Those counselors aren't dumb, just patient.

I was sorry, when we were breaking up and Liby was explaining that she was flying home early in the morning, that Sarah's family looked more awkward and even angrier than ever, but I was glad that Doctor Bob's gang was kissing enthusiastically and behaving in general as though happy days were here again. Maybe for them the skies above were clear again. Father Tim and Sister Mary Carlotta, I decided whimsically, needed a good stiff drink. Father Tim had told me he had invited her out to dinner on Pass Night, tomorrow night, and I told him it would be good for both of them if he would order her a scotch on the rocks while he had his Diet Coke. He said something that sounded roughly like "*Et cum spiritu tuo,*" but it might have been "Up yours."

It hadn't been a bad day. It hadn't been a bad week. I said goodbye to Liby when she got into the van to go back to the hotel and to dinner alone. Whose fault was it that she had to eat dinner alone tonight and fly back to New York alone tomorrow? There is no prize for the correct answer; the prizes were all given out long ago and the trouble was I didn't know what to do with mine after I unwrapped it.

Once Liby left it all seemed like weekend to me, a weekend two days too long. Thursday, Liby flew home. Friday, Denny and John left. Saturday and Sunday, I tried to program what I would do with the week that was left. Walk a lot, I decided, and read a lot. Finish Nora, anyway. Write some journal notes about what had happened here so I would never forget it.

I didn't want to forget that Father Martin had said the heaviest drinkers tended to be left-handed Irishmen. That made me feel secure. I'm right-handed all the way.

And I didn't want to forget the nurse who told us that one of her patients had complained that he thought he had become an alcoholic because his mother hadn't nursed him when he was a baby.

"So," she said, "I asked him what he thought would be useful therapy for him here."

I would be glad to have my journal, and to keep adding thoughts to it, when I got back into the real world without Debbie to hold my hand and watch out for me anymore.

Denny looked more than ready for his reentry when he appeared in blue blazer and gray flannel slacks for his medallion ceremony Friday morning, fresh from his Fifth Step. Even John looked like a cabin boy carefully turned out for Captain's Mast. They both said the last ritual of the St. Mary's calendar hadn't been so bad. Especially for non-Catholics, the idea of a full and complete confession sounds terrifying, and no matter how many times the counselors say it isn't confession it still sounds like confession. "And if it sounds like confession," Dr. Bob said, "and you have to tell all your sins like they do in confession, then it's probably confession." But Denny, who told us immediately what it had felt like, said it was more like being urged by your best friend to open up and tell him exactly what had happened.

"What happened where?" Mark, who was confused about where his problems were centered, wanted to know.

"I guess that's the point," John said unexpectedly. "It was about what happened anywhere."

For a change, Father Tim didn't say anything. Confession was his business and he wasn't working here.

Debbie reached for her medallions. "It's always a mixture of feelings when people we've all come to love leave the group," she said. "You're glad for them but you hate to lose them. Denny and John have, in their own very different ways, meant so much to the group that it's hard to imagine us without them."

"It's not that hard," Doctor Bob said.

"Yes, it is," Debbie said. "I'll bet Ed, who is better with words than I am, will be able to express it more clearly, but the plain fact is that when we meet for group this afternoon we're going to start out by waiting until Denny and John get here, only they're not going to come, and then suddenly we're going to be glad. Glad that they came here, needing help so badly, and glad that they left healthy and happy. Well, a lot healthier and a good deal happier. That's how I feel, Denny, passing this medallion, which you've so richly earned, around the circle of your friends, until it comes back to me and I will put it in your hand." Denny had asked her to make the presentation, a wise idea, I thought, not only because of how much she had meant to him but also because it made it unnecessary for him to choose between Mac and me.

Everybody said something. Nobody said a lot, and there were no tears, but everybody said in their own way that they felt better for having known Denny. "I'll miss you very much," Sarah said. "I feel about you the way I felt about the boy who took me to the senior prom in high school."

Debbie said, when she gave him the medallion, that she thought he ought to do some new things when he got home, some physically hard work that would use up his energy and take his mind off the things he used to do. "Like mowing the lawn, for instance," she said. Denny looked more shocked than I had ever seen him. Not even Emma's telling him that she wanted him to go to church with her every Sunday had made him turn so pale. He straightened his shoulders. "I do not mow lawns," he said. "We have a man at the company who does that."

John took his medallion from Debbie, too, and said that she didn't have to worry about him working hard. "I have to," he said. "I'm going to the halfway house and I can't stay there unless I have a job, and it can't be working for my father." He loosened up a little. "Thank God," he said. "But I'll work, and I'll be glad to do it. It'll be better than being in jail." He didn't seem to know what else to say, but then he finished quickly. "I'll miss all of you," he said, "even if you do use too many big words."

I told Denny I would see him again, even if I had to go to Odessa, Texas, where nobody had gone since Lyndon Johnson when he was running for election.

Mac and I walked the long walk without saying much. He said he was glad we had met each other, and happy that he had been sent to St. Mary's. The only thing he was sorry about was that

Denny and I were finished with ours but he still had to do his Family Week. Saying good-bye to Denny, he said, was tough, but at least it meant we were that much closer to going home, weren't we? I said, yes, we were, and I was ready.

Father Tim came by to say good night, carrying the inevitable box of chocolates. After he let me pick out a couple of coconut creams, he said I would find consolation in the church at times like this if I wasn't so stubborn. "You're smart," he said, "but you're not above help."

"The church doesn't believe in giving help," I said. "If you're a poor young woman who needs an abortion because some guy took advantage of you and knocked you up, you'd better not ask the church to help you out."

"Edward, Edward," he said, "you choose such outrageous examples."

Thinking about the Holy Roman Catholic Church was exactly what I needed to take my mind off my troubles. "To the present pope and the kind of cardinal we've got in New York," I said, "Calvin Coolidge would be considered a dangerous radical. This pope and Cardinal O'Connor would call you a Communist for giving alms to the poor. Although they certainly wouldn't be opposed to the poor having twelve babies per family. But their conservatism allows no room for human kindness. They would probably bring up St. Francis of Assisi on charges."

Feeling better, I went to sleep thinking of something else Joseph Campbell said, about heaven: "If you're going to get it, you'd better get it here because this is where it is."

I thought that I had better start paying attention.

16

There's a Few More Lonesome Cities that I'd Like to See

Lying in bed I could look up at the long row of west wing windows on the fifth floor where the hospice was. The darkness of almost every room was streaked by flashes of light from the television sets that stayed on all night. The little lavender ladies, melted down to the size of tiny Madame Alexander dolls, couldn't sleep without the comfort of the sounds of the world they had left behind. At this hour of the night they were probably watching James Cagney and Pat O'Brien fighting with Humphrey Bogart in *Angels With Dirty Faces* or maybe Clark Gable and Spencer Tracy teasing Myrna Loy in *Test Pilot*. That was the one in which Spencer was always sticking his chewing gum on the side of Clark's airplane when he took off on a dangerous flight and then forgot it the time Clark got killed.

Thinking about the little old ladies who look so brave going to get their hair rinsed blue and set once a week so they'll look nice for whomever comes to see them makes you realize that women know more about pain and suffering than negligence lawyers do.

Everybody says that if we go back to drinking or drugging when we get out of here we'll be dead in no time at all. But I can't die yet. There's too much I haven't done yet. I've never sailed around Manhattan on the Circle Line, I've never broken a hundred at Leewood Golf Club, and I still haven't found out why they call Madonna the Material Girl.

Red Smith was right when he said that "ninety feet between bases is the closest to perfection man has yet achieved." But even Red didn't know why writing men drink so much. All he knew was that he wrote, and he drank.

Why are so many of the happy times associated with booze? And, for that matter, so many of the sad times, too? It's as though you can't do anything important without a drink. How am I going to manage? Polly says by disconnecting events from drinking. They're two separate things.

Maybe I should join Al-Anon. I like their slogan, "If you're not satisfied, we'll refund your misery."

I liked the young woman at the AA meeting who said, "It's crazy, you're always saying go to meetings, stay late, and collect phone numbers. But that's exactly what I used to do when I went to the bars." The same kid said, "Where am I supposed to go when I feel shitty, to the fucking public library? I'll tell you what I did the last time. I went to Bloomingdale's and I tried on a real outlaw dress."

When Bill Bradley was playing basketball instead of being a senator, the Knicks showed the world what New York basketball was like—move without the ball, give and go, defense, and above all, Hit the Open Man. They were beautiful to watch. They reminded me of the Original Celtics and the Harlem Renaissance Five, basketball as poetry. What I want to know is, how did I become the open man?

If I end up disappointed with my life, I want it to be because of what I did, not because of what I didn't do.

I just thought of what T. S. Eliot said in "The Love Song of J. Alfred Prufrock":

> Would it have been worthwhile
> If one, settling a pillow or throwing off a shawl,
> And turning toward the window, should say:
> That is not it at all,
> That is not what I meant, at all.

17

Thoroughly Mashed Potatoes

My last Saturday morning at St. Mary's was dismal, overcast and urgently threatening. It suited my mood exactly. Not even my seven-thirty reading of one twenty-four over eighty-two made me feel good, but it did give me an idea, which might or might not work out, but anyway was something to do. I called Dr. Amer's extension after breakfast and asked if I could see him if he was going to be in this morning. His assistant came back on the line after a short delay and said, "He says sure. He'll be in his office in room 441 at nine o'clock. He'll be glad to see you then."

I skipped the morning lecture, which was another Father Martin film doubtless sprinkled with more Irish drunk jokes that I could easily live without this morning, and walked out to look for a while at the river without any boats before going up to the fourth floor. Knowing that the first thing Dr. Amer, like Jerry Shevell, would do was wrap the sleeve around my arm and take my blood pressure while he was saying hello, I was careful to take the elevator. I wasn't going to give myself a bad number by walking up all those stairs. I was at his office a few minutes before nine, and when I saw that the office, which I noticed he shared with the St. Mary's Alumni Association, was empty, I ventured into the hospice lounge at the end of the hall. The only people there were a white-haired man in a wheelchair and a woman nurse's aide, probably a volunteer. I tried not to stand too close to them but I deliberately memorized their conversation:

Patient: "I can't find my glasses."

Volunteer: "I don't see them. Maybe they're in your room."

"Maybe."

"Want me to take you there to look for them?"

"No."

"Well, what's your room number? I'll go look for them."

"It don't matter. Don't bother."

"It must be hard for you to see without them." (sympathetically)

"It is."

"Well, I'll go look for them."

"Thank you."

MINUTES LATER. "I just couldn't find them. I looked everywhere."

"It's all right."

"Let me feel around your chair." Nothing. "Try sitting up. Oh, there they are. You were sitting on them."

As I was leaving I saw a hand-printed notice tacked on an easel by the door. "There will be a piano sing-along Friday eve at six o'clock after dinner. Leave requests for favorite songs in box underneath."

My friend the baseball-fan doctor was in his office and was satisfied with my blood pressure; it was only a couple of points higher than it had been when Leona Geilfuss had taken it earlier. "That's what I wanted to talk to you about," I said. "I'm only going to be here one more week and I've been wondering if it wouldn't be a good idea to see if I can get along without the Tenormin for the rest of the time. I'd like not to have to take it when I get home, and I thought if I stopped now you could keep an eye on me and see if it's all right."

Dr. Amer didn't seem to mind my playing doctor. He was used to that from the Rehab patients. After all, we were constantly playing psychiatrist, so why not doctor? He checked my chart for the last week and saw that most of my readings had been around one twenty over eighty. "It's worth trying," he said. "I'll change the order at the nurses' station and we'll see how it goes." He seemed to be in no hurry to throw me out, so we sat and talked for a while about the Rehab.

He said most of their new arrivals were in pretty bad shape and had to be sedated for the first three or four days. He had given me Ativan because it takes two or three weeks for Librium to be eliminated from the system and he wanted to avoid that stretch-out if he could. Then, when my pressure stayed high he had given me the Tenormin, which had done everything he had hoped it would.

I was interested in whether or not the intervention patients were harder for him to deal with than the ones who, no matter how far down they were, had at least come to St. Mary's voluntarily. "Well," he said, as he had told me once before, "they're sure angrier. We can't do anything much with them until they calm down and begin to examine their consciences."

When I asked him, he said that despite the bad shape most of their patients were in when they came through the doors, they only had a few seizure cases a year. "Three or four, I suppose," he said, "thank God." Then he saw the director of the Rehab, Jay Hauge, walking into his office across the hall and he said, "Let me introduce you to Jay. He's a man you ought to know."

Jay welcomed us into his office and I quickly formed the impression of a cheerleader type of executive so bursting with energy you could tap it and give shots of it to three or four other people. I saw that there was a picture on the wall of him running across the finish line in a foot race and I asked, "Marathon?" He said, "Yes, that was the Pillsbury Marathon here. I also ran the New York Marathon in 1987, and then I retired. I'm forty now, too old for that stuff." He looked more like thirty-five, and I didn't think he was too old for it at all. Unless maybe he didn't want to risk doing worse than the very respectable 3:53 he had done in New York.

That was when I decided he was the Lou Holtz of the Rehab, smart, good at leading the conversation, a true believer in his cause, and a born evangelist. He reminded me of Frank Leahy, who was always taking Notre Dame to the national championship when I was editing *SPORT* magazine. Aside from being able to sell refrigerators to Eskimos, football coaches on that level share another rare trait; they are so likeable you don't even envy them their success. The only thing you had better not take at face value is their humility. It's there, but it's used like another weapon in their arsenal. Anything for Notre Dame, anything for St. Mary's. I'm for that. I liked Jay.

Before I left and went back downstairs where I belonged, I found out that Jay's first job at St. Mary's, while he was still a senior at the University of Minnesota, was sorting laundry. After he was graduated, and knew he was interested in the chemical dependency field, he got a regular job as an orderly. That was in 1970. Fourteen years later, he became the boss. Horatio Alger wouldn't have had the nerve to dream up a story like that.

It was typical of Jay that he spent most of the time I was with him telling me how wonderful Maureen Dudley is. He was, on his way up, the first person to hold the job that Maureen has now, so he knows what he's talking about when he says she's the Rehab's greatest asset. "She has a sixth sense for hiring stars," he said. "If somebody tells Maureen that his problem is that he's a perfectionist, she hires him. I admire that."

Me, too. I always tell people that the best thing you can do when you're the boss is hire people who are good enough to take your job away from you. And if I were on the St. Mary's board I would make sure I knew exactly what Jay wanted next and have it wrapped up ready to give to him before he asked for it.

Jay told me a story that eloquently illustrates his zeal for his mission. He was flying back to Minneapolis from New York when he noticed that a man across the aisle from him ordered a second vodka on the rocks before he had quite finished the first one, then a third, and in all, downed six vodkas before the captain said they were beginning the descent into Minneapolis and they shut off the bar. Jay couldn't contain his curiosity; he was certain this traveler must be on his way either to Hazelden or St. Mary's, and he was dying to know which. But, no, he was just a businessman making a routine trip to Minneapolis. "Only a day trip," he said. "I'll be back home tonight." Thinking of another half dozen vodkas on the flight home, not to mention whatever he managed to put down at lunch, Jay gave the man his business card and said, "Call me up some time and let's talk."

I was a few minutes late for the Saturday morning no-counselor group meeting, but Doctor Bob, who had elected himself chairman because he had gotten to the Rehab five minutes before Sarah did and easily ten minutes before I did, waited for me to show up before they read the Thought for the Day. I told him the only reason he had gotten there ahead of us was because he was practically under armed guard and that shouldn't count, but he was undisturbed. "You may read the thought if you wish," he said. I told him what he could do with the thought and Father Tim, wanting to cut off further sacrilege, took over the responsibility. It was a message that made every one of us smile, especially as we considered the bulky messenger delivering the sacred writ:

"We should remember that all AA's have clay feet. We should not set any member upon a pedestal and mark her or him out as a perfect AA. It's not fair to the person to be singled out in this fashion, and if the person is wise, she or he will not wish it. If the person we single out as an ideal AA has a fall, we are in danger of falling, too. Without exception we are all only one drink away from a drunk, no matter how long we have been in AA. Nobody is entirely safe. AA itself should be our ideal, not any particular member of it."

"I think," Mac said, "we should make an exception in Ed's case."

"My hands are clean," I said. "I have never aspired to such high station."

Father Tim asked if he had ever told us his story about clean hands. "I'll tell it to you anyway," he said. "Actually, it's not about clean hands, it's about consecrated hands. You know, when we're ordained, our hands are consecrated so that we may always be ready to perform the transubstantiation of the bread and wine into the body and blood of Christ. Well, there was this chilly day when the pastor wanted a fire laid in the fireplace in the rectory and he asked his assistant to bring in some wood and make the fire. 'With these consecrated hands?' the young priest asked, shocked. The monsignor looked him up and down and said, 'Consecrated hands, is it? And what do you use to wipe your ass?' ''

We talked about what was on for next week, Mac's Family Week and Mark's, and maybe another round of Father Tim vs. Sister Mary Carlotta if the Sister was still here on Monday. "I don't think she will be," Tim said complacently. "I think she finally has to get on to her new job. I don't plan to do anything to dissuade her from it."

Tim had another problem he was more eager to talk about. Monseigneur Saltzman had told him during their last telephone call that he wanted to take all of the wine out of Father Tim's sacristy and replace it with grape juice. "I told him," Tim said, and the folds of his usually relaxed face tightened with anger, "that he can't do that. I said it would require a special dispensation from Rome for me to say Mass without wine for the Eucharist, and Rome doesn't look very kindly on that sort of thing. Anyway, I told him I just won't do it, and if he takes the wine out, I'll put it back in. You know, if I was reduced to drinking that stuff, I'd just pour it into the toilet and eliminate the middle man."

Typically eager to lighten the common mood, Tim changed the subject abruptly. "You know, Edward," he said, "I always tell my older parishioners that sex over sixty-five is dangerous. They ought to pull over to the side of the road first."

Father Tim liked the fact that we had managed to talk our way through an hour and could with clear consciences declare the meeting over. Now, except for the wing meeting at six-fifteen to elect officers, the rest of the day was ours. God knows what we were going to do with it, but it was ours. Going downstairs, I saw a tall, balding man with a reddish face and friendly eyes walk through the front door, a canvas tote bag in his hand. He stopped right in front of me. I knew him. He was Tom Danneman, a lawyer from New Orleans, whom I'd met here last summer, and he was back for a second try. I said what everybody says when that happens at the Rehab. "I'm glad to see you, Tom, but I'm sorry to see you."

"I've got to check in," he said, as if he were picking up his room key at the Holiday Inn, "but I'd love to talk to you. Will you look me up later? I've got to be either on the second floor or the third floor, right?" I introduced him to Mac, promised I would see him later, and tried to give Mac a thumbnail description of him as we began our walk.

Tom Danneman had been a leader of the group when I was an outpatient. He seemed to feel the way the rest of us did about almost everything, and, accustomed to being an advocate, he had spoken up for us whenever it seemed appropriate. Debbie didn't always think it was so appropriate, and Violet, the regular counselor for whom she was substituting, thought even less of it when she came back from her vacation, but the rest of us admired Tom's intellectual quickness, his wit, and his courtroom respect for the very authority he was cheerfully challenging. The trouble was, his determination to choose as he wished from the Rehab's program and ignore or throw out whatever he didn't like apparently hadn't seen him safely through the hard first year. Mac said, "They have rules because they've found out they work. It never works when the inmates take over the asylum."

It sure hadn't. When I saw Tom after lunch, he had a copy of my book, *A Nickel an Inch*, with him, although I was the last person in the world he had expected to see. "I just thought it would be a good book to reread here," he said. "I remembered that there was a lot about drinking in it and I thought I'd try again to figure out how you managed to make the drinking mix with your work, why it was okay for so many years, and then what happened when you retired and took up drinking full-time."

"When you figure it out," I said, "I'm in room 349."

"You said something," Tom said before I left "about me having had trouble making it through the year. I made it through exactly sixteen days before I had my first drink. Then I set out to prove that a so-called alcoholic could drink like normal people if he was smart and he put his mind to it. So, here I am."

We talked about Tom's favorite complaint against St. Mary's. "Everything they do is aimed at making the families feel better and the patients feel worse," he said. "I remember once you and I both got sore when one of the family counselors asked Victor's wife—remember Victor?—if she didn't sometimes think she would be better off if he was dead. Jesus, that's therapy?"

I told him what Maureen Dudley had said about the patient's need to learn that he hasn't got a corner on the pain. I also said that I was beginning to see that, no matter how hard it was for the patient to allow such a heretical thought to intrude on his view of the world as himself as New York City and everything else as Hoboken, there were other claims on the Rehab's attention. In essence, they were in business to treat our addiction, not our depression. That would have to wait for after-care. First, St. Mary's had to get us clean and sober. If they could do that in twenty-eight days, they were doing a hell of a good job.

When I left, feeling just a little bit like an evangelist for the holiest of causes, Tom gave me a prick of guilt when he picked up my book again. I hoped reading about all those dry martinis didn't do him in. They sure had done me in.

Mac and I walked for an hour in the hundred-degree wet heat of the late afternoon because we couldn't stand sitting any longer and we thought it would do us good to get so tired we'd be able to take a nap before dinner. We were feeling better about tomorrow, the last long weekend day we would have to spend here unless they found some reason to confiscate our passports, because we had signed up for a bus trip to the Metrodome to see the Twins play the Milwaukee Brewers. Jim Maki was going to chaperone the group and we were the eighth and ninth men to sign up when we put our names on the list pinned to the bulletin board. No women had signed up. Maybe they thought it was going to be too hot; they probably didn't know it's never hot in the Metrodome. Or any other dome. Anyway, we would be leaving at eleven A.M. for a one o'clock game, and that would take care of a big part of the day. It didn't matter much whether it was a good game or not, and anyway, we could keep busy checking out the ball park. It would be worth the twelve dollars it was costing us for the ticket and the bus.

Meanwhile, there was a movie tonight that I'd already seen but Mac hadn't and I was willing to see again. It was a Robert Duvall

picture, *Tender Mercies*, about a western singer who threw away
his career and his marriage by trying to drink all the whiskey in
Texas, and now has met and married Tess Harper, the prettiest
young widow in the state. Like *The Morning After*, the Jane Fonda
movie I'd seen with Denny, it was an odd choice for a hundred or
so alcoholics and drug addicts trying to stay straight, but I remembered it with pleasure and I was looking forward to seeing it again.

Dinner was Saturday-night quiet except for a rare showstopper
by Clark, the head man behind the counter. Murphy, the pretty
kid who sat in front of Tim in the lecture hall and who had taken
it upon herself to find him and let him know when there was mail
for him—"You'd better go pick up your mail, Father," she would
tell him, "there's a ton of it there"—had been hesitant about taking
any of the mashed potatoes with her roast turkey. "I don't know,"
she said doubtfully, "maybe I'd better just stick with the string
beans." That kind of hesitation usually brought down the wrath of
our resident Craig Claiborne on the offender's head, but Clark was
in an awesomely good mood. "You don't want to miss these," he
said, balancing a heaping spoonful of mashed potatoes over Murphy's plate. "First we mash them partially. Then we add the butter
and the milk, then the salt and pepper, and then we throw in a
little parsley while we beat them and beat them and beat them
until they're as fluffy and creamy as they can be. These are thoroughly mashed potatoes." Murphy took them, and so did we. "We
may as well eat them," Mac said. "After this week we all feel like
thoroughly mashed potatoes ourselves."

My blood pressure at eight o'clock was one fifty over ninety-two,
not great. We'd know more tomorrow morning.

The movie helped. It wasn't exactly the same as taking your girl
to Loew's on Saturday night, but it was a lot better than watching
television in the lounge. There's still something about that big
screen that makes the people more alive and the photography twice
as exciting. The whole scene, not just the fact that once again the
plot was built around the troubles of an alcoholic, was the same as
the first time I'd gone. The stage was packed with kids wrapped

up in their blankets, head on somebody's pillow, it didn't much matter whose, hands greasy with buttered popcorn, and cans of soda sitting next to them. The crackling unwrapping of candy bars was just like home, even if the uninhibited participation of the audience in the dialogue and the action was different.

"Give me the bottle!" was the first bite of dialogue we heard as the opening scene unfolded behind the credits telling us that the stars of this Antron production were Robert Duvall, Tess Harper, Betty Buckley, Wilford Brimley, and Ellen Barkin, the screenplay was by Horton Foote and the coproducers were Robert Duvall and Horton Foote. Everybody winced on cue when Duvall woke up in the morning on the floor he had fallen down on in the first scene and looked at himself in the mirror. They checked out the fact that the bottle next to the bathroom sink was Gordon's and they argued about whether it was gin or vodka. "Whatever," somebody said with authority, "it did the job. Look at him." But after that, things got steadily better. Duvall married Tess, who was everybody's girl next door only better looking, and he fought the good fight. He went into a bar once, and he even bought a bottle once, but he didn't take a drink. This was encouraging. If he could do it, we could do it. Then, at the end, after he had written a couple of new songs and had sung them himself on a record that looked like it was going to be a hit, and his new wife was so proud of him she could bust, his daughter by his divorced wife the famous singer was killed in an auto accident caused by her drunken husband, and he beat himself up with the unanswerable question, why? "I don't trust happiness," he said. "I never have. I never will." No jokes from the audience. But then the picture ended with Duvall outside throwing a football with his little stepson, and you could see a new life was beginning because he wasn't drinking anymore and his music was good and his pretty wife loved him, and there wasn't a dry eye in the house. We all went to bed thinking good thoughts. Murphy winked at us as we were going out and asked, "Did you old men like that one?" We went to bed feeling good. In the Rehab, that's no small thing.

Marjorie Noonsong did my pressure in the morning and it was
one forty over ninety.

I hated the ball park but I loved the Sunday afternoon ball game.
There was an exuberant feeling of release and a charge of antici-
pation about leaving the hospital grounds; even the park and its
landmarks and the streets on which we walked had become ach-
ingly familiar. We knew where the roses were having trouble and
where the impatiens were thriving, we knew where the cars with
the most provocative bumper stickers were parked, and we knew
where the pretty girl with the big dog lived. We were ready for
strange sights, new people, and unfamiliar sounds. The ball park,
any ball park, was the place.

The first shock about the Metrodome was that the playing field
was in a hole in the ground. I'd been going to major league stadiums
since I was sixteen, beginning with Yankee Stadium, the Polo
Grounds, and Ebbets Field, and the universal experience was that
you walked upstairs and looked down at the playing surface on the
street level. Here you walked in on the street level and looked down
thirty-six rows to the playing field. It was an eerie feeling, as if you
had been dropped without warning into another world and, amaz-
ingly, they played ball there, too. Furthermore, it couldn't be hell
because it must be thirty degrees cooler in here than it was outside.

It didn't look like baseball, either. What it did look like to my
formerly professional eye was a surrealistic game of Ping-Pong
played on a gigantic table covered by a sprawl of loosened parachute
silk. Even the clicking sound you heard whenever a bat struck a
ball was more reminiscent of Ping-Pong than of baseball. During
infield practice you could hardly make out the ball being thrown
from one man to another. You knew where the ball was, and where
it had been, only by watching the movements of the fielders. We
were only in the twenty-fourth row of the left field stands, there
were plenty of people farther from the field than we were, but we
might as well have been in Bloomington. No wonder they had
television sets in the sky-box suites we had peeked into on our way
here. No wonder they had bars. They certainly couldn't see the ball

game. Maybe the devil had just figured out a different way to torment us.

I heard one boy say to his father, "Dad, they look younger and they look smaller." Well, I thought, they sure as hell look smaller.

But there were compensations that were as old as when the game was played in simple wooden ball parks like Ebbets Field in Brooklyn, Shibe Park in Philadelphia, Sportsman's Park in St. Louis, League Park in Cleveland, and the memorable Polo Grounds in Harlem. There were hot dogs, with or without sauerkraut and mustard, beer and Cokes, and ice cream already oozing out of the paper cups when you seized it from the last person handing it along to you from the vendor standing in the aisle. There was the band playing, "Take Me Out to the Ball Game" and "In the Good Old Summer Time," with a barbershop quartet in straw hats singing the words you knew as well as they did, and there were the retired uniform numbers, in these cases belonging to Harmon Killebrew and Rod Carew, hanging from the outfield balconies. The field was fake and the temperature was fake but the game was still the game, the best game man ever conceived. In the last of the fifth, with a man on, Kirby Puckett proved that a home run is still a home run. We didn't have any trouble seeing it because he hit it right out toward us, on a rising line. It was caught by a boy in the fifth or sixth row who had worn his fielder's mitt to the game and went out of his mind with joy after he made the catch, running up and down the aisle showing the ball to everybody who would look at it. If he did that in New York, I thought, the ball would be gone in ten seconds.

A few of the guys had bought Twins hats or T-shirts, but whether we had a souvenir or only a memory, we were all happy when we got off the bus at 2512 South Seventh Street, in time for a rest before dinner. It had been a good afternoon. I was even willing to forgive the announcer for calling Puckett's shot a Domerun.

Dinner, mulligatawny soup followed by tuna loaf smothered in cream of pea soup sauce by Campbell's, was exactly what I needed to make me feel ten again. I wasn't drinking then, either.

The AA meeting was as bad as I had expected it to be. But what kind of a world would it be if we couldn't count on a few certainties, like AA meetings and big league ball games?

How come at AA meetings they never talk about trying to hit a home run or making an unassisted double play or pitching a no-hitter? Do you think Joe DiMaggio ever let go and let God?

18

Baggage Claim

The best thing that happened on Monday of Graduation Week was that Mac's son James brought us a copy of Sunday's *New York Times*. I liked James. Besides the fact that he had taken the hint in both hands when his father had mentioned that I died a thousand deaths without my Sunday *Times* fix, he was a good-looking blonde twenty-three-year-old with an endearing shyness but the authority and poise of an All-America quarterback. You got the feeling that nobody was going to talk out of turn in his huddle.

Because they were busy with the usual Monday family counseling commitments of the visitor who has to take the ritual *mikvah* bath of the mind before mingling with the inmates, we didn't have more than the usual fleeting lunchtime glimpse of James and Mark's wife, Carol. We spent most of morning group prodding Mac and Mark to review all of the things they wanted to say about why they had lost control of their drinking, and a good deal of that time telling Mark we thought he was a pretty poor excuse for an alcoholic anyway. "You don't drink enough in a day to carry me through lunch," I said. Almost all of the others agreed with me; Sarah stayed out of it because she knew that her white wine addiction already put her in a different category from the rest of us. "But we're not giving out medals for consumption records," Debbie protested.

"Whatever is too much for you to drink is too much, and if you persist in drinking that much, or more than that much, you're an alcoholic. The point is, you've lost control."

That discussion, and the afternoon argument that Father Tim triggered with a sarcastic dismissal of the disease concept, helped kill the time and keep my mind off my morning blood pressure reading, which was a dismal one sixty-four over one hundred four. I didn't know if I should call Dr. Amer and concede defeat or wait for him to call me and tell me to start taking the pills again. Either way, I didn't have any doubt that I would be taking them at least until I got back home. I blamed part of the inordinate rise in my pressure on a futile struggle I'd fought with myself before I fell asleep last night over a key element of the plot in the novel I was writing in my spare time, but I wasn't Saul Bellow and there was no logical reason why a problem with a book that stood a good chance of never seeing print should cost me almost thirty points on my pressure reading. When you're in the hospital, I decided, you behave like a patient, that's all. It wasn't all, but it was the best I could do. The rest was up to Dr. Amer. I hoped he had watched Kirby Puckett hit the home run yesterday afternoon.

Father Tim's thunderbolt, which he reported with satisfaction he had hurled at Father George Coyan, a Catholic priest who was one of the family counselors, was, "If alcoholism is a disease, how come we make them confess it like any other sin? We don't make them confess cancer."

"Ah," I thought, reacting with the lively pleasure of a crossword puzzle nut who has just been told that it's okay to use Latin words that have achieved sufficiently common circulation in English, "why indeed?"

"If it's a disease," Father Tim went on, "why does the Rehab go to so much trouble to nail the alcoholic's hide to the wall during Family Week? I mean, if he can't help it, if it's no different from scarlet fever, which is what they tell us when it suits their purposes, why is he guilty of anything?"

What Father Tim was saying, of course, was why are *we* guilty of anything? But good for him.

"It's a disease," Debbie said, reciting the party line without even taking a deep breath, "because it fills the basic requirements for the definition of a disease. It has serious physiological consequences, once you've got it it becomes progressively worse, and unless checked it is ultimately fatal."

Perversely, I said that one of the few arguments that had impressed me was one I'd found in Nan Robertson's book *Getting Better—Inside Alcoholics Anonymous.* She quoted Dr. Donald Goodwin of the University of Kansas Medical Center as saying that alcoholism is as much of a disease as lead poisoning because they are both diagnosed by a specific set of signs and symptoms and the best treatment for both of them is abstinence. "Why or how a person 'catches' a disease is not relevant," he said. "If some people enjoyed lead and ate it like popcorn, it wouldn't change the diagnosis of lead poisoning. Diseases are known by their manifestations as well as their causes, and why alcoholics drink is irrelevant to the disease of alcoholism."

Speaking for myself, I said, "so what it comes down to for me is that it may not be important whether it's a disease or not. What I'm learning here is that why I drink is less important than the fact that I can't stop drinking once I start, so I've got to find a way to live happily without starting. Mac and I have talked this over a million times, and we did with Denny while he was here. We've got to disconnect our desire to drink from the things that happen in our world." I waited to make sure everybody—well, everybody except Mac and Father Tim—was suitably impressed that I was beginning to see the light. "But," I finished, "I still don't believe it's a disease."

Mac had his own last word. "Well, if all the disease concept does is get the bills paid, and thereby give poor people access to the medical system where they can get help, that's a good thing."

Even Father Tim was willing to agree with that. There were no theological distinctions at stake here. In fact, nobody's pride was at stake. We were all alcoholics and we were all in this together.

My last Monday night dinner in the Rehab—I was beginning to think like that and I encouraged it in myself because pretty soon it would be my last Thursday night dinner and I would be going home the next day—was a classic hospital choice between Salisbury steak and a macaroni and cheese casserole. I went for the Salisbury steak on the ground that it would do less damage to my cholesterol count and I eased my conscience by taking two helpings of the green beans and passing up the lemon meringue pie in favor of the canned fruit salad. I was getting close enough to home to pay attention.

Arlene Larson wrapped the sphygmomanometer, a frightening word for that harmless looking black sleeve, around my arm and said, cheerfully, "It doesn't make any difference what it says, Ed. Dr. Amer says you're back on the pills anyway. I don't think he wants to lose you a few days before you go home." I didn't blame Dr. Amer. It was one fifty-two over one hundred, a little better than this morning but not much. I swallowed the Tenormin pill without complaint. When you've got high blood pressure, you've got high blood pressure.

We spent the evening in the lounge having an informal, un-counselored group meeting. There wasn't anything worth looking at on television, the Twins were home so there was no chance of a road baseball game, and we ended up with almost everybody in the group talking about AA. I defended myself against the general feeling that I hated it. "I only hate it for me," I said. "I met a lot of people at the Freedom Institute who swear by it. They like the fellowship, which is pretty much the main thing I don't like. I'd rather be alone with my troubles if I can't choose the people I want to talk to about them, and there's no way I would ever choose more than one or two. The way it's been here. I don't think there's much that I haven't talked about with Denny and Mac and Father Tim. I can't do that with a group of strangers, and I don't want to, but that doesn't mean I can't see value in it. Listen, you know I hate the AA slogans. I feel they were written by the kids in the third-grade class when the teacher was out to lunch. But one thing they say does make sense to me. What works is what works for you. Obviously, AA works for a hell of a lot of people, a million and a half of them the last I read, and who would want to change that?

And, of course, it's free. Most members, at most meetings, throw a dollar in the pot but nobody pays any attention if you don't put in anything. That's the cheapest hour of psychiatric help you can get anywhere. I'm not against AA. I'm only against AA for me."

I couldn't resist one last shot. "I knew I was right about AA and me," I said, "when I found out that Bill Wilson hated Franklin Roosevelt and thought he was a menace to the country. It figures. H. L. Mencken was right when he said there's no such thing as a one-track nut. If you've got one aberration, you've got them all."

Doctor Bob said, " I think the main thing is finding a group you can feel comfortable with. I have a friend who tried three before he found one he was willing to stay with. But now he likes it a lot. I expect I'll have to do the same thing and I just hope I'll be as lucky as he was. But I'll try. Anyway, it'll be an excuse to get out of the house once or twice a week."

"Well," I said, "all I can think of is the college girl who said once, 'AAA meetings are the ones you're driven to.' "

Doctor Bob told us one thing he had never mentioned before. He said he got a lot of help from a few books he read religiously. "No pun intended," he said. They were *God Calling* by A. J. Russell, the *Twenty-Four Hour a Day Book*, and the Hazelden book, *The Promise of a New Day*. It was interesting that our resident iconoclast embraced such reverent and at the same time cautionary works. I remembered that the thought this morning had begun with the declaration that "we are living on borrowed time. We are living today because of AA and the grace of God." I didn't remember the rest of it exactly but it had said that we ought to make the best use we could of the time we had borrowed and try to pay something back for all we had wasted while we were drinking. I had no quarrel with that.

None of us had ever seen Doctor Bob so reflective and philosophical. He must have been reading one of his books before he came out and joined us. When Mac teased him about what sounded like a conversion, he said, "No, it's nothing new. Maybe one thing is that I'm finally getting over being sore about the intervention." He perked up. "Did I ever tell you," he said, "that that woman not only wouldn't let me go upstairs for my toilet articles and some clothes, she pushed me in the back seat of the car between two other people like I was a common criminal?" His face was going from pink to red.

"Take it easy," Father Tim said. "You're getting unconverted."

Doctor Bob laughed. "I'm a disciple of St. Francis," he said. "St. Francis was an apostle of humility but he was also a fighter for justice."

Mark said, "I remember the way your wife described you when she was here. She said you think you know more than the therapists do, and actually, you think you know more than anybody."

"I sure know more than she does," Bob said. "Oh, hell," he said, "I know I'm bad about people. But, damn it, ninety percent of them bore me and nine percent of them piss me off. That doesn't leave much."

"I hope we're in the one percent," Mac said.

Betty-Lou joined us just as Sarah was saying, "Most of the time I don't know what you men are talking about, but tonight I thought I did. Maybe we're ready to go home now."

"You are," Betty-Lou said. "I've got a lot to do yet. A lot of work, as Debbie says."

"Who hasn't?" Father Tim said. He was on one of the brisk walks he liked to do before he went to bed, up and down the length of the hall from the lounge to the lecture hall and back again, a dozen times. Even that much exercise made his breath come faster, I was sure, than Dr. Amer would have liked. "As a matter of fact," Tim went on, "I'm working right now, while I'm walking, memorizing the homily I'm going to give at the first Masses when I get home. Would you like to hear what I'm going to say?"

Sure, we would.

Father Tim arranged himself not so much for an oratorical effort as for an intensely personal conversation. "You all know where I have been," he said, "and why I was there. But you don't know that I directed a great deal of anger at my superiors for placing me in that situation, I caused them an awful lot of embarrassment, and I want to apologize to them for that. The people at St. Mary's said

I was a hard nut to crack, and I guess I was. It was hard for me. It was the first time in my thirty years as a priest that I had to admit there was something in my life that I couldn't control. But with the help of a wonderful counselor, whose name happens to be Debbie and who has a loving and caring personality but who can be tough when she has to be tough, I finally admitted it. First I gained an awareness of my problem and then I came to the acceptance of it. It's only when we accept the reality that we are able to reach out for help. That help came to me from my superiors, from Debbie, from my friends going through treatment at St. Mary's with me, and from all of you. I won't waste time thanking you for all of the hundreds of letters of encouragement you sent me. I will only tell you that I am happy to be home and I will continue to work and to serve all of you." Tim waited for our approval and seemed satisfied that we meant it when we said we thought it was wonderful. "Good," he said. "Then I plan to end by telling them that I expect to be busier than ever working for the parish because, after all, I will have more time to be busy in."

"Only the drinkers," Mac said, "will know what you mean."

"But," Tim said, "there are a lot of them."

I suddenly remembered a question I'd been meaning to ask Tim for weeks but had never thought of at the right time. "What," I asked him, "is the name of your church?" The good father, who would laugh with open pleasure telling us an inconsequential story like about the nun who believed in scourging herself with a wire brush on the first Friday of every month but bought her underwear from the Victoria's Secret catalogue, didn't even smile. "Saint Edward's," he said, and I was certain he hadn't made that up.

My morning reading of one thirty-two over seventy-six encouraged me to feel that at least they would let me go home. Thank God for Tenormin.

Another thing that gave me a good feeling was picking up the large-size *Twenty-Four Hour a Day Book* in our meeting room—the regular one, room 355, because we weren't expecting such a big crowd today—and seeing for the first time a collection of personal messages scribbled to Debbie inside the front cover:

Dear Debbie:

Well, I'm finally leavin'. You have a lot of shit inside you got to get out if you want to stay sober. I have this strange feeling if I write for two weeks in here I'll have a novel. You're a beautiful person. Who said beauty is only skin deep? You got it inside and out.

Love from Sue

Debbie:

You are one of the sweetest lady I ever met.

Love,
Jim

Deb:

I'll never forget you. I guess I can't if your a part of me. I'm happy we got the chance to get close. I'll never forget you.

Love ya,
Lonna

There were eleven of us when everybody was assembled for the Family Week trials. Mac's son James was introduced to Lacey Fredericks, the senior lay member of Mac's church, at the same time the rest of us were, and we all met Mark Clements' wife Carol as we were fitting ourselves into the circle of chairs. Miss Fredericks, a maiden lady who couldn't have weighed more than ninety pounds but was a bundle of fierce energy despite her wispy size, won everybody over instantly with her obvious concern for the well-being of her pastor. Anybody who liked Mac that much had to be all right. I liked Carol, too. She was an outgoing, shapely woman in her early forties who gave you a strong handshake and looked you right in the eye when she met you. She seemed to care about what we thought of her and I wondered if she was trying to guess how much Mark might have told us about her.

It didn't matter because in the next hour we learned a lot about both of them, from her. Debbie stuck to her practice of having the family members talk first while the patient listened, and Carol didn't hold back. She was convinced that Mark was a bundle of insecurities, loosely tied together, and that he drank because he didn't give himself any rest. When a few of us made brief comments that it didn't look to us as though he drank all that much, she said pretty much what Debbie had said, that if it's too much for you, it's too much. "Mark is fine with a bottle of beer before dinner and maybe even another one with the meal," she said, "but he can't handle liquor, and when he tries, which he only does when he's upset about something, he comes apart." She was candid to the point of being, I thought, almost sadistic in her unconcern for Mark's feelings. Well, not sadistic, because that means taking pleasure from the act of inflicting pain, but certainly disarmingly callous. But she knew her man; the expression on his face while she talked freely about their troubles and his weaknesses showed his gratitude for her willingness to open up the closet doors and let the skeletons out. So far, though, there was only one skeleton—his.

But I was wrong about that, too. She brought up the A word herself. "I don't think I would ever have committed adultery," she said, "and I did, which I know Mark has already told you people in the group, if he had done more to control our marriage and me. I suppose I felt that if he didn't care enough about me to look after me, I'd just go ahead and do whatever made me feel good. I wanted somebody to want me and to care about what I did."

There was an equally stunning climax to James Mackenzie's story. He told us somberly about his mother's swift decline after her cancer was diagnosed, and his father's parallel slide into daily drunkenness. "He began by drinking too much before and after lunch and dinner," James said, "but then it was obvious that he was drinking all the time. There was never a time you would be with him when he didn't smell of liquor." He talked about his younger brother needing looking after, and his mother worrying about things not getting done around the house, and how he would get scared wondering what was going to happen to them all. He felt it was up to him to keep trouble away from their door. "In two years," he said, "from fourteen to sixteen, I went from being a son to being the father."

Whatever we saw in Mac's face when James said that, it wasn't gratitude.

"I feel a lot of shame," Mac said when he got a chance to respond. He must have burned with it when Miss Fredericks told how much she and the other members of the church board had known about his drinking. "I know he thought we had no idea," she said, "but we all knew. He would forget about meetings he had promised to come to, sometimes he would even go to a conference in another city and then not show up at the meetings, and worst of all, sometimes he would show up so drunk he could hardly speak intelligibly. That's why we were driven to organize the intervention. We owe a lot of that to James because we could never have done it without him. But we all, James, too, knew it was necessary."

"I can see now," Mac said, "that I deliberately went to some of our own church meetings drunk because I wanted to show that I was defying them. It was a little different when we went on trips. Then it just seemed like too good a chance to pass up to get off by myself and drink and feel sorry for myself."

He made me think of me sitting in the bar at the Intercontinental on the corner of Lexington Avenue and Forty-eighth Street, drinking two goblets of martinis so big the hotel charged seven dollars and fifty cents apiece for them. Drinking slowly but deeply, picking the cashews out of the bowl of mixed nuts that the bartender, Mister Riley, put on the bar in front of me so that I would put something in my stomach besides the vodka, and feeling sorry for myself. No wonder Mac and I had found each other brothers under the skin. We carried the same security blanket in our backpacks, self-pity, and we fed it with the Miracle-Gro of Smirnoff 80.

There wasn't much that I hadn't heard before in what Mac told James and Miss Fredericks about his gradual acceptance of his alcoholism, but there was a unity and a finality to it that made it different. All of the days we had talked about these things our recovery was happening; now Mac made it sound as though it had happened, and I felt that I could share the glow of hope you could see in his face.

"I think real recovery began," he said, "when I stopped trying to defend the image of myself that I wanted to believe in but no longer could, when I realized that I wasn't drinking because of the things that were happening to me but because I wanted to drink. I had sort of absolved myself with the excuse that my life was being screwed up by a lot of things I couldn't control. But then, not suddenly but gradually, I began to realize that it was the drinking I couldn't control. Most people adjust to difficult life situations that are out of their control, but I was dealing with them, or running away from them, by drinking myself into a state of anesthesia. I saw myself clearly for the first time, and it hurt. The first look at your real self is a million times more uncomfortable than hearing your voice on tape or seeing yourself on television for the first time, but it has a cauterizing effect, too. I'm a much less troubled person now, and that's better than being happy because I was never sure what happy meant, anyway. I'm beginning to think that maybe happy just means untroubled."

Mac went through the whole history of his grief therapy at St. Mary's. He told how Debbie had encouraged him to sign up with the special grief group and he said he'd had private sessions with our group's helpful spiritual advisor. "It was she," he said, "who uncovered the fact that I was distressed because I had never said good-bye to Martha. It had been Martha's wish that we keep a positive attitude. She never wanted us to admit defeat. By the time she gave up herself, it was too late to say a proper good-bye. I recited the usual psalms, gave her the usual assurances, and told her from the heart what a wonderful life she had given me. The trouble is, I'll never know if she heard me."

All during their married life, Mac, who liked to write poetry in his spare time, had made a habit of writing Martha a sonnet every Valentine's Day. He thought that would be the right way for him to say good-bye to her. "So I did it," Mac said. "I wrote her one last sonnet, and that way I was able to get out a lot of grief without beating myself up too much. My Christian faith helped me, I'm sure, find a measure of hope in what I had done. I felt better than I had since Martha died."

Mac was candid about his experiences with the grief group,

which as I knew, had been at best mixed. But he went into it in more depth than he ever had with Denny and me. "I heard more horror stories at the first meeting than I ever wanted to hear," he said, "and it seemed to me that nothing was being resolved for anybody. I went away from there feeling pretty depressed and I told Debbie I didn't want to go back. But she urged me to give it one more try, and I did, and it was better. The counselor seemed a lot more perceptive than he was the first time. Maybe the first time he'd been overwhelmed by the weight of some of the loads those people were carrying, I don't know. Anyway, after he heard my story, he said what I ought to do was write a letter from Martha to me, having her say good-bye to me. Well, I struggled with that assignment for a whole week, but when I finally finished it I was surprised to see that I had managed to remember a lot of the good things I had done that were positive contributions to our marriage and even to Martha's own personal growth. I had fully expected that the letter, if it was honest, would be negative and very hard on me. But instead I really believe it was the way Martha would have written it, and it made me feel that she had liked a lot about me. The letter did a lot to get rid of the layer of self-pity I had wrapped around my grief and it made it possible for me to deal with myself and my future in a positive, instead of a self-destructive way. After that it was easier for me to understand what Debbie had been trying to tell me, that I had let self-pity take me over under the disguise of grief. When I was able to separate my self-pity from my grief, when I knew it when I saw it, could identify it and turn away from it, I got rid of my main reason for trying to drink myself to death."

Mac laughed a little. The minister in him must have worried that he was being too hard on his congregation. "I have to admit, though," he said, "that every once in a while I still wish I could have a drink. Scotch, I think."

Before I fell asleep that night I thought how lucky Liby and I were that neither of us had had to write an imaginary good-bye letter to the other. She would be sleeping alone tonight on her half of the Hollywood bed we had switched to from a regular double bed because I was a six on the electric blanket and she was a four, but on Friday night I would be home with her. You couldn't walk with Mac on his personal stations of the cross without thanking your own lucky star. Mac was a Protestant and he didn't know about the stations of the cross but he knew a lot about pain.

The last thing I remembered was the day I'd told the publisher of *SPORT* magazine that I wouldn't run an ad personally written by Colonel Elliott Spring of the Springs Mills showing an Indian brave climbing into a bed already occupied by a black-haired squaw with the headline "A buck well spent on a Springmaid sheet." It hadn't been much fun but I was certainly spent.

I was even more spent after I had done my Fifth Step with one of the veteran spiritual counselors on Thursday afternoon. It was the final examination before graduation, and I had been apprehensive about it because I didn't know how much of a religious commitment he would want from me. After all, the Fifth Step did require admitting "to God, to ourselves, and to another human being, the exact nature of our wrongs." How much God would be involved in this? Mostly I didn't want to weasel my way out of St. Mary's by telling a lie I hadn't been willing to tell all the time I'd been here, so I hoped he wouldn't press me to declare myself a true follower of the cross of Alcoholics Anonymous.

He didn't. The counselor was a warm, compassionate listener who contributed his own thoughtful insights to our rewarding hour. Right away he liked Liby's suggestion that, as nonbelievers, we should adopt as our power greater than ourselves the union we had made together in the chapel at Fort Jackson forty-six years ago. "You can put your energies to work rebuilding that union," he suggested. "If you want it more than you want your separate selves, you'll make it."

We talked comfortably about touchy subjects that mean a lot to Liby and me, integrity, unselfishness, charity, honesty, and high on the list, a sense of obligation to our fellow man. I said that I believed in the virtue of self-sacrifice and I believed in the promise of following the highest star you can see in the sky above you.

We agreed that I wouldn't be able to do any of the things I cared about most if I kept on drinking. I said I intended never to go back to where I had been and to make amends to everybody I had hurt by doing better than I had ever done before. We shook hands firmly and he said he thought I had a good chance to make it. He said he hoped we would meet again, but not here.

I said Amen.

At our last Rehab dinner Mac and Sarah said their Fifth Steps had gone well, too. They didn't have my problems with the religious quotient but they had problems of their own, and I was glad to see that they both looked serene. Father Tim didn't look very serene because they had delayed his Fifth Step date until Monday because they were trying to talk him into going to a Halfway House for some more work and meditation before he went back to his parish. He wanted them to leave him alone and let him go home and he suspected that Monsignor Saltzman was behind this latest assault on his privacy. Mark was happy because Debbie had decided he wouldn't benefit from any more time here and ought to go back to work and get busy with an AA group as quickly as possible. Meanwhile, she had arranged for him and Carol to have a guest room in the main hospital over the weekend. In addition to whatever else they did, they could see some of Minneapolis and talk about what they had learned during Family Week.

When Mac and I got back to the Rehab after our walk, happy that we had seen a long line of people boarding the Showboat and that we were less jealous than we'd been before because we knew that if we wanted to go to a restaurant for dinner tomorrow night nobody would stop us, we watched a knot of newcomers lighting up their cigarettes at the front door. We looked at them with the wise eyes of first-classmen sizing up a platoon of plebes. It wasn't so much that we felt sorry for them as it was that we were glad we had already done that. I had felt the same way watching kids from the replacement depots report to a bleary-eyed first sergeant on Okinawa. I couldn't help but think of Bill Mauldin's Willie brushing away the Purple Heart and telling the medic, "Nah, I already got one of them. Just gimme a couple of aspirin."

We went to bed early but I didn't do much sleeping. I lay awake most of the night watching the TV lights on the fifth floor and thinking how glad I was that Connie Murray had sent me here and how glad I was that I was leaving. I could hear Jimmy Durante singing, "Did you ever have the feeling that you wanted to go?" Yes, I did, but I didn't have the feeling that I wanted to stay.

Debbie asked Mark to read the Thought for the Day when we met for nine-thirty group, and it didn't take long to realize that she had done her homework.

"There are two days in every week about which we should not worry," Mark read, "two days which should be kept free from fear and apprehension. One of these days is yesterday, with its mistakes and cares, its faults and blunders, its aches and pains. Yesterday has passed forever beyond our control. All the money in the world cannot bring back yesterday. We cannot undo a single act we performed. We cannot erase a single word we said. Yesterday is gone beyond recall."

It was hard to believe that the *Twenty-Four Hour Book* could have come up with so suitable a message for the day of our leaving. "Before we go on," Debbie said, "I want you to take a look at the thought for tomorrow." She read it herself, her midwestern sound working like a key in a familiar lock. "The other day we should not worry about," she read, "is tomorrow, with its possible adversities, its burdens, its large promise, and perhaps its poor performance. Tomorrow is also beyond our immediate control. Tomorrow's sun will rise, either in splendor or behind a mask of clouds, but it will rise. Until it does, we have no stake in tomorrow, for it is as yet unborn."

It wasn't even a quarter of ten yet but I stole a look at my watch to make sure I stayed alert to the time. I wanted to leave the Rehab before noon because I knew the trip to the airport took at least a half hour, once the promised taxicab finally showed up, which seldom was when it was promised, and I had told Liby that I had gotten a seat on Northwest Flight 192 leaving at one-twenty Minneapolis time. That would get me to La Guardia at four-fifty-three New York time, no bargain because we'd have to fight the rush-hour traffic going home, but I didn't want to miss it. I also knew there was no reason to worry; Debbie had seen a lot of her graduates rush off to the airport and I was sure she kept track of the time. But I was a world-class worrier when it came to being on time, and I kept my sleeve pushed back so my watch was never hidden.

With Father Tim's graduation held up by the calculated delay in his Fifth Step, there were four of us up for medallions, Mac, Sarah, Mark, and me. I was glad that Debbie was giving one to Mark; it wasn't his fault that his sentence had been reduced. He had certainly suffered a medallion's worth of Rehab pain.

His was the first Debbie gave out, and the ceremony inspired a wife's remarkable instruction that moved all of us. Mark had told us how much better he felt than when he had come here, torn by the uncertainties that had been fed by the discovery that his natural mother was a mental patient and worried about his loss of control over his drinking. Carol said she owed St. Mary's an immense debt because she thought she was getting back a husband who would give her the security she needed as both wife and woman. She turned to Mark and said, "I want you to promise me one thing, Mark. When we get home, I want you to ask me every single day to do something for you. I don't care what it is, just something you want me to do for you. It will mean a lot to me."

Sarah couldn't stop crying. "I feel as though you've all become part of my family," she said. "I'm sure we'll see each other again. I couldn't leave if I wasn't sure of that. You all took me in so generously when I first came, and I know I was a mess. You did everything but feed me. I'll never forget you, and I'll keep this medallion where I can see it every day and remember you."

"Just keep it where you used to keep the bottle of wine," Father Tim said, and we needed the laugh. But you couldn't look at this Sarah, well dressed in a navy blue suit with a ruffled white silk blouse, looking ten years younger with her hair pulled back and tied behind her neck, and not want to leave something to St. Mary's in your will.

I was glad that Debbie didn't make me wait until last. "I'll miss you," she told me. "I've come to count on your wit and your wisdom."

"They'll give you another man as old as I am," I said, "and you'll never notice the difference."

"I'm worried about you," Debbie said, "not because I think you want to drink but because I don't think you're going to be happy unless you find a way to put all of your energy to work. And I don't want you to be sober and miserable. So get to work doing something worthwhile. You're not one of the people who can be happy lying in the sun. Do something useful that's hard work, and you'll be all right."

"I'll write a book about St. Mary's," I said, "and tell them how to do it right." I hadn't planned to say that. It just came out.

"You really ought to do it," Debbie said. "You like to say you're an irreverent alcoholic, as though that makes you an outlaw, but actually that's the perspective ninety-nine out of one hundred alcoholics have when they face the prospect of going into treatment. What you say is realistic. It doesn't pump a lot of sunshine up people's asses about how wonderful it is. It tells it like it is, and people need that."

Betty-Lou said, "Well, if you're going to do research on the book by coming back to talk to us, you can stay at my house any time you want. I'll send you a key for those new locks."

Mac was the right person to give our valedictory. "I went to an AA meeting last night," he said, "and the discussion was about loneliness. I was interested to hear all of them say they were lonely while they were drinking but they weren't anymore. Now that they were sober they could see that self-pity was what had made them feel so lonely and made their lives so negative. They understood that being alone wasn't the bad thing their loneliness had been when they were drinking. I can see now that the primary thing St. Mary's has done for me has been to help me separate my self-pity from my genuine feeling of bereavement. I've learned that I need time to be alone, and that there is nothing wrong with that. When I'm back at work I can actually look forward to being alone after a long day of dealing with other people's problems." He looked around the room, stopping for a second at each one of us. "But, oh, boy," he said, "that sure was a hard lesson to learn."

Debbie kissed each one of us as she gave us our medallions and, when we were all decorated, we kissed her back. Fair is fair. Then everybody stood up and joined hands in a big circle and we said the Serenity Prayer:

"God grant me the serenity to accept the things I cannot change, the courage to change the things I can, and the wisdom to know the difference."

After I called the taxicab company that makes it easy for alcoholics by using nothing but threes as one of their numbers, I picked up the carryon bag I had already packed, signed my discharge papers at the nurses' station, said good-bye as quickly as I could, and hurried past the gift shop still resisting the T-shirt that said "I survived #* + %#* Family Week."

But I had, and now I could go home.

I had tried to talk Liby into having our friendly neighborhood taxi driver, Fearless Phil Farley, meet me at the airport but she wouldn't hear of it. She had insisted, when I made my last call to her from the day room, that she would meet me herself. If she couldn't get to the gate, she would find me at the baggage claim carousel. I said at least the baggage she was claiming would be in better shape than the last time she saw it. She said she loved me even when I was in bad shape and she would be there with bells on.

Liby had met me at the airport more times than we could count. She had met me when I had come back from Doubleday trips— sometimes, with Sargent, they were more like excursions—to London and Paris, to Frankfurt, to Geneva, to Amsterdam, to Los Angeles, San Francisco, El Paso, Denver, Chicago, and Boston. Then, when I went to work for the McCall Publishing Company, I came back from centrally located sales-meeting places like San Juan and Nassau and Miami. When I worked for the Book-of-the-Month Club, we told everybody, I came back from Harrisburg. But Liby met me no matter where I came back from, and this time she would meet me coming back from the Rehab, which was an even less desirable destination than Harrisburg.

She was the first person I saw when I walked out of the gate, thinking how much stronger I felt than when I had walked slowly onto the flight out. All she said was "Hello, love," while she held on to me and kissed me, but it was enough. In the car, she told me she had held off the rest of the family and all of our friends who wanted to come to the house tonight and had invited the kids to come for dinner tomorrow night. "I thought it would be better for you to have some time to rest," she said, "and not have to talk so much." I was grateful, and as she threaded the car through the traffic on the Hutchinson River Parkway, I tried to say how much I appreciated her constant support.

"I gave you some bad times," I said.

"I think about it a lot," she said, "and it wasn't all your fault. But you're such a different person when you're not drinking. That's the person I want back."

My first shock of awareness of how different things were going to be came when we followed years of habit and sat in front of the television set in the family room to watch the "CBS Evening News." This was when we always had a drink together. I remembered Tracy Cravath asking plaintively, "What's there to do at five o'clock, anyway, except have a drink?" I had fixed myself a Coke but Liby hadn't made up her mind what she was going to have and I suddenly realized she wasn't going to make herself a drink. "That's crazy," I said when she admitted she thought she shouldn't. I got emotional about it.

"Everybody out there said I shouldn't," she said. "They said it would make it that much harder for you."

"Liby," I said, "the world is full of liquor stores and bars. If I decide I'm going to drink, it won't be hard for me to get something to drink. You're only going to make me feel twice as bad if you make yourself suffer just because of me. How is that going to help me?"

"We're not even supposed to have it in the house," she said.

"Then what do we do when some of our friends come by, or when we have people in for dinner? Nobody can have a drink because I can't have one? Why don't they put a sign on me and make me walk up and down the street with it? Nothing doing. I'd rather close the front door and not let anybody in, ever." I got up and went into the kitchen and looked in the liquor cabinets. They were empty.

We had it out. She said she had given most of the stuff to Kevin to keep while she decided what to do, even the good wine from the rack in the dining room, and had stashed a few bottles in an old toy chest in the cellar. I made her go get a bottle of vodka and make herself a martini, which is what she has been doing ever since except when she feels she would rather have a glass of white wine. When we eat out, she has a drink before dinner and maybe a glass of wine with her food. Liby is one of the lucky people who can drink a little and enjoy it without looking around for more; she has no compulsion to drink everything in sight. She has never hidden a bottle in her underwear drawer. And this way I am able to live without the sad guilt of knowing that my family and friends are doing without one of the graces of life just because of my trouble.

Beginning with that first night home, when Liby made us a simple but delicious broiled filet of sole, and she had a glass of Fontana Candida with it while I stayed with my Coke, she has understood that it's easier for me to protect my abstinence when the people I love aren't being punished for my sins.

My second night home, after a good night's sleep and a quiet day, was like Christmas. Kevin and Linda drove over from their house in East Yonkers, not far from Sarah Lawrence College, and Eileen and her husband Paul came up from West Ninety-second Street with their year-old baby, Leona, whom Eileen had named after my mother. We had one of the family's all-time favorite dinners, Mama Libuse's pot roast and potato pancakes, and I opened a bottle of Lynch Bages for those who wanted it. Kevin, who hadn't had a drink for five years, joined me in a Coke. Sometimes he gets adventurous and has a ginger ale or a Sundance; I stick to the Coke. I felt less conspicuously the returned sinner because so much attention was lavished on the baby in her highchair and I felt comfortable in the blanket of warmth that surrounded the dining room table. The month at St. Mary's had been worth it.

Kevin told us about his trip to Seattle, after he left Minneapolis, to supervise still photography for an HBO movie. Eileen told us about her latest adventures in developing her dissertation on drug-addicted mothers and their babies, Linda told us about the newest account loss at her ad agency, and Paul talked about what was going on in the music world he lives in. Leona did her active best to steal every scene and Liby inconspicuously kept the platter of potato pancakes full.

I was learning already that a distinct plus to life without alcohol is that the food tastes better than it has in a very long time. Living without guilt gives you an appetite.

When everybody was leaving, kissing a lot and everybody talking at once at the front door, little Leona made uncertain attempts to walk across the lawn. She wasn't quite ready, though, and she ended up crawling up the hill to the car.

I thought that if she could crawl that tenaciously before she learned to walk, so could I.

Postscript

I can easily remember the worst moment I've had since I left St. Mary's. It wasn't dinner at the golf club with seven other people drinking martinis, scotch, and two bottles of Pouilly Fuisse. It wasn't having lunch with my old friend the writer who drank four Johnnie Walker Reds while he explained to me why, after a whole month off it, he had gone back to drinking because he had had a fight with his agent. It wasn't Thanksgiving or even Christmas with its eggnogs in the morning, martinis before dinner, and two bottles of Gevrey-Chambertin with the turkey. It was an ordinary Tuesday when I'd taken the train in to Grand Central for my weekly date with my counselor, Polly McCall, at the Freedom Institute. I walked back to the terminal after a good discussion with Polly. It was a nice day and I didn't have to fight for a cab with all the good-looking young women in short skirts on Park Avenue, so all was well with the world until I noticed that I only had about three minutes to train time and I began to hurry through the Pan Am Building. I ran out of luck at the escalator; the down staircases were too crowded to allow a step-skipping substitution of self-propelled speed for the safe but slow pace of the technological marvel the Pan Am's architects ineptly christened the People Mover. By the time I had checked the Departure Board and rushed to Gate Thirty-two, feeling every one of my years in the thumping of my protesting heart muscle, I got there just in time to have an unsympathetic conductor slam the sliding door to the platform shut in my face. I had missed the one o'clock train. The next one was one-thirty. I started instinctively toward Charlie Brown's spirits emporium, located conveniently at the top of the escalator that had just betrayed me. Isn't that what every red-blooded man in America would do? What else is there to do when you miss a train and have to kill half an hour waiting for the next one?

If it weren't for that goddamn cholesterol problem, I could have gone into the beckoning Haagen Dazs shop across from Track Thirty-two and bought a half-vanilla, half-chocolate sugar cone. Shit. A powder-dry, bitter-cold martini has zero cholesterol.

The AA persons are dedicated believers in bumper stickers like "A Day at a Time" and "Let Go, Let God." But I've never seen one that said what I needed to remember just then. I remembered it, though, the one that says, "It Isn't Worth It." I ran through the first few slides in my Personal and Confidential carousel and remembered the time I fell down and passed out cold alone in my room at the Hay Adams Hotel in Washington; the time I couldn't control my hand enough to sign the American Express charge when we were leaving the Dorado Beach after a winter golf vacation; the day I backed into the car behind me in the parking lot of a riverfront restaurant where I'd had a martini lunch; and the night I fell asleep over a two A.M. breakfast with Nelson Doubleday and Duke Ellington.

It really wasn't worth it.

Then I thought about the winter day six months after I'd left St. Mary's when it took me twelve hours to get from the lobby of the hotel on Sherbrooke Street in downtown Montreal to home. Three airplanes were cancelled from under me by the snow, one after I'd sat in it on the runway for three hours, and when everybody rushed for a drink, I took a deep breath and had a Coca-Cola. When they finally opened up La Guardia and they were able to sneak us in from Boston, I felt good. I was going home late but I was going home sober.

Thank you, Debbie.